Protection has its price,
but so do fantasies...

A CRAVE
NOVEL

NEW YORK TIMES BESTSELLING AUTHOR
STEPHANIE TYLER

WRITING AS

SE JAKES

For the readers who couldn't get enough of the guys from Men of Honor.

CHAPTER 1

CADE O'SHEA APPROACHED Crave's Fantasy Week with a wariness usually reserved for enemy combatants.

He didn't know his fantasy ahead of time, but he'd steeled himself, fully expecting it to be something he hated, something that didn't fit with his preferences. Something that was likely going to test his limits in a bad fucking way. And still, he'd made his choice to show up, to keep Theo out of trouble. They'd looked after each other from the time they'd been in grade school. That was never going to change, and *that* was the only reason he was holding the damn fantasy card in his hand as he walked toward the main entrance of the club.

Fantasy Week. *Jesus Fucking Christ*, he could think of a few, and none of them involved what he was likely about to endure.

The man who guarded the door was big—built like a tank, like he was born to be a bouncer. No one was going to fuck with him unless they were stupid, and at that point, they'd deserve what they got.

Cade shoved the card forward and Tank glanced at it,

gave Cade a once-over before moving aside to let him enter. Then Tank handed off the card to a dark-haired man whose translucent blue eyes were set off by a dark-blue denim shirt, buttoned to the top and untucked over leather pants. He also wore several heavy silver rings on the fingers of both hands.

Denim and Leather led him to a raised, cordoned-off section across from the bar that appeared to be a reserved VIP area and motioned to a table. "Have a seat and I'll be right back."

Cade did as he was told, which was a rarity.

He was the only one seated there. He took a deep breath and glanced around out of habit, marking potential exit strategies and looking for general threats. It was a routine he'd never fully break, no matter how old he got. And at twenty-five, he felt far older than his years.

A bartender sauntered over and handed him a water with lemon, and although Cade wanted something stronger, he'd read the rules—there was no drinking allowed before you played here.

He'd heard the rumors that the club was owned by ex-military guys who did merc work. It didn't seem implausible that the man who'd commandeered this fantasy for him would know them as well, and it made his resolve to make them pay for their part in this even stronger.

Finally, Denim and Leather came back over to the table and sat close enough for their conversation to be private, but not close enough to invade his personal space. He held a clipboard with a card and a paper attached, and he put it in front of Cade before handing him a pen. "Please check your card to make sure it's correct. I'm going to tell you what the other paper says, but I encourage you to read it yourself. You got a copy with your envelope as well."

The five-by-seven card spelled out the fantasy. Cade didn't want to read it, but he forced himself to skim it, catching words like *four men* and *paying a debt* and pushed it aside in favor of the other paper. He'd familiarized himself with that one—basically he was signing away liability, which was fine since he'd take matters into his own hands when all was said and done.

He signed and quickly pushed the clipboard and the card back toward Denim and Leather. "I'm good."

"Signing this agreement doesn't mean you don't have the right to say no once you're in the room."

"Are you the club's lawyer?"

Denim and Leather remained unperturbed. "My name's Oz."

"Like *The Great and Powerful?*"

Oz's odd eyes studied him, and Cade suddenly felt exposed. "I'm here to make sure what you do here tonight is safe, sane, and consensual. Fantasy Week also includes a healthy dose of reality beforehand. Your scene includes non-con—or non-consensual sex. By signing, you've agreed that you consent to the non-con. That it was your idea and that, by definition, you've given your consent."

Cade rolled *non-con* around in his head. He wasn't against fantasies as a whole and he'd fulfilled his fair share of them, although the pleasure factor on his end was minimal. This particular scenario wasn't so much a turn-off...but the reason behind him coming here was, so separating the two seemed next to impossible.

Cade nodded and Oz continued. "Once your fantasy

starts, you can stop it at any time by simply saying 'red.' If you need things to slow down, use 'yellow.' Think of a traffic light. I realize it sounds simple, but when you're in the moment, panic happens easily."

"Got it. Red for stop and yellow for slow." Cade's impatience was growing. There was no stopping or slowing for him, so this speech was all bullshit.

Oz nodded slowly, his eyes searching Cade's face. "You're all set. Follow me, please—and you can bring your water."

Cade took his glass and walked through the crowd, feeling eyes on him. Because he was new, and maybe because people knew he was here for Fantasy Week, or maybe because they just wanted to fuck him. He stared straight ahead because if he didn't? He'd bolt.

Just when you thought you'd gotten away from this shit, you're back in.

Oz stopped in front of the door marked Room 4 and handed Cade his card. "Give this to the first man you see inside the room—that's when your fantasy starts, so now's the time for any last-minute questions or concerns."

"I just need to do this." His heart thudded in his chest. He took a long gulp of water, and Oz put a hand on his arm.

"Hey, it's normal to be nervous, but this is supposed to be fun. Freeing. Nothing happens that you don't want. Remember, red and yellow, okay?"

Right—fun and freeing. Cade wanted to tell him that this was an obligation for someone he loved, because of someone he hated who, for all he knew, might show up behind this door...but instead, he simply nodded, handed off his glass... and walked inside.

The door closed behind him as he waited for his eyes to adjust to the low lighting in the room. Later, he'd notice the bed in the corner, the bench, and various BDSM tools, but his immediate focus couldn't help but narrow, with a laser-like intensity, on a man who took up all the space in the room.

That force of nature stood casually, leaning against the wall, his gaze bent on exposing and seducing and *Jesus*, he was goddamned beautiful in that hot, badass kind of way with short, spiked, almost white-blond hair that made him look fierce. He was taller than Cade and broader, but his body was honed from whatever work he did for a living and not simply gym muscles. Cade could definitely tell the difference. This man was capable.

This man would break him. And he'd have fun doing it.

Cade shifted, not sure what to do next. Finally, he held out the card and said, "Hey, I'm Cade." Like maybe the guy didn't know who he was, or why he was here.

The man's dark-blue eyes caught him, held him in place. "Hey, I'm the one who's going to make you scream."

His voice was a deep drawl that ran like warm honey down Cade's spine. He fought a shudder and lost, and the man graced him with a wicked smile.

Man up. Get it over with. Cade straightened his spine and waited for the order.

It came far too quickly.

"Strip. Now. There's no reason to keep your clothes on for what you're here to do."

But something—*someone*—distracted him from following the command. He hadn't clocked the other man, didn't know if he'd just come in or if he'd been there the entire time, but once Cade caught sight of him, he couldn't pull his gaze away.

His eyes were dark, like his hair, and his entire countenance screamed, *Threat: make contact at your own risk.* There was no couching or hiding it. It was in his eyes, the way he moved as he walked across the room toward Cade and took the card, read it, and dismissed it with a flicker of a gaze.

If it were possible, he might be more dangerous than the first man.

"You need to pay your debt, lad. Time to give us what you promised." His brogue was heavy, Welsh, maybe and fuck, who the hell cared?

But Cade was spinning, struggling to stay afloat in all this. His fingers shook as he tried to take off his jeans. He'd jumped out of helos under fire, been shot at point-blank range, been through things no normal human would think of signing up for...and this would be the thing to take him down.

He'd expected to hate this. He'd wanted to hate this. But now that he was in here, with these two men...it was nothing like he'd thought.

The man with the accent moved Cade's hands out of the way and hooked his fingers in Cade's front belt loops. Cade kept his eyes down, couldn't look at him. Finally, Cade forced himself to ask, "Your names?" but it came out as more of a mumble.

"What's that, Cade?"

Cade raised his head. "Your names. I need..." He stopped as the obsidian eyes locked on to his, then managed to draw in a deep breath. "What are your names?"

The bigger man sauntered to his other side, and Cade was boxed in. "I'm Tegan. He's Vic."

Even as he spoke, Vic was sliding the leather jacket off Cade's shoulders. It landed on the floor with a *thunk*. "Following orders isn't your thing, is it?"

Fuck, his mouth was dry. "No. Not really."

Vic smirked. "After tonight, I don't think that's going to be a problem." He tugged at the hem of Cade's T-shirt, then pulled it off before skimming his hands down Cade's sides. He tilted his head to glance at the barbell piercings in Cade's nipples before dragging his gaze up to Cade's face as adrenaline buzzed through him like a goddamned drug.

He wanted Vic to touch them, roll them, wanted him to take them in his mouth and suck, use his teeth and tug the piercings. Hard. But all Vic did was run fingertips along his abs down to the waist of his jeans before quickly freeing Cade's cock. Tegan helped by pushing the jeans down from his hips and finally, Vic bent down to take off Cade's boots, socks, and jeans, all while Tegan held him steady, his rough touch digging into Cade's biceps.

Vic glanced up at him. "He's going to make for a fun ride —I can tell." His words were directed at Tegan, but his eyes never stopped roaming Cade's body, and Cade was never more aware of being naked in front of these two fully clothed forces of nature.

He hadn't ever been particularly modest, had been told all his life that he was handsome, with clothes or without, so the naked part didn't bother him. Neither did being sandwiched between the two men. No, it was all about how he was feeling—the fact that he wasn't able to numb himself to get through this. He couldn't escape, couldn't get the emotional distance he needed and *fuck*—he forced himself to just goddamned breathe.

It wasn't supposed to be like this. He wasn't supposed to be wanting or aching with need. But he was, and both men seemed to know it.

Tegan let go of him and walked around him, and Cade felt himself flush at the visual inspection. But when Tegan's hands went over him roughly, Cade fought to stand still and take the touches without groaning, each brush of the man's fingertips on his skin like a lick of flames...and nowhere *near* enough. The sensations it brought made his synapses fire and he was going to need for Tegan to tie him down and *soon*, or else his body would take over and run.

"Are you ready to start paying us back, boy, just like you promised you would?" Tegan's voice was a growl, heavy with lust, and it did as much to Cade as his hands had.

"I, ah...I'm not sure..."

Vic chuckled, a gruff sound that went straight to Cade's cock. "He's not sure. His dick looks sure."

Tegan went around to his back again. "Payment's coming out of your ass, baby." Tegan's fingers slid into the cleft of his ass, and Cade fought the urge to gasp like a goddamned virgin. "I'm not sure you're taking this seriously enough, Cade. Do you have any idea how much trouble you're in? How you're going to pay, over and over? How you're going to think you can't possibly handle any more of what we've got to give you...and then we're going show you how wrong you are."

Jesus, the promise in those words shot through him like a current. His dick twitched and he felt Tegan's hard cock press and rub and grind against him.

"I think he's starting to understand." Vic gave a lazy smile as he moved closer and took Cade's cock in his rough palm.

Cade attempted to bite back a moan...and failed, which earned him another smile. "His dick's leaking. He wants this. Wants to take whatever we give him and more. Don't you, Cade?"

Cade swayed under Vic's expert stroking, and he might've nodded, but he couldn't keep his thoughts straight. Everything was pure sensation, his skin hot, the wet of his precum being swirled around, the pressure of Vic's finger pressing into his slit. "Yeah, you're going to be taking cock everywhere tonight, baby." Vic assured him. "And you'll love it."

Cade went to shake his head because that was his role, to pretend he didn't want this...but his cock wasn't agreeing at all. Vic was going to make him come, right here, and what would that mean?

Vic's rough palm stroked him with just the right pressure as Tegan nuzzled Cade's neck. Cade found himself leaning back against Tegan, heard his harsh pants in the otherwise quiet room and watched Vic studying him intently. "I think he wants to come."

"Is that true, Cade?" Tegan's voice murmured against his cheek, his hand sliding along the seam of his ass. "You want to start coming already? Because once you start, we're not going to let you stop."

Fuck, Cade—answer him. Play the goddamned game. Because this wasn't real...no matter how real it felt. How real the look in Vic's eyes seemed...the desire, the concern for his pleasure.

And suddenly, coming seemed like the worst idea ever. He'd never be able to stop himself from reliving it, and he'd never allowed himself to live in fantasyland before this. It was already almost too much for him to handle, and so he shook his head and managed, "I've got to pay my debts first."

Vic stroked him a few more times and released him. "You don't get to make the decisions, boy. Gave that up when you walked through the door."

As Tegan continued to hold him, Vic took what looked like a small remote out of his pocket and hit a button. The walls along the back section of the room receded like pocket doors, revealing floor-to-ceiling glass panes that let him see into the club below. Another button pressed and Cade could hear the people, many of whom were staring up and cheering.

It took him a second to realize that it was one-way, that they couldn't see or hear him. It didn't seem to matter—they cheered because they knew something was happening in here, and their stomps and whistles shot straight to his dick.

He flushed hot again at the idea of being on display. The only thing that stood between him and total exposure was Vic's thumb hovering over a couple of buttons on the remote he held as he laughed. "I think baby boy here wants to put on a show for everyone."

He tried to grind out something like "Not your fucking baby boy," but Tegan answered Vic with, "Looks like he's about to."

Tegan shifted his body, so he faced the crowds and he heard himself mutter, "Fuck. *Fuck*," and then Vic reached out to roll one of Cade's nipples between his thumb and forefinger before tugging on the barbell and yes, *finally*. Cade jumped, moaned, pushed into Vic's hand for more friction, more of the touch, more of anything. So fucking needy. Maybe the water had been drugged.

Maybe these men were just that good at seducing him, and *that* was not on the goddamned card.

Tegan's hand caressed the back of his neck. Vic moved in closer and kissed him, open-mouthed, tongue playing along the roof of his mouth, sliding along his as Tegan's hand fisted in his hair and held him there, against Vic's mouth. God, he'd never known a kiss could be that intimate or erotic, and he couldn't help but give as good as he got. When Vic pulled away, Cade groaned in protest, but Tegan shifted him slightly, hand still in his hair, and took his turn at Cade's mouth and again, the best goddamned thing. Cade's dick throbbed, Vic played with his nipples and his cock again, and this wasn't at all what he'd expected.

The crowd was yelling, stomping, and the floor vibrated under his feet as Vic tugged and stroked and fuck, Cade was going to come and they didn't care—obviously wanted it to happen, because they held him in place as his orgasm ripped through him. He reached out to grab Vic's arm, and Tegan claimed his mouth through it as his knees weakened and Vic steadied him...and this was why he hadn't wanted to come—he was already too goddamned vulnerable and now?

And now...he clung to Tegan and Vic like lifelines.

And maybe for tonight, for this, they were.

Tegan finally broke the kiss. Cade struggled to pull in air as he watched, fascinated as Tegan's eyes left his to bore into Vic's, watched as Vic licked his fingers that were full of Cade's cum. Both men were breathing hard, staring each other down, and if they'd kissed—or fucked, right then and there, Cade wouldn't have been surprised. Actually, he hoped he'd get to watch.

And then they'd both be tasting you. Fuck, it was enough to get his cock hard again.

But that wasn't part of the deal. He was the main course, and he'd agreed to be the one who got fucked, over and over. Any way they wanted him.

That was when Tegan led him over to a flat leather bench and put pressure on his shoulders, his voice a rough touch in and of itself. "On your knees, baby. Lay your chest on the bench and spread your legs."

Cade gripped the sides of the bench, his cock still heavy and hard. *Fucking traitor.* His entire body buzzed with need as Tegan's hand stroked down his back, between his legs. He heard the clink of metal handcuffs before he saw them placed close to him, and he knew they'd be used. *Fuck.*

He turned his head away, his cheek down against the cool leather...and that was when he got the wake-up call.

He saw the first camera, pointed down at him. He glanced around and spotted another, had to guess that there were more of them hidden from sight. They were no doubt there for safety reasons, but they also sealed his fate...and served as a freezing-cold dose of reality.

The earlier message he'd received played over in his head.

"Oh, and Cade? Don't even think about not going. I've set it up to watch the scene in real time, with the help of the men who own the club. They were very accommodating, and they promised to send me a recording as well, so I can experience it over and over again."

He'd be watched tonight—and it would be captured for posterity. His gut clenched, along with his fists, as he resigned himself to his fate. According to his card, two other men would be joining them....

Stop. Don't go there.

One step at a time.

He knew from past experience that it was the only way to get through hell. And when it was all done? He'd make the owners of this place pay for allowing him to enjoy a little piece of heaven on the trip there.

CHAPTER 2

VIC SLOWLY WALKED around the ruggedly good-looking man on the bench, studying him. Cade's jaw was clenched, his dick had gone slack, and his eyes were screwed shut like he wanted to be anywhere but here.

The change had come down as sharply as a guillotine. Tension rolled off him in waves. Nerves were to be expected but this was a whole other level, especially after how responsive he'd been just moments earlier. Tegan seemed to feel it too, looked confused as to how to handle this—and Tegan always knew how to handle anything.

Those first moments had been electric, like a current ran between the three of them, and what the fuck had happened? Either Cade was really playing his role...or he was well out of his comfort zone, and not in the good, life-affirming BDSM way.

"What the hell are you waiting for? Take it out on my ass," Cade snarled suddenly and normally, Vic would reprimand a sub during a scene for doing that, punish them...but this entire fantasy seemed like a punishment already...and not the kind Vic was up for doling out.

His eyes skimmed over Cade's body—the tattoos on his back that covered the scars, his tight ass and sculpted muscles from years of military training. His dark-blond hair was perfect for fisting, the way Tegan had done to him earlier when they'd kissed him. Vic itched to do it now, to control Cade's mouth while he sucked him, to force Cade to watch him with his goddamned hazel eyes—complete with gold flecks and ringed with black—that Vic knew he'd get lost in.

A firm knock on the door just before it opened pulled him from his thoughts. Tegan had pulled in Colin, one of the bouncers, and Asher, a dominant who worked here, to come in and help them. Vic wondered if they'd been watching on camera, but he didn't think they'd come in looking so eager if they had.

But now they almost immediately appeared to sense the tension in the room. Vic's distress in and of itself was probably the most palpable—his instinct was to grab Cade and get him out of there.

Tegan just looked sick. And angry.

The requested scene was spelled out on Cade's Fantasy Week card, along with his limits. It wasn't elaborate, but it involved a level of careful planning, as non-consent scenes always did. Cade's background for the fantasy was simple enough: he was unable to pay a debt and was forced to trade himself as payment to four men for a night, and he wanted to be fucked until his orgasms stopped. As fantasies went, it wasn't an uncommon one.

Vic had been looped in because Tegan knew he liked the

rougher scenes. And Vic? Liked Tegan, if his dick's constant response to the man was any indication.

Colin let his gaze drop over Cade and murmured, "I saw him come in. He seemed eager enough."

Asher added, "He's compliant."

"They're here for you, Cade, waiting to collect. Look at them," Tegan instructed.

Cade's eyes remained closed. Vic reached down and grabbed hold of Cade's hair again to force his gaze upward. "Open your eyes, baby."

And finally, Cade obeyed, his gaze taking in Vic before shifting to Tegan when he began to speak.

"You're going to take all four of us, one right after the other. We're going to ride you, have our way with you, until you come...until you stop coming. That's tonight's goal." He and Tegan waited for something—anything—to flare in Cade's eyes, but they were flat and lifeless. His body remained in a perfect pose, his legs spread to the men behind him.

Normally, by now, Cade should be moaning, hard and wanting this. Teasing the men into taking him. Into it, the way he'd been at first. Because fuck, he'd most definitely been, and Vic had hoped his change of attitude had been nerves. But Cade was still throwing up red flags a mile wide around his perimeter.

Vic shook his head at Tegan.

"Just do it, okay? I'm ready to be fucked. Give me a dick to suck." Cade's eyes blazed, hate, anger, and pain flashing through them at a rapid pace until his expression settled on haunted. He was obviously white-knuckling his way through, and that wasn't what Fantasy Night, or anything in this club, was about.

"It's not happening." Tegan jerked his head, motioning for Colin and Asher to leave. Vic released his grip on Cade's hair, and Cade turned around when he heard the door close. "This is over."

Cade got to his feet and was in Tegan's face, a bold, swift move that Vic would've expected coming from the former Army Ranger. "You sent them away. You can't do that—you can't make the decision to cancel this. I have a card. I signed the papers. And I consented."

"And I'm an owner of this place and I'm shutting this down. It also said that on the paper you signed."

Cade closed his eyes, then opened them, his eyes snapping fire before the anger suddenly extinguished as he muttered, "I just need to find someone else who'll follow through." He glanced at Vic. "Help me—find three other guys."

"I'm an owner too," Vic told him and something odd flashed behind Cade's eyes. Disappointment, but not just because Vic said no, but also a new wariness.

He took a step away from them, and Vic fought the urge to grab and shake him. "I don't understand—it's obvious you've stopped enjoying this, and that's okay. Tell me how to help you."

"It's not okay and I'm not meant to goddamned enjoy this," Cade shot back.

"Then you're in the wrong club," Vic ground out.

Cade dropped his head like the finality of this news could break him. His cheeks flushed when he realized he was still naked in front of them, and he began to dress. When he was done and halfway out the door, he told them, "I'm going to go find the right one."

Before they could stop him, he was gone, disappearing into the crowds of the club like a puff of smoke.

CHAPTER 3

TEGAN KNEW there was a goddamned good reason he hadn't wanted any part of this goddamned fantasy. Oz had decided he needed an attitude adjustment or some shit like that, and so he'd added Tegan to a card that included Vic, of all goddamned people. The FNG (the fucking new guy), the brother of their dead teammate, and an all-around general asshole.

"I figured you'd be able to relate," Oz had deadpanned.

"Go fuck yourself, Oz!" he called now. "How's this for relating?"

Now, as he'd been doing for the past month, Vic leveled him with a gaze. Perceptive asshole acted like he could see right through him.

He doesn't know shit. Doesn't know you've been jacking off thinking about him.

But hell, after touching him tonight when they'd been standing around Cade...Vic looked at him like he knew. "We should go after him."

"He's not our problem. Let him go," Tegan insisted.

Vic shook his head. "You heard him—he's going to find someone on the strip to fuck him."

It had been so goddamned intense, but the second Cade had fought it, seemed scared, Tegan's need had turned into something different, and he'd gone from protective to angry. Now, standing here with Vic, Tegan's need ramped up again, the way it always did when they were in each other's presence.

They'd been circling each other for years like lions who hadn't decided if they could actually be friends or if they needed to kill each other. "So let him go. Getting fucked is why people come to the strip." Tegan sounded irritable, even to his own ears, and he couldn't figure out why the hell this thing with Cade had him all wound up.

"You're a cold motherfucker," Vic muttered. "But you weren't when you watched me lick his come from my fingers."

Tegan's dick throbbed, tight against his jeans. "So?"

"So you need to get laid, and soon."

"You gonna be the one to do it?"

Vic's eyes flashed. "If you were done playing games, I'd bury my face in your ass right here and you'd shoot, and you'd love every second of it."

Fuck me. His words, that accent, like drags of glorious nails raking his spine.

Vic leaned in to kiss him, the way he'd kissed Cade, an all-encompassing, curl-your-toes-and-make-your-dick-impossibly-hard kiss.

"You still taste like his come."

"Now you do too," Vic murmured. "Want more?"

"From you or from him?"

Vic's smile was lazy. "So you do want to find him."

"One of you needs to, so we can ask him why someone tried to hack our feed to watch him," Oz said from behind them.

Well, shit. That changed everything.

"Fuck you for not securing this place." Vic's anger was sudden, swift, and aimed directly at Tegan. He pushed forward off the wall toward Tegan, but he pinned Vic back with a palm across his throat, knowing the only reason he'd gotten the drop on him was sheer surprise, coupled with Vic's anger.

Anger always got you fucked over in the end.

"Read the card, Vic. That's all we can do. We took our usual precautions," Oz told him, seemingly unperturbed at the impending death match. He'd handled Vic well from the second the man stepped into their building, if not their lives. "If you're going to kill each other, do it quickly, please."

Tegan stared at Vic, his body reacting to the proximity of the man, the way it had been for the past month and goddammit, this was the most inappropriate timing. He tried to turn it around by saying, "We'll get him back and figure it out."

Vic nodded and Tegan stroked his palm down Vic's neck, feeling the electricity tingle between them. When he turned back toward Oz, Oz simply rolled his eyes at the obvious *fuck or fight* theme running between them.

Vic remained against the wall, but he shifted when Tegan glanced between his legs. His countenance changed, and he put his hands up in the air, palms out, as if to apologize. Every time he looked Tegan in the eyes was like a physical stroke to his cock.

Isn't that why Oz picked him to help you with this fantasy?

He reluctantly moved farther away from Vic, who shot him a this-isn't-over-yet look and yeah, it definitely wasn't. Vic pushed past him, hitting Tegan's shoulder with his purposely, all that strength coursing through him.

"I'll ask Colin to put out feelers," Vic called over his shoulder as he walked out of the room.

"Yeah, you do that," Tegan muttered and headed to watch the crowds by the bar from behind the two-way mirror in the hall. He watched Vic talk to Colin, saw Josie greeting customers. Business as usual, except it seemed like everything was changing. Again.

"Didn't mean to disturb your wank session," Oz said.

"Did you see my dick out?" Tegan asked as he followed him into the aptly named war room.

Oz merely smiled before inquiring, "Are you two going to fuck and get it over with or what? Asking for several friends... because I'm not the only one who noticed."

"Maybe," Tegan admitted, and that apparently satisfied Oz enough for him to refocus on the other business at hand.

"I dug a little deeper into Cade when I found the hack in the feed. I knew he'd been an Army Ranger. He's been out for two years."

That was why Oz had greeted him instead of Josie—Oz handled all the military men who came through this place, and for good reason. Many of them had agendas, whether they were looking for work or had a beef against them...and some of them were simply looking for a fight.

Cade didn't fit any of those slots. "He was nervous, but

into it. And then a wall came down when he caught sight of the cameras," Tegan murmured.

"He's got juvie records that are sealed. Recently, he's been making money cage fighting and working at fight club—the legal fights and some underground ones through them too. Beyond that, he's clean."

"Right—clean *and* hacking into our systems," Vic said, taking his life into his hands by criticizing Oz's tech skills and dammit, Tegan hadn't even heard him come in.

Judging by the look on Oz's face, he hadn't either. "We don't know if he's the one doing the hacking. Even so, the only hack that occurred was in Room Four—and our reservation schedule, which only contains first names. He's not getting anything off our main systems. The feeds for the club are very different than the mainframes that house our personal information and the intel on our missions," he explained.

"That underground fighting ring has mob ties," Vic added.

"Did anyone stop to think that it's Cade doing the hacking—for whatever reason—and we're about to bring him back into our private space, just to make sure he's okay? Because I definitely did," Tegan said loudly, to no one in particular.

"Noted," Oz told him.

"To that end, Colin's got a lead on Cade," Vic added. "If we're doing this, now's the time."

CHAPTER 4

NORMALLY, Cade would head to the Underground to get his fix, but The WHIP was more anonymous and therefore the best place to do his duty. Then he'd figure out how to put an end to this shit.

He'd forgotten to steal back the Fantasy Week card, and so he'd been faced with the humiliating task of explaining, step by step, exactly what kind of BDSM experience he'd wanted to book for the night once he got to The WHIP. To make matters worse, he'd had to pay for it and ask if they would record it for him.

He figured Courier would probably love the extra layer of humiliation, the way Cade had behaved like a good soldier.

Luckily, he'd managed to get a private room rather than a public space. He'd been stripped roughly, forced onto his hands and knees by the four men who surrounded him.

He'd been actively trying to block out their words from the beginning, but he'd been unable to. Their taunts ranged from, *"He definitely wants this"* as they fingered his ass to

"He wants all our cocks inside of him tonight—I'm betting a slut like this can take us two at a time."

He immediately tensed. That wasn't what he'd asked for, but beggars couldn't be choosers.

You could still get up and leave.

But the end result would still be hurting Theo irreparably. And so, he stayed, felt one of the men lining up behind him with a hand on his shoulder and a cock rubbing between his ass cheeks before he heard, "Come on in, Tegan. There's enough of him to go around."

Tegan? Cade looked up and met Vic's gaze first, and then Tegan's, before he looked away quickly as humiliation burned fresh and hot through him.

The man behind him didn't pull away but didn't enter him, and Cade was forced to remain in position, even as Tegan bent down and put his hand on Cade's head gently. "There you are, boy," he said to Cade before addressing the other men. "I see you found our sub."

"*Your* sub? He's already bought and paid for," the man behind him said.

Cade fought the urge to hyperventilate as he saw Tegan pull a now-familiar card from his pocket. "He was at Crave's Fantasy Night. Still is. Escaping from me and coming here is part of the fantasy—and it needed to feel realistic to him. I have to rescue him from a situation like this one...and bring him back with me."

The men looked doubtful, and Cade's expression was stony.

"It's been cleared with Jai," Tegan added. "He's being refunded as well. We needed you guys to be part of the fantasy."

The men grumbled a little but most of them laughed—and promised payback and cockblocks and blue balls.

"Hey, if you want to be punished even more, you know where to find us," one of the men said. "We could even come back with you to Crave and help finish him off. We've already got the beginning on video."

That was the last thing Cade heard before he saw Vic go full metal jacket on the man who held the camera, and all hell broke loose.

Vic ignored Tegan's yells and grabbed the camera—and the man attached to it—and slammed both to the floor for good measure. He blocked another guy who rushed him with a fist to the solar plexus, and pushed him away before erasing the video of Cade. He also ripped out the memory card, crushing it beneath his heel before pocketing the pieces, ignoring the men who continued to curse him and the rush of the bouncers who hovered at the door.

Tegan helped by taking on a couple of the men and putting them down on the ground.

In the melee, Cade had gotten up off the floor, managed to yank on his jeans, and move to the corner of the room. He met Vic's stare, betrayal written on his face.

What the hell did this guy want from him?

And why do you care?

He'd taken part in one other fantasy that week, but it'd been more about Asher than him and *nothing* like this. His reaction to other men touching Cade was primal, and he was ready to rip the entire fucking room apart for a boy who was staring at him insolently, begging to be spanked.

Now Jai was there, telling them all to "Calm the fuck down," and informing Tegan that he owed him. Tegan was grabbing Cade's gear while Vic gritted his teeth and manhandled Cade outside, shirtless and barefoot.

There was a fierce, raw energy emanating from the younger man. Vic studied him under the fluorescent lighting, committing him to memory quickly, indelibly, noting the way his hazel eyes stood out against his golden skin, the way his dark-blond hair was long enough to fall into his face and curl around his ears. He was lean and strong, and he smelled like sunshine and hope, two things Vic barely recognized anymore, which was why he'd latched on to them immediately. Now, his need was even fiercer, and it was beyond desire—it was protective. And it threatened to overthrow anything in his path.

As soon as they hit the open air, Cade attempted to bolt just like Vic assumed he would—no shirt, no shoes, no problem. He didn't count on Vic being faster than he'd anticipated, and Vic was glad about that because being underestimated made for the best of surprises.

He grabbed Cade's biceps and jerked him into the alleyway two stores down from The WHIP. He pinned Cade to the brick wall with a palm on his chest.

"What the fuck do you think you're doing?" Cade snarled. "I'm not going anywhere with you."

"Cut it out—unless you want them to let anyone who pays enough come in to fuck you. Because that's what they'd do—they won't limit it to what you ask for. They let people watch."

Cade still looked furious and not sure if he should believe Vic, but just then, Tegan's truck pulled into the mouth of the alley. Vic ignored Cade's protests and instead strong-armed him into the back seat, which wasn't easy since Cade fought the entire time.

"That went well," Tegan called back to him. Cade stared mutinously between both men, obviously plotting his next escape move.

"We've got a big problem," Vic told Cade as Tegan drove away—which was good because it would be hard for Cade to jump out of a moving car.

Hard, but not impossible, so Vic didn't take his eyes off him.

"There's no '*we*' in this situation. Just let me go. None of this is your concern."

"It's a big fucking concern when someone hacks our club feeds." Vic's palm pressed his throat even as Cade shook his head. "So you need to start talking. What's your game? Because I'll get my answer—I always do."

"Prepare to be disappointed." Cade's voice was hoarse, and a twinge of arousal shimmered through him at Cade's baiting.

Fuck or fight was Vic's calling card, and if he could combine the two, so much the better. The energy in this truck alone was enough to make his dick hard. Again.

He'd need to take the edge off soon, or else he'd end up ripping something—or someone—apart. Instead, he kept his palm to Cade's throat, feeling the man's pulse beat rapidly against his skin until Tegan pulled into the lot and called Oz, telling him, "We're bringing him in."

As soon as he heard that, Cade went nuts, attempting to

kick out the windows of the truck. Vic had no choice but to knock him out in order to get him inside without attracting attention, using a quick pressure point spot on Cade's neck to do so. Then he slung Cade over his shoulder in a fireman's hold and walked him through the club's back door.

"This is *not* good," Oz murmured as Vic strolled by him on his way up the stairs.

" '*Take part in the fantasy, Teegs. It'll do you some good, Teegs,*' " Tegan began mimicking Oz's earlier words. "Never listening to you again."

Oz rolled his eyes. "You say that *every* time."

"This time I mean it," Tegan shot back.

Vic listened to them bickering as he went into one of their common living areas that doubled as a guest apartment, where he deposited Cade into a chair and zip-tied his wrists, then levered them up over his head with a rope he'd pulled over the high beam.

"And if that doesn't keep him in place, what's next?" Tegan asked.

"I'm thinking a taser," Vic said evenly.

"Well, now we've kidnapped him." Oz sounded halfway between pissed and exasperated.

"He hacked us," Tegan pointed out.

"Allegedly," Oz added.

"And we *allegedly* kidnapped him," Vic added, looking pleased with himself.

"I think he's in trouble," Oz stated.

"I think he *is* trouble," Tegan corrected.

Vic stared at Cade's sleeping form. "Well then, he's certainly in the right place, now isn't he?"

Cade woke and quickly realized he was immobilized in a seated position, his arms pulled above his head, wrists zip-tied together and threaded with a rope that hung over one of the ceiling beams. He was uncomfortable all around, and his head ached like a bitch.

Bastard had knocked him out.

He blinked a few times, and as his vision began to clear, Cade saw the bastard in question, sitting across the room on a bed, staring back at him. He swept the rest of the room and clocked Tegan leaning against a countertop in the open plan loft area.

He swallowed hard, his throat dry, and Vic was slowly walking over to him, opening a bottle of water. He put his hand on Cade's chin and fed him some of the liquid. Cade wanted to spit it out, in case it was drugged, but *fuck*...he was so thirsty, he needed it.

"Why am I here?" he managed finally.

"To stop you from doing something stupid," Tegan told him.

"I thought I did that when I left this club," Cade shot back.

"I definitely didn't hit him hard enough," Vic said.

"You didn't hit me, asshole—you used pressure points. Didn't even have the guts for a good punch." Cade glared at him and tugged at his wrists...and then he glanced up, pushed his wrists outward, and broke the zip tie.

As if he'd seen it coming, Vic was already on him, grabbing his arms and pinning them down by his sides as he wrestled Cade to his belly so he couldn't punch anyone. Tegan was behind him with the handcuffs. Once they'd immobilized his hands yet again, Vic pulled him up and put him back into the chair and stood close enough to stop him from doing anything else stupid.

"Listen, you need to talk to us. We might be the only ones who can help you." Vic leaned in and for the first time, Cade noticed the scars on the left side of Vic's face bore evidence of a semi-recent run-in with a wicked knife...and down the side of his neck and shoulder, more evidence of a fight gone bad.

Then again, he was still standing here, so Cade guessed that Vic won the battle, if not the war. "Christ, if you're help, I'd hate to see my enemies."

"You could think of us as both." Vic smiled. "And I'm offering that punch you mentioned, anytime now."

"Go for it," Cade goaded.

Because you want him to touch you, you stupid asshole. And Vic probably knew it, too.

"Cade, come on now—you need to let us help you," Tegan reasoned and he moved closer. Too close. Cade felt the heat radiating off his body, and he didn't need a goddamned white-horse rescue.

"Help? You're in on it," Cade told them, his voice sounding raw and angry to his own ears. "And I don't take fucking orders from you."

"So who do you take orders from?" Vic demanded. "Because you didn't seem to mind it earlier."

Cade stared between the two men surrounding him, realizing that, even if he took them out, there was still Oz...and others beyond him that he'd have to get through.

He sagged under the realization of how he'd fucked up, and Vic caught him before he fell off the goddamned chair, lowering him to the floor. He was aware of both Vic and Tegan kneeling around him, tending to him, telling him to "Breathe, dammit."

Finally, propped by the wall behind him and hemmed in, he calmed. After several minutes, he managed, "I didn't hack into your feed."

"Who did?"

"I don't know," Cade shot back.

"*Bullshit* he doesn't know," Tegan muttered.

"You gonna waterboard it out of him?" Oz asked.

Vic snapped his fingers. "Thanks for the suggestion."

"Look," Cade started tiredly, "it's just some asshole I fucked a couple of times. He's got some videos of us, and he said he'd delete them if I came here and did this."

Tegan leaned in. "Nope. Try again."

"It's all I've got."

"You don't agree to a fantasy you didn't choose and fight that hard to make it happen unless the fallout's going to be bad," Tegan informed him.

"Fine. I shared a little too much with him."

"That's closer, but it's still not right," Tegan said.

Cade sighed. "It wasn't my idea—the fantasy thing."

"No shit?" Vic deadpanned.

"Joining in, or the fantasy itself?" Tegan asked.

"Neither," he admitted. "That guy—who has the video of me—submitted it on my behalf. I didn't know about it until I got the invite."

"But you came anyway." Tegan's voice was calm and made Cade want to spill his secrets. Not doing so would just force these men to chase him harder—like predators to prey... and the last thing he wanted to do was make them suspicious.

The last thing he wanted to do was tell them his secrets too. "Yeah, I came anyway."

"Because you didn't have a choice?" Tegan asked.

Cade's voice sounded low and angry to his own ears. "I had a choice. And I made it." He felt the anger run hot through him. "You agreed to let him watch the feed. You agreed to let him record it." He shifted and went for his back pocket, and Vic's hand shot out and grabbed his wrist. "I'm just getting my phone."

"I'll get it," Vic told him. Cade nodded and let Vic move his hands away so Vic could get his into Cade's pocket and pull out his phone. Then he got Vic to unlock the screen, find the original message, and play it on speaker for them.

"*Oh, and Cade? Don't even think about not going. I've set it up to watch the scene in real time, with the help of the men who own the club. They were very accommodating, and they promised to send me a recording as well, so I can experience it over and over again.*"

Both men's expressions hardened, and the tension in the room was palpable. They were pissed, but not at him. The tide had turned, as evidenced by Vic unlocking his wrists from the handcuffs. Now, he just had to keep them on his side and not mention Theo...and then he'd figure out a way out of all of it.

Vic stood and walked away, visibly upset before doubling back, getting in Cade's face to demand, "Do you know what we would've done to you tonight...against your fucking will? What those guys at The WHIP were prepared to do?"

Cade's gut clenched. He hadn't considered the position he'd put all these men in, his endgame his only concern. "I didn't..." But he stopped because he'd planned on making these men pay—at least the men from Crave—once he was done. "I'm sorry."

"That's not good enough," Tegan told him.

"I've sold myself before, so fuck you and your lecture about *Do I have any idea what I was getting myself into*. Fuck yes, I knew exactly what I was walking into. I know how to close my eyes and pretend." Cade jumped up and slammed Vic with his fists against his chest.

"That's not a way to live." Vic's hands closed around Cade's wrists. "You've been taking care of yourself for a long time," he said, like some kind of fucking soothsayer, even as Cade struggled in his grasp. "But whatever situation you're in now? You're not getting out of without help."

"Maybe I don't know any other way," he ground out. The things he'd seen growing up had been beyond the pale. The military had been a way out, with a controlled violence he'd learned to appreciate, if not completely embrace. Fighting on the regular helped ease the urges inside of him, and it allowed him to no longer sell himself for money.

Until you slept with the wrong guy.

"What does this guy have on you?" Tegan asked him.

"Does it matter?" Cade knew he was being purposefully difficult, but these men couldn't help him...and even though he was pretty sure they weren't helping Courier, hell, he couldn't be sure of anything. There was no way he was mentioning Theo.

"Was it part of the fantasy?" Tegan persisted. "Because we don't know the guy who left you this message. The fantasy came in couched as a favor to one of our friends. We checked with him—he had no clue about it. We have cameras in the room for safety reasons only, but nothing is recorded. Nothing. They're spot-checked only."

Cade wanted to believe them, and hell, maybe he did, but what did it change? "I want to go home, okay? I won't bring any trouble to Crave. I didn't hack into your feed. I won't come back."

"Good. Don't." Tegan's tone was gruff, and Vic released his wrists and shook his head like that wasn't the outcome he'd been looking for.

Cade shoved his disappointment down deep at the withdrawal of contact—like he did every other disappointment in his life—steadied himself, and walked out the door.

CHAPTER 5

"THAT WENT WELL," Oz said after Cade left. "Any other bright ideas, you two?"

"You said to find him," Tegan pointed out.

Oz sighed. "Fucking impossible."

Vic shrugged. "I'll watch him—make sure he gets home all right."

Oz walked over and put a hand on his shoulder. "Thanks, Vic. We'll figure this out."

Tegan watched Vic walk out of the room and head down the stairs. "Maybe we need to rethink Fantasy Week."

"Yeah, you tell Axel that." Oz handed him the file he'd been holding since they'd come in with Cade.

"Do I want to see this?"

"No, but you have to. So does Vic, when he gets back." Oz looked troubled. And tired. He was the smallest out of them, which wasn't saying much, considering they ran anywhere from six foot five and below. Oz was just shy of six feet, on the thinner side, but no less deadly. He'd been a former comms director in the Air Force, and then he'd moved into criminal investigation before landing here, with Tegan.

They'd met on a mission nearly ten years ago, when Oz's skills had saved Tegan and his squad from certain death by getting them air support—and it had been something of a miracle. Oz had been formally reprimanded, and it tanked his career...and he hadn't cared a goddamned bit.

Tegan stared at the innocuous blue folder. "I don't want to read this."

"I know."

Tegan sat heavily in the chair across from his friend and opened the file. The first thing he saw were ER reports, and memories flooded back to him. He shut it without actually reading. *Not yet. Don't go there yet.*

"I know you're thinking about just letting Cade figure this out on his own, but we were involved the second you and Vic touched him." With that, Oz slipped out.

Tegan didn't bother to ask where he was going. Oz ran the club and the business tirelessly. But tonight, he didn't need to do that alone—Tegan saw the haunted look in his friend's eyes earlier, and Oz hadn't bothered to hide it. He followed Oz into the war room, watched him finish his nightly routine of checking on the feeds before calling down to Colin, Asher, and Josie to ask if they were good to lock up. They stayed open later than normal during Fantasy Week, and half the time, the club closed as the sun began to rise.

He'd bought Crave from his friend Damon—they'd been in the military together, and when Damon gave the club up eight years ago, he'd grabbed the building with the intention of making the space purely a landing place for his new business venture, Gray Ops, Inc. They were mercenaries, pure and simple, and they chose their jobs based on their individual skill sets. At one time, he'd had twenty or more men in play in different parts of the globe...and they were all men who'd served with him, Oz, Axel, Trevor, and Brian. Brian had been Vic's twin brother, also in the SAS when Tegan had been with the SEALs, and during their military careers, they'd worked together on several joint missions. He'd been one of the original owners and had worked and played here until his death five months earlier, gunned down on a job senselessly. Caught in the crossfire.

The loss of one of their core triad had been like losing their center. Brian had been a combination father / priest / commander / shrink to all the men who worked for Gray Ops. And well before his death, they'd begun transitioning Gray Ops into something different. Both Brian and Tegan had started noticing that more and more of their friends needed a safe spot to land post-military—or even a place to lay low while they found a way to get them out of their service. Tegan had also realized he needed less of the merc work himself, but Brian continued doing it, because to him, it was like breathing.

Tegan understood men coming out of the military had a particular skill set that wasn't always appreciated in the civilian world, and that those skills could command a high price for those who craved danger and weren't picky about their life expectancy. Even so, his company's philosophy had always been more about the well-being of their talent, and to that end, they'd decided to deal more with domestic matters, although they'd take on international jobs if they felt the mission was in their wheelhouse.

To that end, he and the other owners decided to buy the

warehouse next door and connected it to the upper floors of the club that served as apartments and meeting rooms and war rooms, but the general club area remained similar to when Damon and Law had run it. It was still BDSM themed, but it was also a bar where pickups for even the most vanilla of sex could happen. But what Crave had become most known for—thanks to a moment of sheer brilliance from Axel —was Fantasy Week.

Fucking Fantasy Week. He swore he could hear Brian's laughter echoing in his ears.

Now, he caught sight of Casey on the monitors as he walked into the club. He was the resident night owl, and he'd man the video feeds until morning and facilitate with closing, along with Colin and several other senior staff. He and the others were only a call button away.

"I'm tired, Teegs," Oz finally admitted, and he wasn't just talking about general lack of sleep.

"Your head again?"

Oz rubbed his eyes. "Yeah."

Without Brian around to tell him to get the hell off the computer, Oz often lost himself in the war room and work in general, for hours on end. It was easier than thinking about Brian.

"Going to see a doc about that?"

"So he can tell me I've got headaches?" Oz stood and Tegan got him to his room, which was one floor up. Damon's old apartment. Oz stripped down to boxer briefs and climbed into bed as Tegan brought him ice packs.

"You don't have to stay."

"You're not the boss of me."

Oz snorted. "Keep telling yourself that. By the way, Jai's taken care of—I gave him a fantasy with Taz."

"That's something I never want to think about."

"I always feel the need to share my misery with you."

Tegan rubbed his friend's back. "Let it out, Oz."

"Ah, fuck, Teegs. I'm so goddamned tired of letting it out. It doesn't help shit."

"Yeah, it does."

It started as a slow rumble, the way it always did. Oz was so deep in mourning Brian, who'd been his lover for six years, that he didn't know where to begin, and all the men willingly took turns comforting. Because Oz would fucking die for any of them.

Tegan worried that his friend was dying of a broken heart, and he had no real way to help, except letting him cry and wiping his tears. Oz sobbed into his pillow.

Part of this was brought on because of Cade's background —Tegan knew that Oz had read through each and every piece of intel in those files, no matter how bad it was.

"Tell me about you and Vic," Oz managed finally when he caught his breath.

Tegan wiped the tears from Oz's cheek. "Nothing to tell."

"Right. Not what I saw tonight. It's been years of you two eye-fucking. You even eye-fuck over the phone," Oz grumbled, his voice thick with tears. "Just go stick your dick in him."

"You watched us with Cade, didn't you?"

"Couldn't help it—it was fucking hot. And I'm not getting any."

Tegan snorted. "Fine, you can live vicariously through me."

"You keep getting cock-blocked. Sure, it's funny but frustrating as hell for me."

"For you?" Tegan shook his head but Oz's response? A light snore. Tegan gently touched his friend's head and pulled the covers up. "Sleep well, Oz. Sleep well."

Cade grabbed his truck from the parking lot behind The WHIP without incident, although he couldn't shake the feeling that someone was following him. If anything, it was probably Vic or Tegan.

Or maybe that's who you want it to be.

His phone rang as he drove toward his house. He didn't bother answering, mainly because he saw the unmarked police car sitting at the curb, waiting.

He listened to Courier's message when he pulled into the driveway.

"You didn't follow your end of the bargain. There are consequences to every act, Cade. You're going to find out what yours are very soon."

"Motherfucker." He shoved the phone into his pocket, opened the truck door, and kept his hands where the officer could see them as he approached his house.

"Cade O'Shea?" The officer was out of his car, meeting him halfway up the walk.

Cade glanced at the tall man in the suit and tie. "Yes, sir."

"Detective Rourke."

Great. Maybe they could bond over good Irish names. "How can I help you, Detective?"

Be polite. Don't give the authorities any reason to do

anything more than they need to. He'd learned early that being a smartass rarely got you as far as a pleasant "sir" or "ma'am."

Rourke was tall, maybe six foot four, and well-built, with blond hair falling over his eye. He was good-looking and he held himself with the awareness of someone who utilized his body like a weapon and kept it in shape as such. "Cade, I've got a few questions. Can I come in?"

"Sure." He pointed to his pocket. "Just grabbing my keys."

"Do you have any weapons?"

"On me? A knife. Inside—my two weapons are registered." He pointed to his pocket where the knife was, and Rourke closed in and pulled it out. He was pretty sure Rourke gave him a once-over that had nothing to do with his badge.

"I'm going to hold on to this while we talk, okay?" Rourke asked.

"Fine with me." Cade headed to the front door, and Rourke fell in step behind him. The house was quiet—too much so without Theo and Sway here. Cade hadn't been out very long, and he didn't miss the military nearly as much as he did spending time with those two.

"You're former Army, right?"

Bonding over military service—right out of the playbook. Cade went with simple. "Rangers."

"Marines."

When Rourke didn't immediately rattle off a unit, Cade suspected a special forces designation. "It's hard to leave the military behind."

"My knee made the decision for me." Rourke followed

him to the back of the house and into the kitchen and sat at the table. "You live alone?"

"I've got a couple of roommates. They're still in the military—and they're currently deployed."

Rourke nodded and make a few notes on the pad he'd pulled out of his jacket. "You didn't ask why I was here."

"I work over at the fight club. I see the police there nightly," he said honestly.

Outwardly, Rourke seemed to accept the bullshit. "I'm not here about the fight club. I've got some questions about a man named Donald Dolentz."

Theo's stepdad. Cade couched his surprise easily and shrugged. "Okay, but I'm not sure how much I'll be able to help."

"Last time you saw him?"

Cade made his best thinking face. "Christ, it was years ago. Before I went into the Army. I was seventeen at the time."

Rourke didn't ask about Theo, and Cade wasn't volunteering shit, but the fact that, after all these years, someone was looking for Dolentz? Meant that Courier was following through on his threat.

Yeah, Cade knew how to follow through on threats too.

"You're not going to ask why I'm checking up on Dolentz?"

"I've learned it's best not to ask questions about things that don't concern me."

"But Dolentz is your roommate's stepfather, correct?"

"Yes."

"And he never mentioned being concerned about Dolentz's disappearance?"

"No."

Rourke studied him for a long moment, then stood and put Cade's knife on the table between them, along with his card. "If you think of anything else, give me a call." Cade frowned because Rourke was looking at him not so much as a suspect, but... "You can use it for personal reasons, too. I've watched you fight, Cade. It's definitely why some of the officers go to the club."

As Rourke slid the card toward him, Cade's cheeks heated. "Okay, sure."

Rourke chuckled. "Stay out of trouble."

"Always trying."

"Try harder," he advised.

CHAPTER 6

AN HOUR LATER, Tegan slid out of Oz's bed gingerly, padded out of his apartment, and found Vic sitting on the floor in the hallway.

"Everything okay?" he asked, keeping his voice low and shutting the door halfway behind him.

Vic rose. "Yeah. I was just checking. I heard..." He motioned toward Oz's door. "I fucking hate feeling helpless. Too much of it in one night. I didn't mean to intrude."

"You didn't. You're not." Tegan wasn't surprised that Vic was worried about Oz. From the first, Oz hadn't minded Vic's questions, didn't bristle the way Trevor and Axel—and Tegan himself—had when Vic asked them. They'd known he'd inherit Brian's share of Gray Ops and its various holdings. They'd offered to buy Vic out, told him he could also remain a silent partner...but he'd been interested in retaining his brother's share of the club and working for the merc business as well.

Vic had been newly retired from the SAS, which turned out to be a nice way of saying that he'd been branded a traitor by his team and dishonorably discharged—after surviving a brutal capture and beating—and was looking for a way to fill that void. At the time they hadn't realized the extent of what he'd been through on that final mission, how badly he'd needed this place and his brother's friends.

Hadn't realized that Vic's best friend and lover of ten years had been the man who'd actually betrayed Vic and the rest of the team. A double blow that had cut Vic as deeply as the physical scars on his body and left him claustrophobic and unwilling to trust most everyone.

Axel and Trevor were naturally suspicious of strangers, even those who were blood relations of their friends, and they hadn't been happy bringing Vic in straight away...but they'd settled in with him quickly. More quickly than Tegan had, and that annoyed him to no end.

Now, Tegan motioned for Vic to follow him down the hall, to where his apartment was, so they didn't disturb Oz. "Oz pulled some intel on Cade you need to see."

Vic took the file but didn't open it, just sank down on Tegan's couch instead. "There was a detective waiting to question Cade. Went inside, stayed for about fifteen minutes. Got a plate number."

Tegan pulled out his phone. "And I've got someone who can get us information about that." He sent the text and watched Vic as he began to look over the files. "I think it's time for Cade to tell us what he's up against."

Vic looked up, his eyes troubled, and he was barely a quarter of the way through Cade's past. "That's not going to happen without some...pressure."

"Good thing we know how and when to apply it."

Cade watched Rourke's lanky body stride out the door, shutting it behind him. He listened through the open kitchen window and didn't move until he heard Rourke's car drive away and even then, it was reluctantly. He'd lived a fucking thousand days over the past hours, and it was nearly four in the morning.

Rourke hadn't seemed that concerned about Dolentz, but Courier wasn't going to give up that easily. Cade would see Rourke again, and the next time he might not be all that nice.

He stood, his muscles sore from being shoved around tonight. He swore he could still feel Vic's hands around his wrists like a goddamned brand, could hear Tegan's murmurs in his ear.

It'll fade. It wasn't real.

He stripped as he walked toward his bedroom. But before he slept, he'd check in with Theo. They'd text first, and then they'd make contact by SAT phone since it was protected—secured. Theo made sure of that.

Because sometimes, what the military didn't know wouldn't hurt them. And Cade would die before he hurt his brother. Because that's what Theo was, even if it wasn't by blood. What they had was stronger.

After ten minutes, Theo called in. Cade settled into bed, listening to Theo's voice telling him that everything was just fine where he was.

"A little warm, though."

Cade snorted. "I'd imagine so."

Tonight, Theo had time. There was noise in the background, which probably meant Theo was on a military base, not out in the jungles. "You sound not okay."

"Just tired."

"Uh-huh." Theo paused. "I'm here, Cade. Talk."

"Sometimes...I just feel like I'm so fucked up," he finally admitted, not sure of how else to put it.

"Ah, Cade...you're not any more fucked up than anyone else. We've all got our shit. You handle yours well. You do good things, so you gotta just remember that," Theo told him. "You saved my goddamned life, more times than I can count."

"Yeah, well, ditto." His throat was too tight to say anything else.

Theo chuckled, his voice husky and hoarse, the way it always seemed to get when he was far away, doing things Cade wasn't supposed to know about. Having been a Ranger, Cade knew. "You're such an asshole." And then he got serious. "Say the word and I'll come home."

He would too. Cade knew that, which was why he'd never ask. "I'm okay. Just a rough night."

"Care to elaborate?"

"Nope."

"Cade—"

"You've got to concentrate on you now. You deserve this, okay? You worked hard. And I'm fine—really."

Silence. "I still remember sleeping in Pat's truck during that storm. Before that, I always hated thunder...until you explained that it's the universe losing her temper when bad things happened, just like us."

"She's pissed for us. She's raining down hell because she knows it shouldn't have happened. She's crying for us. She wants someone to make it right, and they will."

Fuck, they'd been young and semi-innocent, and Theo had clung to those words all this time, even though he was no longer young and nowhere close to innocent. Hell, if Cade were honest with himself, he'd clung to the damned words too.

"And someone did make it right," he said now.

"You did," Theo reminded him.

"Fuck, you're getting maudlin. Get some sleep."

"I'm going to eat the Fruit Loops I found in my ruck."

"Wonder how those got there, in the middle of nowhere," Cade said. "Love you, man."

"Love you, Cade."

It was the way they always signed off their calls, because they were family. And family loved you no matter what.

He put the phone aside, satisfied that his brother was okay for the moment. That he'd done what he could...that hopefully Theo would be far enough away when the shit hit the fan, and Cade could hold the wolves at the door at bay.

And he would, by any means necessary.

Vic shoved the folder to the side. He didn't need to know about Cade's shitty childhood to want to help him. And even though it had been compiled with the best of intentions, he still hated the invasion of Cade's privacy. It was obvious after only knowing Cade a very short while that he had a lot of pride, wanted to fix things on his own, and Vic would rather learn all about the contents of that file from Cade himself.

He glanced at Tegan, the man's gaze boring through him

as usual. He hated the way Tegan watched him like he was still figuring out how much he could trust him.

Isn't that how you feel about trusting anyone but yourself?

His nightmares had been getting worse since he'd arrived, not better, as he'd hoped, all flashbacks to being kept in a coffinlike, underground cell for nearly two months, only pulled out to be tortured for intel he didn't have. Intel his oldest friend and lover—Danny—had already handed over to the enemy, long before the op even started. Now that man was dead, and Vic shouldered all the blame.

Oz had discovered him in the throes of one such nightmare a week into his residence. Ever since, whenever Vic had woken up from those dreams, Oz was sitting on the bed next to him, calming him. Since then, they'd often sleep in the same bed like puppies, bonding in their grief. Sometimes, they'd talk about what happened to Brian, and Vic would share bits and pieces of what had happened to him. Oz was a friend—a confidant.

On the other hand, Vic's attraction to Tegan had been intense and immediate, but he hadn't been able to bring himself to do anything about it...until tonight, when the need threatened to overwhelm him. Between that and Oz being unavailable, sleep wasn't happening.

Unless...

"You need something else?" Tegan asked.

You. "It's nothing. Never mind."

"Tell me."

Vic stared into Tegan's intense gaze and went for it. "I was going to stay with Oz tonight. For me, as much as him. I sleep with him sometimes—next to him," he clarified. "I need some rack time and..."

"The nightmares. You'd rather sleep next to someone. And I'm available."

Of course Tegan knew about them—because Trevor and Axel also knew...but they also came in to help him when Oz wasn't available. Tegan never had. "You don't have to do this."

"I know," Tegan assured him.

"You never have before."

"But I am now."

———

Anyone else might've been waiting for Vic to shake his head and retreat, but Tegan knew better, which was why he'd made the offer. Even if Vic didn't want Tegan to see what he considered a weakness—his nightmares—Vic never retreated from the difficult.

Instead, he took it as a dare, was already stripping off his shirt and jeans as he walked into Tegan's bedroom, then lost his boxer briefs. Tegan's gaze followed him, raking down the scars along the left side of his body, wondering how long it would take to trace all of them with his tongue.

"Picture would last longer," Vic called over his shoulder.

But it wouldn't quite capture the way Vic shifted and stretched like a big cat, his movements lazy to the untrained eye but to those in the know, nothing short of deadly.

The scars were less than a year old. Vic had been through hell...and he'd come back to discover his twin brother had been killed.

He and Brian hadn't looked anything alike—Vic was dark to Brian's light, and their personalities were different...but they'd been close. Maybe it was the twin thing, but Tegan remembered Brian not talking to Vic for weeks and then suddenly picking up the phone mid-conversation because of a feeling.

He'd never been wrong. Even when he'd been bleeding out, his last text to Oz had been "Something's wrong with Vic."

Oz, of course, made it his mission to discover what that was.

And here you are.

He followed Vic to the bed, leaving the main door to his apartment open so they could hear if Oz called. When Vic noticed, he nodded and then he climbed into Tegan's bed, where he watched Tegan strip down with a small smirk on his face.

He knew Vic was exhausted—mentally and physically—and even so, Tegan knew he'd find it hard to keep his hands off him.

He turned off the lights before crawling into bed. The shades were pulled, so it was still dark in there, even though soon people would be getting on with their morning routines.

Vic stared up at the ceiling, an arm behind his head. "It's going to happen."

"I know."

"Wouldn't mind Cade being here."

"Me neither," Tegan admitted.

"Fucking hot. So confusing."

Tegan laughed. "All of that, yes, Vic." Both Vic and Oz were goddamned delirious from lack of sleep, but hell, they spoke the truth. "Do you want to protect him or fuck him?"

"Both," Vic said honestly. "Is that wrong?"

"I'd give the same answer." With that, Tegan rolled toward Vic, who did the same and, with their bodies flush, he began to nuzzle Vic's neck and cheeks. The rough of their stubbled cheeks scraped against each other, which shot spikes of pleasure through him.

"Fuck yeah," Vic groaned as Tegan caught both their cocks. Neither of them was going to last long enough to fuck unless they took the edge off first, and Tegan stroked them fast and hard. Even though he knew that drawing out his pleasure made for better orgasms, right now his dick didn't give a damn about that.

Their gazes locked, neither man able to look away from the other. Both were panting as their orgasms hovered, and Tegan had no doubt they were both picturing Cade there with them.

"Fuck, s'good, Teegs," Vic murmured. "Don't stop."

"Don't worry." Tegan's balls drew up and his rhythm increased. Vic's back arched and he hissed, and it wasn't going to be much longer...

But the unwanted combo of throat clearing and a sharp rap on the door took care of that shit—and fast.

The door was still wide open, and even though the bedroom was behind the living area, Paulo could see straight through to the bed. Which Tegan realized when he let go of Vic to see who the hell was disturbing them.

Vic groaned and buried his head in the pillow, and Paulo laughed and Tegan cursed.

"I'll just wait on the couch. Take your time," Paulo told them.

"I hate him." Vic's voice was muffled by the pillow.

"I'd hate me too," was Paulo's response.

"He's got our intel—about Cade's detective visit," Tegan told Vic.

"Fuck." Vic sat up and ran his hands through his hair, his cock still hard. "Only because it's that. And we're finishing this."

"Not getting an argument from me." Vic used the back exit out of Tegan's apartment, naked, clothes in hand. Tegan stared after him for a long moment before pulling on sweats and a T-shirt and meeting Paulo in the living room. He was a retired detective who'd opened a PI business with his partners, Styx and Law, the latter of whom was one of the former owners of Crave.

Paulo smiled. "Sorry about my timing."

Tegan rolled his eyes in response. "I appreciate how fast you got back to me."

Paulo's blue eyes looked sharp, despite the late hour, and his light-blond hair looked like he'd been running his hands through it. "Law and Styx are both working—and Styx is away, so I had time on my hands."

"You didn't mention this to Law, did you?"

Paulo gave him an I'm-not-fucking-nuts look. "He'd be here right now if I had—and he wouldn't have waited for you guys to get dressed." He paused. "So...you and Vic? That's new."

"Very," Tegan agreed.

Paulo handed him a file. "Where does Cade fit in?"

Cock-blocking us at every turn. "That's what we're trying to figure out. Any insights?"

"Cade's been interviewed because of an anon tip about the murder of a friend's stepfather. Guy's been MIA for years. According to Rourke, the records for both Cade and his

friend, Theo, show abuse. I've got CPS files. Juvie records."
Paulo pointed to what he'd handed to Tegan. "Both are
sealed, so I never saw them."

Tegan didn't bother to mention that Oz had already
pulled some of them. "Person of interest?"

"Besides Cade? Theo, most likely." Paulo shook his head.
"But I'm betting Cade's got another name to give you."

Theo had to be the one Cade was protecting with his
silence. And yeah, the asshole who left Cade the message was
the name they needed—Tegan would make sure he and Vic
got that intel out of Cade, one way or another.

"One more thing. Theo? Delta Force." Paulo had more
than a few contacts in that world, including one of the men
he lived with, so Tegan knew it was the truth.

"Think Theo's in trouble?"

"I'm betting Cade's going to do everything in his power to
make sure that doesn't happen," Paulo speculated. "How'd
you get involved with this, anyway?"

Fucking Fantasy Week.

CHAPTER 7

TEGAN FOUND Vic in the gym and stood in the doorway, frankly appraising the big man as he worked out his frustrations.

Vic was shirtless. He'd pulled on a pair of loose-fitting shorts and he was hitting the bag relentlessly, no doubt trying to rid himself of the pent-up frustration that had reached the boiling point for both of them.

He watched the muscles bunch in Vic's back, the thin sheen of sweat making them stand out. His forearms were corded with muscle, and the tattoos on his biceps seemed to take on a life of their own under the thrown punches.

Tegan had sparred with Vic several times, and each time he'd reminded himself that it was a bad idea...and not because Vic was practically unbeatable. He was, but fighting with him brought him too far into Tegan's personal space, and he'd been unable to control his hard-on.

The only saving grace was that Vic had the same problem. Tonight, none of that was an issue—their cards were on the table.

"I told you we're finishing this," Vic called above the *thwack* of his punches.

"And I told you that you're not getting an argument from me."

Vic gave several one-two punches, followed by a solid roundhouse kick with his bare foot and then threw his gloves to the ground and stalked Tegan. "You dug into Cade's past, and that was bad enough. But then you had the cops do it too?"

"Paulo's not a cop anymore—and besides, the police are already involved." Tegan stared into Vic's eyes that were so dark they looked nearly obsidian tonight. His longer hair was half-pulled away from his face and he looked fierce. Intent. And angry. "You're really pissed."

"Just figuring that out?" Vic shoved him, both palms hard against his chest, and Tegan stumbled back.

He ripped his own T-shirt off and threw it to the side. "We're doing this?"

"We are." All the aggression Vic held was going to come down on Tegan, and fuck, he welcomed it.

"Did you really think Cade's early life would come complete with the white picket fence?" Tegan bounced on the balls of his feet. Vic smiled and then, like he was on fast-fucking-forward, his body was slamming against Tegan's, a bowling ball to Tegan's pin.

Tegan went down to the mat, Vic's heavy body half on him, pinning him. "I think that he's entitled to some privacy."

"You were pissed as fuck that someone hacked our system —for all we know, it's him." Tegan leveraged his lower body strength, bucked up, and wrapped his leg around Vic, rolling them. For a moment, Vic's body was under his, but he didn't keep the advantage for long, and they ended up rolling until they hit the wall.

Vic's arm went across Tegan's throat, not hard, but enough to keep him in place. "I don't like it."

"Because you like him?" Tegan was aware that he suddenly sounded jealous as fuck, and maybe he was. "You just met him."

Vic started to say something, but then he stopped. Tilted his head. And smiled. "Ah, Teegs." He brought his mouth down on Tegan's, slid it down in order to capture Tegan's bottom lip in a suck-and-bite move.

"I just got you, Vic." He heard the words come out of his mouth before he could stop them, and he hadn't even realized he'd felt that way, that possessive of him, until he'd said them.

He'd expected Vic to pull back, maybe even recoil because he was barely six months out of losing the man he'd spent years with. Instead, Vic took his arm off Tegan's throat and brought it up to tenderly caress his face. "You've got me, Tegan. I'm not going anywhere."

Tegan's tongue darted out to lick his bottom lip. "Sorry. I just..."

"Yeah, I know. That scene was intense," Vic admitted as Tegan's finger traced the scars on his jawline, followed them down the side of his neck. "You need some reassurance?"

"Fuck you." Tegan tried to push him off but Vic wasn't budging.

"Yeah, you do." Vic leaned in and captured one of Tegan's nipples in his mouth, biting it and then sucking, hard enough for Tegan to groan and grab for Vic's biceps. He murmured, "Yeah, that's it, baby, isn't it?" before latching back on, his free hand playing with Tegan's other nipple, twisting and rubbing while Tegan watched helplessly. Two men, both used to being in control was a tough sell, and one of them was going to have to back down and give in...and based on everything Vic had been through? Tegan knew it would have to be him, had resigned himself to it the second Vic had walked in through Crave's door, when everything sparked between them. Light-the-building-on-fire spark, which was what threatened to happen now, in the middle of the damned gym, and Tegan didn't want to stop it.

So he wouldn't. He'd just let his body react to Vic and let himself sink into the moment.

Vic's thigh parted Tegan's insistently, and he spoke to him as his hand continued playing with Tegan's nipple. "I saw you rutting against him, Tegan. Saw the way you kissed him. You were hard for both of us."

Tegan wanted to deny it but ultimately couldn't. Because Cade wasn't coming between them here—he was turning them both on more. "Vic—"

But Vic's hand had left his chest and was already down his sweats, rubbing his palm insistently over Tegan's hard length. Holding him hostage, slow and steady, but there was nothing sweet about it. "Going to make you come, so hard that you stop thinking."

This was so goddamned worth it, even if it was out of his comfort zone. The man knew exactly what he was doing, and it seemed like all he wanted was Tegan's pleasure, would force his surrender, and Tegan would march there most willingly.

Vic was going to take him, fuck him, and Tegan couldn't remember the last time he'd wanted anything more...or the last time he was this worried about getting exactly what he wanted.

Vic wanted to take it slow, to worship Tegan's body, but there would be time for that—Vic was sure of it. Right now, they both needed a good, hard fuck, and Tegan wasn't protesting.

Vic was already rutting against him. Tegan arched his body up to meet his, hooked his fingers in the waistband of Vic's shorts, yanking them down without finesse, trying to regain some of the control.

For the moment, Vic let him, tilting his head to meet the onslaught of Tegan's brutal kiss. The kiss swallowed his groans, and Tegan's hand clamped down on the back of Vic's head, holding him in place. Vic took the opportunity to jerk Tegan's sweats down as well, and together they twisted and kicked free, so they were bare-assed against each other, with Vic's body between Tegan's spread thighs. He grabbed Tegan's free hand and wrestled his arm over his head, holding it on the mat as the kiss intensified—it was more like a goddamned claiming as Tegan's body stretched out under his, yielding slightly when Vic bit his bottom lip, then sucked on it hard before pulling away.

Wordlessly, Tegan's hand fell away from Vic's hair and joined his other above his head. Vic caught both Tegan's wrists in his and held them there for several moments, wondering if he'd comply. Deciding that no, he probably wouldn't, he grabbed Tegan's abandoned T-shirt and wrapped his wrists together before flipping him onto his belly.

"Fuck—Vic," Tegan huffed as Vic tugged his hips into the air while pressing his hand between Tegan's shoulders to keep his chest down. Seeing Tegan submit like that, even briefly, made his dick pulse heavily.

"Beautiful, T," Vic murmured as his hand stretched over Tegan's ass cheeks even as Tegan snorted at the comment. Vic ignored it, rubbing, owning, leaning in to bite and mark because, soon enough, Tegan would be moaning his fucking name.

In the old days, he might've let Tegan take him, but now, he was still too fucking fragile. It wouldn't work—he'd be flashing back to those days in the pit, and everything would go to shit. Tegan obviously knew it, which was why he lay pliant but definitely not fully submissive.

He was fucking beautiful anyway. Vic would make sure to remind him of that, over and over. Because if this was a mistake, it was one he should've made years ago, and more than once...if for no other reason than to *never* learn his lesson. "You remember what I told you I wanted to do to you?"

Tegan's breath caught so yeah, he did. Vic forced his legs wider and buried his face in his ass, his tongue immediately focused on Tegan's hole.

"Jesus Christ, Vic." There was surrender in Tegan's tone —a beg as well, and Vic wanted all of that and more. He held Tegan's ass open as he ate him, licking and tasting and rubbing his stubble along the sensitive skin until Tegan's tied fists drummed a rhythm on the mat in an otherwise quiet surrender of his body for Vic's pleasure.

It started off a slow, dirty grind, with Vic's cock rubbing the seam of Tegan's ass, Tegan rutting back against him, his hands fisted, his wrists tied together, and Vic wanted to bind him to something—anything—to force him passive. He found his target and slapped Tegan's ass. "Wait here."

"Funny," Tegan grunted. "Ah, Vic, come on—we don't need to do that."

"I definitely do." Vic carried over a twenty-pound dumbbell and settled the bar over Tegan's bound wrists. Tegan could, of course, get out from under it, but it was a heavy reminder that Vic wanted him still. He grabbed his shorts, because he'd put lube and a condom in them earlier, and asked now, "Protection?"

"I'm clean, Vic. It's been a while for me."

"My last test came back clean but—"

"Do it," Tegan instructed.

Vic threw the condom to the side, squirted and then warmed the lube with his fingers before pressing them to Tegan's hole. Tegan groaned as Vic's finger breached him. "So tight, Teegs. Been a while?"

"You fucking know it has," Tegan bit out.

"Good." Vic's word had definite heat behind it. "This is mine." He smacked Tegan's ass hard, several times, and Tegan's body rocked, his dick hanging heavy. Vic reached around and stroked it, adding lube to make Tegan moan contentedly. He continued palming him as he worked two fingers in and out of him, and when he added a third, Tegan sucked in a harsh breath. "Fuck—can't wait anymore."

He was mounting Tegan, a hand on the back of his head, holding him, cheek down to the mat as he demanded entrance. Finally, slowly, Tegan's body accepted him enough to push through the first tight ring of muscle. "Come on, Teegs. Open for me. Let me the fuck in—you know it's going to be good."

Tegan put his forehead to the mat, and Vic felt his body relax and finally, he was seated all the way in, his balls against Tegan's ass. For a long moment, they both stilled. "I've gotta move, T. Fuck, so tight and hot—can't hold on anymore," he heard himself groan. He leaned forward and grabbed Tegan's hair, holding his head up as he pistoned his hips, slowly at first, until he felt Tegan relax under him. Only then did Vic push Tegan's entire body to the mat, put his hands on his head, grabbing him and fucking him, desperately, hard and fast, until Tegan's breath sawed in and out and he was humping the mat...and Vic drove forward with an inherent need to make Tegan scream his name.

He didn't have to wait long before Tegan shouted his name like a plea. "Don't stop—don't you dare fucking stop."

"Not a chance," Vic assured him, hammering against Tegan, wanting the man to feel him for days, knowing that Tegan needed to. Whether he admitted it to himself or not was a completely different story, one Vic didn't concern himself with at the moment.

No, it was just his dick throbbing in Tegan's tight ass. "Gonna come inside you, baby. Fill you up."

"Yeah, Vic—yeah," was all Tegan could manage, his breaths uneven as his muscles tightened and his body jack-knifed as his own climax hit. His ass milked Vic's cock, and Vic's hips stuttered several times as his orgasm hit, a wave of heat body-slamming him until he'd emptied himself into Tegan's ass.

"Beautiful," he murmured against Tegan's neck, tasting the salty sweat there.

"Almost killed me," Tegan murmured happily. "Let's do it again." After several long moments, Vic half rolled off him, moved the dumbbell and helped Tegan turn on his side, his hands still tied. "Gonna help here?"

Vic regarded him, flushed, bound, but definitely not helpless as he considered the request. "Not yet. I like you like this." Tegan rolled his eyes but didn't protest. "Thanks, T. I know that's not your usual preference."

Tegan ran his bound hands along Vic's chest. "You might just make it that." Vic's gaze searched Tegan's intense one, seeking bullshit and finding none. "You'll get there—with everything."

"Never going to be the same."

"None of us are. Would you want to be?"

Vic considered that. "Some days, I think, definitely. Nights like tonight and I feel like I'm exactly where I'm supposed to be."

"Maybe more feeling and less thinking? Because you are exactly where you're supposed to be. Here with us—with me." Tegan's words were fierce and so was the kiss that captured his mouth and ended with a bite and suck to Vic's lower lip. "This would've happened sooner if we'd been in the same country for longer than fifteen minutes."

Vic laughed. "You know my ex hated you. I guess he sensed it too. I just didn't sense how badly Danny was fucking me over in the end."

"So much loss. We'll get through it. We already are."

"At some point, I'm going to ask you...want you to fuck me."

Tegan smiled. "At whatever point that is, I'll be here. Until then..." He looked down at his dick, which was hard again.

"And that's why I kept you tied," Vic told him before flipping him onto his back for round two.

CHAPTER 8

CADE WOKE with a start to the phone ringing in his ear. Literally, because he'd fallen asleep on it, his body slick with sweat, his dreams restless and feverlike, involving Tegan, Vic and that *fucking* Room 4.

He groaned into the phone. "Yeah?"

"Cade, it's Andrei." Andrei was his manager from the fight club. His voice was heavily accented on a good day, worse when he was stressed, which he obviously was.

"I'm off tonight."

"We need you. I need you. Favor? The money's good."

Cade liked Andrei. Hell, he liked all the guys who ran the underground fight club. Most of them were made men in the Russian mob, but they didn't fuck with him, they paid him well, and they'd definitely offered extra protection when he'd needed it.

Except he'd stopped asking, and he definitely wouldn't where Courier was concerned. Even the Russian mob couldn't help against a CIA spook. "The money's always good," Cade said now, and hell, he wasn't looking a gift horse in the mouth. Probably wouldn't hurt to get out some extra aggression. "Give me an hour?"

"Thanks, man." Andrei hung up and Cade forced himself into the shower, the hot spray cascading over his aches and pains. He didn't jack off because he refused to before a fight. Maybe it was just superstition, but it'd worked so far.

Less than an hour later, he drove into the locked back lot, reserved for VIPs and staff. Billy, who guarded the place at night, called out to him. "Thought you had the night off?"

"I guess they needed a real fighter."

Billy laughed and waved him in. He parked and headed in through the back entrance that was guarded by a burly bouncer named Ivan, who could give Colin from Crave a run for his money.

Hell, he had to stop thinking about that damned club. Instead, he focused on saying hi to everyone he passed, because he'd been working here since he'd been fifteen years old, moving up the ranks of fighters until he'd left for the Army. They'd had the job waiting for him when he'd returned.

These days, he worked at the fight club, bouncing as well as fighting...and at times he was a hitter for the men when they needed him. In between, he found jobs that fit with his skill set—he helped people who needed out of their current situations. So the ultimate irony of not being able to find an escape from his own wasn't lost on him.

You got in with the wrong guy. Fucked the wrong man. And now, the obsessive fucker was hell-bent on revenge.

Andrei was in the main locker room with his clipboard. He managed the fights and usually without incident. "You saved me tonight. Boss was gonna have my head if I didn't replace Knight."

"He's away again?"

"I guess so. He's not answering his phone." These guys employed a lot of men who did the sudden disappearance thing. "By the way, that man you showed me the picture of hasn't been in at all this week."

He'd asked Andrei to keep his eye out for Courier since this was where Cade had originally met him. "Thanks, Andrei. What's on tap for tonight?"

"You're with Pacman."

They'd squared up before. Pacman was bigger, but Cade had managed to best him every time. He didn't take anything for granted though—things could change in the blink of an eye.

He grabbed the supplies he needed and went into the smaller pre-fight room assigned to him, stopping short when he saw that Vic was waiting there for him. But he recovered quickly and moved forward to put his bag on the table, grabbing the white tape while ignoring him.

But Vic? Didn't let that happen. He moved close to Cade, took the roll of tape from his hand, and patted the table. Cade reasoned that he was going to sit there anyway, so it wasn't like he was following Vic's silent but definite order.

"What the hell are you thinking? You were unconscious less than twenty-four hours ago." Vic's dark eyes sliced through him.

"I guess you'd know, since you did it." Cade watched as Vic began taping his knuckles. "I'll be fine."

"Were you fine when the detective showed up at your house last night?"

Cade's gut pulled tight. "You're watching me now?"

"You need watching." Vic's hands moved toward his, and Cade wasn't sure how he felt about Vic watching over him. Or why he wasn't angrier about it.

"I thought you didn't think I should fight?" he asked.

"You're obviously not a great listener, so I might as well keep you safe." Vic finished Cade's left hand and worked on his right. "How long have you worked here?"

"Long enough." Cade was well aware that he sounded like a sullen teenager. Vic also seemed amused by it, and that both pleased and annoyed Cade.

"How's that feel?"

"You're pretty good at this." He flexed a taped hand. "Do a lot of boxing from wherever it is you're from?" Vic smiled and showed Cade his fist, and Cade ran a finger over his knuckles. "Bare-knuckle fighting?"

"It's a big thing back home."

"Where's that?"

"Small town in Wales."

So, Cade had been right about the accent. "Did you like it —fighting, I mean?"

"I didn't have much of a choice." Vic finished with the tape and reached for the blue wrap next. "Fighting was the family business. Do you like it?"

"Yeah, I like it a lot."

Vic glanced up at him. "And you're good at it?"

"Very."

"So I shouldn't bet against you then?"

Cade shrugged. "Unless you like losing your money." Then he paused. "You're staying to watch the fight?"

"Yes. And after you're done, you should come back to Crave with me."

"With us," Tegan corrected, and Cade's head snapped to find the tall man standing in the doorway.

"Motherfuckers," Cade muttered. "I'm not doing that."

"But we can help you. That's what we do," Vic reasoned.

"You're mercenaries." *Just like Courier.*

"Yes, which means we're free to take on the jobs we want," Tegan explained. "We help people without the red tape."

"I didn't ask for help," Cade pointed out.

"But you are in trouble." Vic's dark eyes held him in place until Cade ripped his gaze away and focused instead on the scars that wove their way down his neck. Because how was he supposed to answer that?

"Want to tell us about why the detective visited you?" Tegan asked, casually moving closer to Cade. He leaned against the table, and suddenly both men were so goddamned close to him, boxing him in. Cade refused to speculate on why he found that so hot.

Because he knew. "Not really, no."

"You will, eventually." Tegan's voice in his ear sent a shiver down his spine and fuck, his dick was hard. Again. Granted, it started when Vic touched him. Maybe they drugged him. Maybe it was the hit on the head.

"Your face is flushed. You feeling okay?" Vic asked.

"Fine," Cade ground out. The knowledge that Vic and Tegan would watch him fight made his belly tighten, and he didn't want to think about why he cared, why he needed to prove himself to them.

"You sure you're all right?" Vic pressed.

"Do I look all right?"

"More than." Vic caught his chin with his free hand, forcing Cade to meet his gaze. "We're here for you. Knock 'em dead, kid."

"Not a kid," was all Cade could manage.

"Wouldn't be here if you were."

Vic couldn't deny that Cade was an excellent fighter. Fast. Hit hard. Stayed out of the way of the other man's fists and feet and gave back a shitload of both. His strategy in the ring was methodic and unrelenting. His hits were strong and he thought through his punches and takedowns.

The crowd loved him too, and it wasn't hard to see why. Shirtless, his skin naturally tanner than most and slicked with sweat, Cade looked handsome and fierce. The few women who were here no doubt wanted him, and most of the men either wanted him—or wanted to be him.

Tegan glanced at him like he knew what Vic was thinking. "It's lucky you knocked him out before he kicked out my windows."

Vic nodded. "He's going to be a handful."

"Going to be?" Tegan shook his head.

"Think the guy who's fucking with him is here?"

"Cade's worked here for a long time—and he brings in good money. Why would they let someone fuck with him?" Tegan asked.

"Have you met Cade? Guy doesn't exactly ask for help. From anyone." It annoyed the fuck out of him, even though it was also his MO. But he couldn't shake the look in Cade's eyes when he'd left Crave or when they'd found him at The WHIP.

"We can't just drag him out of here," Tegan reminded him as if reading his mind.

"I definitely could," Vic grumbled, with a glance at Cade. The guy was goddamned beautiful, his form perfect. He took the bigger man down hard and the crowd roared. Vic flashed to Room 4 and the crowds staring up at the glass, salivating for whatever was happening behind it.

Damn, they needed to get Cade into bed with them, and sooner rather than later.

"I checked in with the fight manager—they do record the fights, but it's on a seven-day loop," he said to distract himself.

"I'll have Oz run facial recognition on the crowds from last week. Who the hell knows what we'll pull up."

"I hope he comes to Crave."

"I think he's got major trouble trusting."

"I know a little something about that."

Cade's opponent had struggled to his feet after the last takedown, and Cade circled him like a shark before bringing him to the mat for the last time.

He was bruised and bloodied, badges from a well-won fight, but his opponent fared far worse. Vic remembered his winning days very well—both his and Brian's. The memories were a mix of family pride, a fighting way of life. Violence too, and money. But most of all, it was the camaraderie. The ties to family.

Vic and Brian both gave up the ring when they were recruited straight from the octagon by the SAS. Brian left after five years, wanted Vic to leave and come to work with him and Tegan and Oz, but Vic refused. His team needed him...until he was betrayed by men he thought were family.

As if Tegan sensed what Vic was thinking about, his palm went to the back of Vic's neck, warm and steadying, and it stayed there while the ref held up Cade's arm in victory, until the crowd roared...until Cade's eyes met both of theirs.

"He'll come to us, Vic. Have a little faith."

"How can you still believe in that?"

Tegan leaned in and murmured, "Because it brought you here."

CHAPTER 9

BY THE TIME Cade had pinned Pacman, who'd cursed him the entire time, he was wrung out, in a good way. But a second need began to claw at him. The familiar arousal curled in his gut, worse than ever this time.

Having Vic and Tegan's eyes on him made the entire fight a blur of pure adrenaline, which left him more turned-on than usual. If this had been any other night, he'd have found a guy to have a quick fuck with in the alley out back, and then he'd go home and lie in the tub to bring himself back down to earth.

But he didn't want a random fuck with a random guy, and jerking off in the shower in lieu of that hadn't done a damned thing to help.

Shit. He pressed his head against the metal doorjamb because his entire body ran hot, and it took everything for him to not slam his fists against the cement walls.

A knock on the door a few minutes later made him tamp down his urgency. "Yeah, come in."

It was Andrei. "You looked great out there," he said

before handing him an envelope. "I told you this would be worth your while—there's a nice bonus in there for your help. You need the doc tonight?"

"Nah, I'm good."

"Get some rest—I'm thinking you guys can have a rematch next week," Andrei said over his shoulder on his way out of the room.

Cade shoved his winnings into his front pocket and pulled his sweatshirt on. He pulled the hood up, grabbed his bag, and prepared to leave, still frustrated as fuck, when his phone began to ring.

Private number. His pulse raced, but against his better judgment, he answered the call. "Who is this?" he asked even though he already knew exactly who it was.

"Congratulations on your win tonight, Cade." Courier's voice, graveled and seductive, made his heart pound in his chest. "I hope Theo's that lucky too. You can't be too careful in those small West African countries."

A blaze of hatred burned through him. "Do you want to fuck me again? Is that what this is all about?"

Courier laughed. "It's about you following directions, which you've proved to be completely incapable of doing. I'll be sure to give Theo your best. He won't even see me coming."

Cade's vision swam, so he closed his eyes with the now-silent phone still pressed to his ear. He wanted to punch something—someone—but that wouldn't help shit.

He opened his eyes when an idea hit him that just might.

When he fought, he didn't feel helpless. When he fought, he was in control. Now, he pulled the money out of his pocket and realized how much extra was in there. He stared between it and his phone, and he knew exactly what he needed to do.

"...we can help you. That's what we do....We help people, without the red tape."

His mind raced. He knew he couldn't protect Theo from Courier, and neither could the military—at least not in time, and that was if they even chose to listen to him. And what would he tell them?

But maybe...just maybe...Tegan and Vic actually could help. And Cade would give them a name, just not the *exact* one they wanted.

Suddenly, he couldn't get to Crave fast enough. There was a line out the front door because it was both Saturday and the end of Fantasy Week. So he drove around to the back and parked in the lot meant for employees, because fuck it. What were they going to do—tow him?

The back door Vic and Tegan brought him in the other night—after Vic knocked him out—was locked, but that had never been a detriment to him. He picked the lock quickly and was inside before anyone saw him. He figured he'd be on camera, that someone must be watching, but he was greeted with an empty hallway.

He went up the stairs he'd zoomed down last night after he'd been released. He didn't remember the trip inside but he recalled the way out, so he retraced his steps.

The first hallway contained the main room they'd kept him in, and the door was open. *No one.* He went up another flight slowly, wondering who he'd encounter on the next landing.

There was a doorway at one end and another one down the hall. Both were closed. He had a momentary flare of panic, whirled around and saw Vic, standing in a suddenly opened doorway, leaning casually. "Looking for someone specific?"

He pushed off and moved toward Cade, who retreated toward the wall, showing his hands. "I'm here for a good reason."

"Yeah? Breaking and entering for a good reason when we've got a front door that's open?"

"There's a line. I don't like to wait." God, Vic's body this close to his was too tempting. Like the fucker had trained Cade's body to react to his. All he needed was for Tegan to show up to complete the goddamned magical trifecta of erections and he'd come all over himself.

Again.

Vic was half smiling.

"Stop reading my fucking mind," Cade muttered.

"But it's fun to. Doesn't take much either." He glanced down at Cade's hard cock and back up to his face. "Is that what you came for? Done fighting and now you're looking for a fuck?"

"Yes. I mean, no. *Fuck*—yes, but there's also another reason I'm here," Cade said firmly.

"I'm listening."

"I'm going to pay you to protect my friend. Because you told me that's what you do—you protect people, right?" Cade challenged. "I have money. Tell me how much it will take to protect my friend. If I don't have enough tonight, I'll get the rest."

Oz stared at the monitor that showed the various public places inside Crave. This last night of Fantasy Week had been crowded, and no matter how big of a moneymaker it was, Oz was happy this round was finished.

It was the first one without Brian, which made it extra difficult, but Oz would never cancel it—even though the others offered to do so—because there were a lot of men he knew who'd created incredible memories during Crave's favorite week, himself included.

Which was why, when the monitors that swept the private areas of the club showed Cade picking the lock on the back door, gaining entrance, and subsequently heading toward the stairs, Oz hadn't bothered to stop him. "Good for you, Cade," he'd murmured. "Show them a thing or two."

Because, while watching the immediate chemistry between Cade, Tegan, and Vic had been bittersweet, it had also given Oz a twinge of hope. Tegan and Vic's circling of each other like angry sharks had nearly made Oz handcuff them together until they fucked out their frustrations. But with Cade, everything had suddenly clicked.

Oz had always been a firm believer in magic, because that had happened for him with Brian. He just didn't believe it struck twice for the same person, but he wouldn't have changed the time they'd had together for anything.

Just thinking about his lover made his chest heavy, and he couldn't deny that having Vic here had eased some of the ache. Both men were handsome, their brogues similar, although Vic's was thicker and Brian's had lessened somewhat after living in the States for over ten years.

But the way they laughed—that was similar, except Vic laughed a whole lot less than Brian had.

Vic had come to them shattered, maybe not physically, but he'd been recovering in a hospital at an undisclosed location for three months during his debrief from the SAS. Once Oz had finally been able to extricate him, he'd gone himself to pick Vic up and bring him here.

Vic hadn't spoken to anyone the first week. After that, he'd gradually thawed out as his comfort level increased but still, most nights, they ended up sleeping together, which seemed to lessen the nightmares...for both of them.

Vic was going through hell, and Brian would've done anything to help him out of it. He'd have expected Oz to do the same, and it wasn't a hardship to do so. It was a way to honor his lover and his lover's family.

And, if he had to guess, Vic was doing exactly the same thing for him, because that was what his brother would've wanted.

But Oz was keeping a secret from Vic, from all of them, and that was also something Brian would've wanted him to do.

Because Brian had been murdered. And that was exactly what had happened, except no one else knew it—they were all under the mistaken impression that it was a horrible, tragic accident, a wrong-place-at-the-wrong-time type of thing. But Oz knew differently, even if he didn't have the evidence to prove it yet. He and Brian had both known he was being stalked. Studied. Hunted.

Now, Oz let his fingers fly over the keyboard because it was his best weapon for the moment.

Somewhere on the dark web, he'd find the man he was looking for.

Vic watched Cade carefully. It was obvious that he was worked up, and it was equally so that he was serious about needing help. What had transpired in the last hour to have changed his mind so completely?

Vic would need to find that out—fast. "What does protecting your friend entail? Does it have to do with Rourke's visit to your place last night?"

"Maybe," Cade conceded.

"Oh no, little boy—you're not pulling this 'maybe' crap with me. Not if you're serious about wanting help."

Cade gave him a hard shove which didn't actually move Vic anywhere. But then Cade tilted his head, reminding Vic of a bull that was deciding how—not *when*—to charge. Before Cade could move, Vic was on him, pinning him to the wall, a palm across his throat and this time, it wasn't the way it had been in the truck the other night. Suddenly, it wasn't about a fight. Not at all. Vic's mouth crushed down on his and Cade accepted it. Wanted it, if his openmouthed groans were any indication.

He also wrapped his arms around Vic's shoulders and half climbed him. Vic didn't protest—instead he hiked Cade's thighs up so he could wrap his legs around Vic's hips, held up by the pressure of Vic's body and the wall behind him.

He felt, rather than saw, Tegan's presence. Knowing he was being watched by Tegan made this even hotter and yeah, he was on an adrenaline-fueled search for relief. His skin was tight, his blood hot, and his cock impossibly hard.

"Cock-blocked again." Tegan, in a towel, still wet from

his recent shower, smirked at Vic before turning his gaze to the cockblock in question.

"Wait—I'm the cockblock?" Cade asked. "Wait, you two were...*ohhh.*" He bit his bottom lip...but he didn't move away from Vic at all. In fact, his fingers dug into Vic's biceps as he looked between the two men.

"He came here to hire us," Vic informed Tegan.

"Hire us?" Tegan asked.

"Not for this." Cade finally broke away from Vic, leaving him to wonder exactly who was cock-blocking who in this situation. "My friend needs your help. I'm hiring you to help with that."

"So kissing Vic is like an extra?" Tegan pressed.

"I want that—kissing, and more...with both of you. I'm consenting to that but it's got nothing to do with the situation I'm hiring you for." He held up the cash. "Can you promise me that you can separate the two?"

Both Vic and Tegan nodded, but Tegan added, "And you're promising to let us help? To give us the information we need to help your friend and keep us safe while we do so?"

Cade had obviously already come to terms with his choice, because his words came easily. "Yes. Yes, I'll let you help and I'll give you what I know. In return, you'll take this."

He handed it to Tegan and Vic wasn't surprised when Tegan's hand closed around the cash—because they both understood and respected the need for Cade's pride.

"Deal. How immediate is this danger?" Tegan asked.

"The walls are closing in," Cade admitted.

Vic groaned. "Fucking cock-blocked at every turn."

"What Vic's trying to say is...we're not doing this here.

There's too much room for..." Tegan gave both Vic and Cade a once-over. "Conflict of interest."

"And don't think we're just going to roll over and accept all the bullshit you try to throw at us," Vic told Cade, who frowned.

"Why would you automatically assume I'm going to spend hard-earned money and then bullshit you?"

"Happens all the time," Tegan warned him.

CHAPTER 10

CADE WALKED into the office and saw Oz for the first time since the disastrous Fantasy Night. "Hey."

Oz glanced over at him with a quick nod while Vic motioned for him to take a seat. Tegan closed the door and Cade looked at the bank of monitors that seemed to cover all areas of the club...including the back door he'd snuck in through. He frowned and caught Oz's eye. Oz gave him a small, friendly, yeah-saw-you-and-let-you-go-anyway smirk.

Yeah, he owed Oz one.

At least there were no cameras for the upstairs hallway... but he swore Oz could read his goddamned mind, because Oz clicked one button and Cade saw that the hallways were covered. Great. At least Oz had turned them off instead of almost watching the potential show, and now Cade knew for sure that he'd only gotten as far as he had because Oz had chosen to let him.

Tegan and Vic didn't seem to notice the exchange.

"Welcome back, Cade." Oz's tone held the slightest edge of sarcasm.

Cade made sure to match his tone. "Thanks. I hope it's more fun than the last time I was here and hanging from the ceiling."

Vic snorted, and Oz seemed to catch on to the energy between the men as he glanced around at them. "I'm guessing this has to do with what started the other night?"

Cade plowed forward, ignoring the fact that Oz's words had more than one meaning. "My friend is in trouble and he doesn't know it."

"From the same guy who hacked into our feed and sent us your fantasy?" Oz pressed.

"Yes."

"Because you didn't finish what he started?"

"Yes." Cade clasped his hands together and leaned forward. "I only know him as Courier. J. Courier."

"And how do you know him?" Tegan demanded.

Fuck, he was mad again—maybe not at Cade, but still. "I fucked him."

Both Tegan and Vic looked unhappy with his remark. "Like pulling teeth," Oz muttered with a pointed look at him.

Cade shifted. "Anyway, Courier's a spook. American, but I'm not convinced he's only CIA."

"Tell me why he's forcing this fantasy on you." Tegan crossed his arms, looking more imposing than usual.

"Because he's a fucking psychopath." Vic rolled his eyes at Cade's words. "You're supposed to be helping my friend—not me. I don't need your help."

"That's where you're wrong," Vic said irritably and Cade felt his cock go hard again, because something about these men brought out both his fuck *and* fight instincts.

"Let me rephrase—I don't want your help, outside of helping my friend. That's all I'm looking for. I don't need bodyguards of my own," he bit out. "How long is this interrogation going to be?"

"Are we keeping you from something? Do you have another fantasy to explore?" Vic asked.

"Fuck you."

"You're definitely not ready for that." Vic smirked, and Cade wondered why Vic was purposely baiting him.

Because that's what happens in interrogations. Was he that far out of the Army? Or had he really started to believe that these men trusted him? "Listen, there's nothing Courier can do to me that can hurt me."

"But he can do something to someone you love, which is why you're leaving yourself vulnerable," Tegan shot back, and Cade guessed it was bad cop / bad cop / silent cop. "That's the only reason I can think of for why you're being so goddamned unreasonable. And stupid. People do stupid things—for love and for family. So which is it, Cade?"

Both, Cade wanted to tell him but instead kept his mouth shut.

Tegan wasn't done yet. "You don't want to talk about how stubborn you're being? Fine. How did you meet Courier?"

Cade ran his hands through his hair and thought about lying. But these men were all agreeing to put themselves on the line for Theo. "At one of my fights."

"Why would a spy go to underground fights?" Vic murmured.

"Did you know what he was?" Oz asked, and Cade wondered if silent cop would turn bad or good.

He nodded. "I suspected. This close to the military base... well, let's just say, we're close enough to a lot of HQs. I mean, he never came out and told me."

"And he got pissed when you blew him off and he threatened you and your roommate," Vic continued.

"Yes."

"And when we stopped the fantasy he created, he got pissed."

"Yes. Last night...he left me a new message that said I'd pay." He waited for them to get pissed that he hadn't mentioned the new message before this.

"And that means that your friend will pay too. Why?" Vic's eyes bore into his.

"Because Courier knows that will hurt me." It was only half a lie, and Cade was pretty sure these men knew it, but he didn't care, not as long as they agreed to get Theo out of danger.

"Was your friend a part of why Rourke talked to you the other night?" Tegan reminded him and fuck, how much did these men know?

"That wasn't..."

"About Theo? Really?" Cade tried not to wince at his friend's name, because fuck, how did they know this shit?

How could you think they didn't? They probably knew everything about him as well, probably pulled his and Theo's files. He hadn't felt as exposed during his fantasy as he did now, and the anger burned perilously close to the surface. "You had no right to dig into my life."

Tegan moved in dangerously close, his hands on both arms of Cade's chair, effectively locking him in. "No right?

You compromised our club. You came to us for help. So why are you lying to us?"

"You promised you'd protect Theo—that's all you need to do, and I'll take care of the rest." His voice was a rough rasp.

Vic looked up at the ceiling and cursed.

Tegan hadn't moved. "That's exactly what we're afraid of."

It took everything Tegan had not to pick Cade up and hand him over to Vic to tie up again—for Cade's own protection. From his own stupidity. "Where is Theo now?"

"You seem to know everything else, but you don't know that?"

"You're playing with fire, Cade. I'm very fucking patient...until I'm not," Tegan murmured softly. "Come on, baby. Don't be like this."

Cade looked torn, but he admitted, "He's in the Army. Active duty. On a mission in West Africa."

Vic cursed loudly, still staring at the ceiling, like he was waiting for divine intervention, and Tegan hoped to hell he'd get it, because things were looking murkier by the second.

"Cade, you get that, when you hire us, you're supposed to actually help us do our jobs, right? If we wanted this level of frustration, we'd have stayed in the military," Oz offered.

"He's active duty. He was a Ranger," Cade started. "Now he's a mechanic."

At least he was finally telling the truth. Tegan already knew that Theo was a member of Delta Force, but the elite unit was so secretive that, to anyone else, Theo's job would be innocuous. "Mechanic" was one of those monikers for those in the know.

"This just gets better by the fucking second." Vic was pacing now. He'd known what Theo was, but he was playing his bad cop part to the hilt. Because Cade needed to realize what he was up against. "So your friend, the Delta Force Operator, is on a job in the jungles of West Africa, and you think the man who can't get over you is just going to waltz in there and kill him?"

"Or is this about Theo's stepfather?" Tegan asked and watched Cade slam shut like a vault.

"Not my secret to tell," was all he offered. "I've got a SAT phone number—one I'm probably not supposed to have."

Oz handed him a pad of paper, and Cade wrote the number down immediately and handed it back. For Cade to be worried about a Delta Force Operator, something bad was going down. "Is Theo's team in danger?" Tegan asked him.

"I don't...think so. Courier wants me to pay. I don't know the rest of Theo's team."

Tegan believed that. "You need to stay here until I can make contact with someone who can help Theo—that's important."

"I need to fight tomorrow night. So you've got me until then," Cade offered.

"We're here to help you, Cade. You've got to decide if you can trust that or not." Tegan stared at the stubborn, stubborn man sitting insolently in front of him, the weight of the world so obviously on his shoulders.

He didn't expect Cade to jump out of his chair and stand toe-to-toe with him—again—although he probably should have.

"I don't trust. I didn't trust Courier—that's not why I'm so pissed. I didn't trust myself—that gnaw in my gut that said it wasn't right. I thought I just needed sex—that everything was just pent-up inside. I ignored my instincts." Cade's hands were fisted, his entire body so tight with anger that it made Tegan ache. "You don't understand—you have people you can trust. Probably always did."

"So do you," Tegan told him.

"Don't. Don't you fucking dare. I won't be fooled again. I paid for you to help me help Theo—I didn't pay to trust you with anything else. I won't. I can't. Don't expect it."

There was something so broken and primal and heart-breaking in his eyes—for just an instant—but Tegan had seen it, and he could tell by the sharp intake of breath that Oz had too. Vic closed his eyes like he hadn't wanted to see it, but it was too late.

Cade felt something deep inside of him break again, just when he'd thought it wouldn't have ever healed. Like the time he'd had to have his nose rebroken because it had healed too fast and all wrong. It always hurt worse the second time, and a sense of betrayal from Vic and Tegan coursed through him. Which was ridiculous.

Since he couldn't walk out until Theo was safe, according to the trio of interrogators, he went upstairs to Tegan's bedroom.

Their setup was great—the apartments were light and modern, and everyone had their own space while still being together.

Because they wanted to be. Cade figured they all had more than enough money to live in their own place.

Knowing the strong bonds these men had forged made him feel better about his choice, and it also made him miss Theo and Sway a hell of a lot more.

So instead of staying inside, he climbed out the window and up the fire escape onto the roof. It was huge, encompassing the club and connecting to the warehouse next door. He sat in the middle, staring at the skyline, wrapped in the blanket he'd grabbed from Tegan's closet—because he didn't want one that smelled like those men, needed something clean with no memories.

Be nice if you could clean your brain like that.

He used to sit on the roof of his third foster house like this —it'd been an escape from the constant cigar smoke and yelling. It didn't stop him from getting hit though, and he always waited until the beating portion of the evening had ended, because he'd been afraid they'd cut off his roof access.

Now, Tegan's words rang in his ears.

You've got to decide if you can trust that or not.

He'd tried to trust—in the early days, he'd done what the social workers told him to. *"The nicer you are, the more you let yourself trust, the easier things will be. People will like you— they'll want to be part of your family."*

But it wasn't fucking true. Being nice only made him an easy target, and it got his heart broken more than once. Because fitting in and being accepted by a foster family was about as easy as being reborn into the perfect family.

Not trusting was much easier.

And it didn't even matter—he hadn't trusted Courier worth a damn, but it had come back to bite him nonetheless.

And now these men wanted trust after a fuck? It didn't work that way. The world didn't and he sure as hell wouldn't.

When this was all over, things would return to normal—for him. He'd fight Courier however he could. The men from the club would help him, if Cade let them. Once Theo was safe, he'd take Courier on.

CHAPTER 11

VIC GAVE Cade fifteen minutes alone before settling next to him on the roof. He lit a cigarette and wordlessly handed it off. There was a momentary hesitation, as if Cade was letting him know that accepting it wasn't a fucking truce.

He'd known that anyway.

He lit his own, letting the smoke warm his throat before curling outward. He didn't light up often anymore, but when he did, he was brought right back into SAS training with his friends, his brother, on cold nights that seemed to have no end, when every part of his body hurt, and his brain begged for relief.

It reminded him of the times he'd never thought he'd make it and ultimately, he always did.

"How often did you fight?" Cade asked finally, his voice hoarse.

"For fun or for money?"

"Same thing for me."

Vic smiled as he stared out into the skyline. "Growing up where I did, you fought for three reasons—fun, survival, or money. Sometimes, if you were lucky, it was all three rolled into one."

"When did you fight for money?"

"From the time I was ten," he admitted. "Like I told you, bare-knuckle fighting was a time-honored tradition."

"Sounds like child abuse," Cade muttered.

"Maybe. But it gave me a way to defend myself."

"So you were forced to do it?"

"I never thought about it like that, but I suppose there wasn't a way to say no. Not an easy one, at any rate."

Cade nodded. "Where are your parents now?"

Vic crushed his cigarette under his boot. "I have no fucking idea." He felt Cade's surprise but Vic didn't elaborate, and Cade didn't push. "Do you have any idea what you're up against with Courier?"

"Contrary to popular belief, my head isn't up my ass."

Vic nodded. "And you're going to just go kill him alone."

If Cade was surprised Vic knew that, he didn't let on. "All you need to do is keep Theo safe."

"For how long?" Vic pressed, and Cade didn't say anything, because of course he wouldn't know how long his whole tour of vengeance was going to take. "How long do you think Theo's going to deal with being hidden from Delta Force? You're risking his career—you know that. And how pissed do you think he's going to be with you for all of this?"

"Won't matter. He'll understand." Cade stood and started to walk away.

"So you're going to pay us indefinitely?" Vic called after him and, as expected, Cade walked back toward him, the blanket dropping from his shoulders.

"Yes." Cade was getting angry again.

"Well, that's fucking stupid. But hey, hand it over."

Cade moved closer, which was even stupider than his payment bullshit. "When's the last time you accepted help from strangers, Vic? Tell me that. Were they the same ones who scarred you?"

Vic didn't turn his face toward him—instead, his entire body shot up and caught Cade by surprise. By the time he tried to fight back, which was, admittedly, mere seconds, Vic had him down on his back on the rooftop, a knee in his groin and a forearm across his throat.

He leaned in close, whispered. "The scars are from a man I trusted more than I trusted myself. So I guess he was a stranger all along—it just took me longer than most to realize it. I'll never make that mistake again."

He didn't bother waiting for a response—he pushed off, but Cade came after him, faking him out with a left while getting in a good kick that almost took Vic down.

Almost.

Vic moved in and strong-armed Cade, shoving him to the ground. But Cade dropped and rolled away effortlessly...got to his feet smiling and realized his mistake only after Vic reared back and took him down with a dizzying precision. Cade clawed and attempted to punch, but he was restrained well and good by Vic's body, shoved hard to the ground again and held there by Vic's knee against the back of his neck...as in, if Cade moved the wrong way, he could kiss breathing good-bye.

Vic held him there for a while until Cade stopped struggling, and Vic's own anger waned, dissipated like smoke. He took his knee off and backed away a little, and Cade stayed where he was for a second, then raised his hands as he rolled, first to his side and then onto his back.

It was only a momentary truce—Vic knew that. But hell, he'd take what he could get.

He sat next to Cade's prone body. "So much pent-up in there." Vic touched a finger to the side of his head and he saw Cade stiffen. "Can't be angry when you fight."

"Save your advice." Cade bit his bottom lip briefly, and that was all Vic could focus on. He leaned down and took Cade's mouth—hard, fast. Punishing. Cade kissed him back with a desperation Vic recognized, let Cade moan into his mouth and press his body up into Vic's wantonly...and then he ripped his mouth away. His eyes met Cade's stunned ones before he got up and left the roof, wondering how he could be both victor and loser in the same breath.

Lesson learned. And Cade wasn't under any illusion that Vic had meant to teach him something.

He'd seen the jungle in Vic's eyes, the soldier's instinct, finely honed to be the tip of the spear.

Vic had yet to leave the jungle behind.

Cade's ribs ached when he pulled in breaths, and he stared up at the sky. It'd been a long time since he'd lost a fight.

You lost the fight with Courier too.

But Vic wasn't Courier—on the complete opposite end of the spectrum. And he'd treated him the same. Tegan too.

Speaking of, the big man loomed over him now, his expression a cross of concern and satisfaction. Oz probably played the show over the big screen inside Crave. That bothered Cade more than the video Courier had recorded of them together and constantly threatened him with. There'd been no intimacy with Courier. With Vic? The entire fight had been uncomfortably intimate...which is why it'd hurt so much when Vic made him respond to the kiss, then walked away.

"Theo always tells me I'm too angry." His words were more to himself than to Tegan, but Tegan answered anyway.

"And that doesn't piss you off?"

Finally, he met Tegan's gaze, hating the way they seemed to see right through him. "I know I'm angry. I tell him he's feral—and he knows that. Isn't knowing your own weakness supposed to make it your power, or some shit like that?"

"How's that working for you?" Tegan's drawl was thick with sarcasm. He hadn't offered Cade a hand up or asked if he was okay.

Strangely, that made Cade feel better. "Just fine," he drawled, his Louisiana accent thick. He felt drunk—punch-drunk, probably—and he knew he was playing with fire.

With Tegan, he was far more likely to get burned.

Vic didn't scare him nearly as much as Tegan did. Cade understood Vic because he and Vic were a lot alike, except Vic knew how to calm himself down. Vic had himself under control.

But Tegan? He was always in control—probably didn't even let up when he was coming.

This was all a job for him, and Cade knew if he asked Tegan that, he wouldn't deny it.

What Cade couldn't understand, for all his own protesting, was why this wasn't just a job to him? He'd hired these men. Offered to fuck them, too. He'd done the latter more times in his life than he cared to count.

The words tumbled out before he could stop them. "I hurt Vic."

"You're the one lying flat on your back—he walked away."

"I'm not talking about physically."

Tegan tilted his head, studying him. "And it bothers you?"

"I'm angry, Tegan—I'm not a psychopath." He sat up gingerly, wincing as he turned and pulled himself up to stand. Again, Tegan offered him no help...and Cade would've rejected it anyway.

"You're trying to get us angry enough so we throw you out."

"What? That's not...true."

Wasn't it, though? Fuck, had he been doing that without knowing it?

And meanwhile, Tegan had just stood there, waiting for that realization to bloom.

You're so fucking predictable, Cade. Theo's words, from another time and place, fit so perfectly here.

Theo.

He wanted his best friend to be safe, to not be caught up in this Courier shit. Wanted to take back so much of what happened these past weeks. But the one thing he wouldn't change was what happened between Vic, Tegan, and himself.

It was time to leave before he ruined it any further. "I should go."

Tegan sighed. "You need sleep."

Cade couldn't argue with that. He followed Tegan down

the fire escape and into his window, and Tegan pointed to the empty bed. "You're staying until Theo's in safe hands—that's my sticking point. You leave, we don't help him."

"And you've got someone who can help him?" Cade hedged, not wanting to ask—or know—too much more. In this case, it could make him a greater danger to Theo than he already was.

"I'm headed downstairs to read in a team right now."

"And they're good?"

"Better than," Tegan bit out. "The man in charge? There's *no one* I'd trust more to do this job than him."

With that, Cade marched over and got into bed, yanked the covers over him, and closed his eyes.

Asshole.

Tegan laughed as if Cade had spoken the word out loud. Cade just wasn't sure which one of them he was referring to.

CHAPTER 12

"AND HOW'S OUR young escape artist?" Oz asked when Tegan slammed back into the war room.

"Vic beat him up, so hopefully that will keep him calm."

Oz cocked a brow and didn't ask for details. Probably because he'd watched the entire thing play out, even though the roof monitor was currently dark. "What's your end game here, Tegan? What are you after with him? With Vic? Because from where I'm sitting, you're both in pretty deep."

Tegan deflected that easily with, "Anything on Courier?"

Oz just mouthed *Okay, then* before telling Tegan, "I ran the most cursory of searches. CIA by way of law school. No military—he's a lifer, and he's one of their best and brightest. He's got Russian ties, which worries the CIA, but he's got a font of connections and intel. They'd be stupid to get rid of him."

"Until it suits them," Tegan added cynically. He'd met—and helped—his share of spies along the way. Courier wouldn't be that lucky.

"So his hard-on for Cade is just that? An obsession? Or maybe Cade's not the first one he's done this to? Maybe digging into Theo's past was a way to keep Cade...obedient?"

Tegan snorted. Cade being obedient was a fucking pipe dream. He had him and Vic running in circles.

And wanting to fuck him. Don't forget that.

As if he could. *Dammit.* This shit was all Oz's fault—he'd go to his grave saying that, and judging by the way things were shaking out, that could be sooner than later.

"Can we rule out the possibility that this is part of a plan to get to us?" Oz continued, glaring at him like he knew Tegan was arguing with him inside his mind. "Maybe the fantasy thing's a ruse to get close to us. I mean, look, we've moved him in."

Granted, Oz was more paranoid than most—and had good reason to be, based on his past—but his questions couldn't be ignored. "Yes, *we've* moved him in, Oz. *We* saw him come in on the monitors, and *we* didn't stop him."

Oz shot him the finger. "And if I kept him out? What then? Cade's not exactly the shy, retiring type. And to answer my own question, I don't think Cade's in on this."

"But Courier could be using Cade to tug at our heart-strings and distract us. We need to find out if any of us have a past with this spook."

"If he's doing it to get us to step in and help, it's working," Oz muttered.

"Courier is using us in a personal attack, and Cade's one of us."

"Fine." Oz took a deep breath, ostensibly to keep himself calm. "So what's the plan?"

"Courier's expecting this—that we'd bring Cade here.

That we'd find out," Tegan reasoned. "So we don't disappoint him. He thinks we're just dumb mercs who'll use this kid while we can."

"There's a very real possibility Theo will have his secrets exposed, no matter what we do or don't do." Oz looked troubled. "Think Cade's prepared for that?"

"I think he knows it's inevitable, but he's hoping for a miracle," Tegan admitted.

"We've all been there." Oz flexed his hands again. "Christ, rescuing a Delta Force Operator from his Delta Force team...who the fuck's crazy enough to do that?"

"We definitely know someone who fits that profile," Tegan offered and Oz frowned. "I'll just give Deran a call."

Oz's brows shot up but he recovered quickly. "Oh, okay. Sure. That'll work." He tried to sound completely normal. And failed miserably. "When's the last time you guys spoke?"

Tegan had to think. "We've both been busy." But Deran would be there for him—he knew that the way he knew he'd be there for his brother in a hot second as well.

Oz was already handing him a SAT phone before leaving the war room to give Tegan some privacy. It wasn't necessary —he and Oz had no secrets, but he appreciated his friend's thoughtfulness.

Four rings later, he had his brother on the line.

Like Tegan, Deran was a former SEAL—a wild man who took on wild missions...until he decided that he was too much for the military and its red tape. These days, he helped military men disappear from sight. He gave them a second chance.

It was similar to what Tegan did, but Deran's methods definitely skated the line of illegal. He took far more chances than he should, but Tegan was proud as hell of him.

They'd been thick as thieves growing up, but he knew that the guilt from what happened during their childhood pushed them in different—but similar paths.

Hell, they were far more alike than they were different.

"Everything all right, Teegs?" Deran was asking, concern in his voice.

"Yeah, I'm good. And you?"

"Good. Glad to hear it, little brother. And I'm doing the usual—staying ahead of the shit."

"I've got a job. A favor—for me."

"I'm listening."

He laid out what he knew—gave him Theo's SAT phone number. "We didn't let Cade alert him, just in case."

"Yeah, that's smart."

"His name's Theo Davies."

There was such a long silence that Tegan was sure the line dropped, until Deran said, "He's Delta," with a definite tension in his voice.

Tegan had never known him to worry about the confines of the military when executing a rescue before. "Is this okay?"

"More than. I'm on it. Tell your friend not to worry." Deran paused. "This Cade guy? Is he just a friend?"

"Since when do you get involved in my love life?" Tegan asked and regretted it instantly, mainly because of Deran's knowing laugh.

"Have fun with your love life. I'll check in as soon as I get a bead on Theo and give you an ETA. How dire do you think this situation is?"

"I can't tell, D. But my gut tells me it's going to get a hell of a lot worse before it gets better."

"It always does, little brother. It always does." He hung up and Tegan felt satisfied that Courier wouldn't stand a chance against Deran and his merry band of men.

Now Tegan just had to worry that he and Vic had the same odds against Cade.

CHAPTER 13

VIC HEARD THE WHIMPERS, but he'd spotted Cade's nightmare coming ten minutes ago, and he'd hovered between waking Cade up or letting it happen.

You'll learn more from letting it happen. And so he watched as Cade began to thrash from side to side.

"Get off me. No—I'm not—I won't do that. Get off me. I don't do that—get the fuck off me!" Cade mumbled, but Vic knew that, in Cade's dream, he was screaming.

Tentatively, he put his hands on Cade's shoulders and rubbed. "You're safe, Cade. C'mon—wake up." It was what Oz did with him, and it always worked.

After several long moments, Cade stopped mumbling and he wasn't fighting the touch. His eyes fluttered open and he flushed when he looked at Vic. He didn't throw Vic's hands off him though, and so Vic continued to stroke a palm down his damp back. The touch seemed to be calming him, and Cade's eyes drifted shut for several moments like he was pulling himself together.

And then he opened them and shifted to his side. "Were you watching me?" he asked hoarsely.

"Yes."

"I wasn't going to try to leave."

"That's not why I was watching you." Vic tugged the blanket up over him. "You're shivering."

"Why are you doing this?"

"Giving you a blanket?"

"Helping me."

Vic avoided the question and went to push away from the headboard. "If you're okay now, I'll leave you alone."

But Cade's hand went to his wrist. "Don't. Please."

The plea in Cade's voice cut right through him, and he wondered when he'd become such a goddamned sucker. But even though he remained where he was, he didn't move in closer, because no—if Cade wanted more, he'd need to ask. "Okay."

"Theo would be really fucking pissed at me now."

"Why's that?"

"Because of the way I treated you. He always tells me that I lash out first and think later."

"Is that an apology?" Cade's grip on his wrist tightened for a second before it disappeared entirely. Vic felt the blankets shift and before he could say anything else, Cade was half straddling him, his forehead pressed to Vic's and fuck, yeah, he was a goddamned sucker, because his arms went around Cade's back.

"No, it wasn't." Cade leaned in, kissed his cheek first, then let his tongue trace the scars that ran along Vic's cheek and jaw, so fucking tenderly that he closed his eyes and let it happen. "But this is." Cade continued, trailing his kisses down the side of Vic's neck, murmuring, "Sorry, Vic. Sorry...I didn't mean..."

Vic found himself pulling Cade against him. The emotion that must've been building for days welled up and the dam broke as Cade's body wracked with silent sobs.

———

Cade was exhausted when he finally got himself together. One minute he'd been kissing Vic's scars and the next, crying and holy fuck, he was confused.

"It's all right, Cade. Been a rough couple of days."

"Never fucking cry," Cade sniffed.

"It's not a character flaw. Neither is being vulnerable. You're not the only one who has nightmares."

Comfort and arousal competed for Cade's attention. He rubbed his face against the soft cotton of Vic's T-shirt, and Vic tightened his arms around him in response. Then he felt the bed dip next to him and knew it was Tegan when the hand on his shoulder tugged him away from Vic. And then a warm, wet washcloth went over his face, then down his arms, his back, and almost immediately a towel wiped away the moisture so he never got chilled.

"You were still shivering," Vic offered by way of explanation.

When Cade felt Tegan begin to move away, he reached around and snagged his wrist, held it close. And Tegan remained there, his chest to Cade's back, leaving Cade hemmed in between the two men.

You're safe.

Cade couldn't remember the last time he'd felt safe...but

having Vic's arms around him, with Tegan at his back, he realized he'd relaxed for the first time in months. The only ones he'd trusted with comfort like this had been Theo and Sway, but that had been in a completely different context.

But this? There was no mistaking this context, not with Cade's cock hard as a fucking diamond, even as Vic's hands carded through his hair as if to quiet his mind. Tegan's hand rubbed his hip, and Cade fought the urge to rut between the men.

"Fuck, I'm so much trouble, you should both probably stay away," he said finally, and both men's hands stilled.

"We like trouble, Cade," Tegan murmured roughly in his ear.

Cade's anger attempted to surge again and he bit out, "I won't let you fucking pity me."

"Silly boy—I don't pity you—not at all. I want to give you a safe place to lay down your strength—your fists—and just be."

Cade's breath caught in his throat. The tears threatened but Tegan's palm rubbed down his back soothingly, Vic encouraging him to just *"Breathe,"* and *"We'll make sure you get through this."* That *"This is what our company does."*

"I thought you handed out fantasies."

"Isn't safety the biggest fantasy for some people?" Tegan asked quietly, and Cade turned so he could see his pained expression, a look Cade could place as surely as if he'd lived it.

"You've got our protection. But what else do you need?" Vic asked.

"Right now...I need..." He didn't know how to ask, because he barely understood what he needed himself. The force of his attraction was the strongest, zero to a hundred in no time, during the worst time of his life. All he knew was that he was restless as fuck, his skin felt hot and tight, and his cock reminded him that he hadn't had his usual post-fight comedown. His body demanded it now. "I just *need*."

He leaned in and kissed Vic like his life depended on it. And hell, maybe it did. Tegan shifted him back into position, straddling Vic's lap, and Tegan's cock was against his ass, Vic's against his cock, and he rocked back and forth between them, seeking friction.

Vic let that happen for several long moments before placing a palm on his bare chest and banding his other arm around Cade's waist, simultaneously forcing him onto his knees and holding him in place as he went for Cade's nipple, biting, then sucking. The jolt of sensation made him cry out Vic's name and then wrap himself around the bigger man, pressing his face against Vic's head. "Fuck, please..."

Vic didn't stop sucking his tit, alternately playing with the piercing with his tongue and teasing the tip and *fuck me*, it forced Cade to dry-hump him, cock rubbing Vic's chest, his needs desperate and increasing wildly with each rough lap of Vic's tongue against his taut flesh.

"I think he's going to come from this," Tegan murmured to Vic, who hummed around his nipple and *this*? Was *definitely* going to be enough to make Cade shoot in his pants.

Except Tegan's hand came around to squeeze the base of his cock, hard enough to stop his dick from shooting, but it didn't stop the quakes that shot through his body at the sudden loss. Cade nearly howled but Tegan told him, "Too soon, baby. Delayed gratification's worth it."

"Fuck—no it's not," Cade bit out with a growl.

Tegan gave a low, dangerous chuckle as his palms slid into Cade's sweats to cup his bare cheeks hard before he ran a finger down the seam of his ass. A blunt finger pressed against his opening, and Cade moaned at the contact, which made Vic suck his nipple harder.

"He likes me playing with his pretty ass, Vic," Tegan said, almost conversationally, and the fact that he was talking *about* Cade to Vic? Hot. As hot as the way Tegan was now pressing two fingers against his opening to tease him, and Cade didn't know which end to seek friction—or relief—from. "Fuck, want to bury my face in there and taste him. Eat him. Think he'll like that?" Tegan kept up his running commentary, and Jesus Christ, the dirty talk alone was going to kill him.

Vic pulled back from his assault on Cade's nipple to study his reactions. "Fuck, baby—you blush."

"He's going to blush harder then," Tegan promised, and Cade was lifted off Vic's lap momentarily, stripped of his sweats and repositioned to half kneeling, half sitting against Vic.

Cade felt the rough of Tegan's stubbled cheeks scrape along his shoulders, down his back in sweet fucking torture. Vic's arms wrapped around him and cupped Cade's ass cheeks, then spread them apart, displaying him. Before anything computed, there was once again the drag of Tegan's scruff, lower now, and in a very intimate, sensitive place, teasing him. And then he licked a stripe across Cade's hole and he froze, mouth open, his face heating as Vic studied him.

"Ah, you like that, baby?" he asked, but all Cade could do was offer something that sounded like a strangled half sob of pleasure. Still, Vic persisted in a torture of his own by trying to hold a conversation with him, requesting, "Tell me what Tegan's doing to you."

A simple request but all Cade could manage was, "He's licking...fuck..." as he straightened his spine in a simultaneous attempt to pull away and move closer. But there was nothing he could do about it. He was held. Trapped.

Worshiped.

He was no prude, but he'd never been a slow-fuck, spend the night in bed exploring each other type either. No, he went for the fast and dirty, not your place or mine, neutral territory, using whatever body parts could get him off the quickest and the hardest, but this was the farthest thing from that, and it was obvious that Tegan was getting off from rimming him as much as Cade was getting off being on the receiving end. It made him blush harder, which made Vic's smirk of satisfaction even more wicked as he stared into those dark as obsidian eyes that held more secrets than Cade figured he could ever uncover.

But dammit, he was going to try.

Vic's gaze continued to hold his as he nodded slowly. "That's right, baby—Tegan's eating your ass, just like he wanted to. I'm just helping him—and you—holding you wide open. Forcing you to just accept it. Because that's what you want, isn't it?"

Cade couldn't speak, could barely fucking breathe, and it took everything just to nod the affirmative to Vic's question as Tegan licked and laved while Vic continued to hold him open, immobilizing him. All he could do was kneel there and take it. His hand went for his cock, but Vic shook his head no and Cade chuffed out a hard breath but put his palms on Vic's shoulders instead, his cock throbbing between them.

His breath came in pants as Tegan used his spit to make him extra wet, which made it sound even dirtier. Then Tegan kissed his hole like he would've kissed Cade's mouth, then speared his tongue to gain entrance, which made Cade whimper. *Whimper*, for fuck's sake, and his fingers dug into Vic's shoulders, probably hard enough to leave marks, as he tried unsuccessfully to rock his hips and moaned in frustrated pleasure.

Vic smirked up at him. "Teegs, he looks so fucking hot when he's all worked up and helpless."

Tegan's hand came around to his cock, but instead of palming it, Tegan's finger swiped precum from the head...and Cade watched as Vic bent to meet Tegan's finger, never breaking his gaze as he licked the fluid from Tegan's finger.

A low, protesting keen escaped Cade's throat as Tegan's tongue continued taking him relentlessly, even as his hand remained holding the base of Cade's cock, frustrating him and turning him on even more at the same time. It only got more tortuous as Tegan added his fingers—first one, then two, twisting them, brushing them lightly against his prostate, but too fast for it to do anything but frustrate him in that gorgeous, pain/pleasure-filled way that kept his climax just out of reach. He was hanging by a goddamned thread as they kept allowing him to get to the edge before pulling him back, and he was aware of his curses and protests and moans that filled the air, loud and demandingly, heard himself in a haze, saying things like "*Someone needs to touch my goddamned dick,*" and "*Need to come, please,*" and "*Swear to Christ I'm going to lose my fucking mind.*"

But although those demands remained unmet, he couldn't deny that other needs were being filled to their breaking point. His breath came in short pants, and Vic bent his head to suck his tit again, and his balls tightened as Tegan's knuckles made contact with his gland and rubbed and pressed and *finally*. The pleasure that coiled in his belly spread outward, and his body began to clench tightly as Tegan's hand released its hard grip on his cock completely.

He cried out, Tegan's name and Vic's, and he came in short, hard jerks with Tegan's fingers still buried deep inside of him, pressing, even as his cock and ass throbbed like they had a heartbeat inside of them, beating in time with each other.

Vic released his nipple and let Cade wrap around him completely, his hips jerking, his body flooded with relief as he scrabbled against Vic, needing to hold on to someone, to ground himself as the shockwaves coursed through his body. It was as if he hadn't had an orgasm in forever, which wasn't true at all, but this? They hadn't been anything like this, at least not the ones in recent memory.

"Good, baby—that's good—come all over yourself," Vic encouraged as hot spurts of cum hit his belly, his chest, smearing on Vic as well. "Won't be the last time tonight."

Cade heard himself half laugh, half sob as he sank from his knees to rest on his heels, forehead on Vic's shoulder... until Tegan eased him back and began to lick the come from Cade's stomach and still-sensitive cock.

Vic threaded his hand through Tegan's hair and watched him contentedly, even though his own cock was tenting his shorts. "So dirty. So fucking perfect," Vic murmured, and Cade wasn't sure if he was talking about what Tegan was

doing or Tegan himself, but Cade agreed with both senti-
ments, especially because his dick was making a more than
halfhearted attempt at a fast revival.

He wanted to see them naked too, grabbed the bottom of
Vic's tee and tugged, and Vic obliged him by pulling it off.
His chest was hard—defined—and several tattoos decorated
his arms. Cade leaned in and sucked a nipple, because turn-
about was fair play.

"Yeah, baby, that's it—suckle it. Good practice," Vic told
him. And Cade did, listened to his commands, pushing any
other thoughts from his mind beyond making both men feel
as good as they'd made him feel.

Tegan's hands brushed along his hair, his shoulders.
"Making Vic feel good, baby? C'mon, let's get you lower." He
helped Cade up and shifted Vic so he sat on the edge of the
bed, feet on the floor, then put gentle pressure on Cade's
shoulders so he was kneeling in between Vic's legs. He
buried his face in the soft fabric of Vic's shorts, breathing in
deeply, and then Tegan pulled him back and freed Vic's cock,
hard and heavy and big. Tegan stroked it as Cade glanced up
to see the look of utter pleasure on Vic's face. His head was
partially thrown back, and he had a half smile on his face, his
eyes heavy-lidded and lazy.

Cade turned his focus back to Vic's cock. Tegan guided
his head toward the broad head and Cade opened willingly,
humming around its thickness.

"Jesus, Cade...yeah," Vic muttered, his own hands
twining in Cade's hair. Cade looked up in time to see Tegan
kiss Vic, and holy hell, it was beautiful to see the two men
kiss. It was more like they were sparring, fighting for domi-
nance as their mouths crushed against each other's.

And you were in the middle of that.

One of them would need to submit, at least momentarily. Cade made sure it would be Vic, sucked him down more deeply, causing him to shudder. Vic let Tegan kiss him more deeply even as his hand went between Tegan's legs, tugging demandingly on his shorts. Tegan obliged, pulling them down and Vic's hand circled his cock, which was big and flushed with need. God, either one of those cocks would fucking split him, and Cade couldn't help moaning around Vic's shaft as he reached up to roll his balls with his free hand.

"Jesus, Cade—yeah, baby, just like that," Vic encouraged even as Tegan half shouted because Vic was stroking him hard. One of Tegan's hands remained twined in Cade's hair and the other, Cade noted, was tracing the scarred side of Vic's body, his fingers moving from Vic's cheek to his neck and shoulders and back up again, caressing. Cade used his free hand to touch himself because Christ, he was going to come again, no doubt about it, and he really wanted to see Tegan fuck Vic or vice versa and he wanted one or both of them to fuck him right now...but then Vic shouted and he was coming in Cade's mouth, and Cade came and Tegan followed shortly after, half sagging against the headboard and cursing.

He leaned his cheek against Vic's thigh for several moments as they all just breathed, the room smelling of sex and man and filled with their harsh breaths. There were no regrets or recriminations, and after several long minutes, there were soft murmurs and washcloths and water to drink and he asked if there could be pizza as he was half falling asleep against both men.

He'd wanted them to fuck him, but by not doing so,

they'd immediately set themselves apart from every other man he'd fucked or been fucked by. And they'd raised the bar considerably, high enough that someone would have to be an Olympic-level jumper to even attempt to compete.

Cade didn't want to think about that now. Not when it was dark and cool, and he was half floating like it was all a goddamned dream. Part of him hoped it was, because that would be easier to live with. Dreams would fade...but the reality of what happened and how it made him feel promised to not be erased nearly as quickly, if at all.

All Cade's resistance for the night drained away. Surely, it would make a renewed entrance after several hours of R&R, but for now, Tegan would enjoy the pliant man in his arms.

Vic's chest was pressed to Cade's back. "Think it helped?"

Tegan smiled. "Sure as hell helped me."

Cade laughed softly against his chest.

CHAPTER 14

WHEN CADE FINALLY WOKE, he had no idea what time it was because the bedroom was dark. The fact that he was alone didn't bother him, especially when a quick glance at his phone told him it was close to five in the evening. There was orange juice and a bagel next to the bed with a note that read, *More food downstairs—come down when you're ready*, and one of them had brought in his bag from his truck.

His ass was slightly, but definitely happily, sore, a remainder of the heady experience of last night, and no, it definitely hadn't been a dream. His dick had already been hard when he woke but got harder still when memories from last night came flooding back to him in full-blown technicolor and he stroked himself, wondering what would've happened if he'd woken up in bed with them now.

Something else fittingly filthy, he figured, then pulled his hand away from his cock. He was fighting tonight and he didn't jerk off or fuck on the day of a fight. He figured last night didn't count toward that, not if he didn't want it to, and fuck it, it was his rule.

He was still half cum-drunk, dammit.

He downed the juice and ate the bagel on the way to the bathroom. He showered and changed and then went off to find Tegan and Vic, his stomach doing nervous jumps like he was a school kid with a crush.

Christ. He ran his hands through his still-damp hair, shouldered his bag, and found them in the same room he'd met with them in last night, on the first floor. Oz was there too, typing with his heavy rings in place, and Cade wondered if he ever stopped to sleep.

As soon as Tegan saw him, his expression warmed and Cade's stomach did another small flip, and another when Vic turned to pin him with a gaze. Tegan smiled like he knew what was running through Cade's mind. "Theo's position has been located."

Relief coursed through him, and he dropped his bag outside the door before stepping into the room. "Good. That's good, right?"

"Yes. But it'll take a while to get to him," Tegan cautioned.

"Yeah, I know." The jungles of Western Africa weren't exactly equipped with a superhighway. It was all dirt roads and hard travel. "Listen, I need to go fight tonight."

Oz stopped typing but didn't turn around. Vic muttered something about "Mr. Stubborn's back." And Tegan? Gave a long-suffering sigh.

Hell, it wasn't like Cade hadn't been on the receiving end of those most of his damned life.

"Look, I get it, okay? I'm at risk. But Courier's not going to take me out right in the middle of the club. I need to work." It wasn't just about paying Tegan and Vic for helping Theo—

he had other responsibilities to the man who'd helped him through the worst of times.

"Then we'll take you," Vic offered.

He glanced at Oz, who hadn't turned and fuck it, it wasn't like Oz didn't know what happened between the three of them. "What's happening between us? Scares the fuck out of me. And I guess that's okay...maybe it's even normal. But I don't want to drag you into my shit."

"You're not dragging us," Tegan told him. "If we can do it for total strangers, then what's the point if we can't help people we care about?"

"I don't...how do you know that—that you care about me? And why? I've known you for five minutes," Cade protested and figured they'd be mad, but it was the truth.

To his surprise, Vic looked more amused than upset while Tegan explained, "How did you know to apologize to Vic last night? I'm assuming you don't walk around saying you're sorry to everyone. It's what you do when you care about someone and yes, it can be scary as hell. It's the risk you take when you let people in."

He didn't like risking other people's safety, and he never thought he'd be capable of the intensity of feeling he had toward these men. This place. But... "I'm not going to know if you only want to help me or if you really feel something for me if I stay. That might not make sense to you."

"It does," Vic said reluctantly. "I can promise you, we know the difference. But you need to feel it."

He nodded, ignoring the warning bells that told him he had fucking felt it before, during, and after he'd come and finally conceded. "How about if you guys drop me off at work?"

"And pick you up afterward?" Vic asked. "And you'll come back here?"

"Until Theo's safe," Cade agreed.

"How about we discuss what happens after that *when* it happens?" Tegan suggested.

Cade was already up and heading to the door, but he turned to face them. "I can live with that. But can we leave now? I don't want to be late."

He wasn't angry about it—more like resigned—as he took a step back without turning around, and before he could do anything else, he felt the heat of a body close in behind him.

Tegan saw Strider fill the doorway behind Cade just before the grab, but there was no time to stop him. Strider was an old member of Gray Ops, and he was crazy, but Tegan didn't think he'd bring harm to Cade.

But Vic had only heard about Strider through Brian and never had the pleasure of meeting the man in person...which was why Vic was actually growling and ready to lunge... which would've made Tegan hot if it hadn't been under "Cade in danger" circumstances.

"I'd let go of him now, Strider." He jerked his head toward Vic, whose teeth were bared.

"I don't follow your orders," Strider told him, his tone pleasant, not releasing his iron grip on Cade. Cade was strong, yes, but he wasn't a match for the six-foot-six package the world knew as Strider, who rode the line between handsome and menacing.

Vic went toward him but Tegan grabbed his shoulder. "Stand down, Vic."

"Not until he gets his hands off Cade."

Strider frowned. "Touchy. It's like you've all bonded... like werewolves." His voice took on a peculiar glee at that last word.

"Werewolves?" Tegan asked.

"What the fuck's he talking about?" Vic muttered, the growls abruptly stopping as he frowned, and yeah, that was Strider for you.

"Fucking nuts," Oz added.

"Do *none* of you read romance novels? Werewolves? Fated mates?" Strider shook his head sadly at their frowns. "You're missing some great shit. Anyway...onward. I've come for the boy, so this works out perfectly."

Vic growled at Strider calling Cade boy and Tegan demanded, "What's your business with Cade?"

"The usual. Someone paid me a great deal of money to kill him."

The entire room stilled. Cade went pale before his anger bounced back and he began to struggle.

"Hands off, Strider. Now," Tegan instructed when he was able to breathe again.

Strider ignored him, keeping a strong grip on Cade's biceps as he leaned in to look at him. "You've got all of them turned around. In the old days, they wouldn't have coddled you. So why do you interest them so much?"

"Strider," Oz said harshly, and Strider met his gaze with his own oddly colored, nearly amber eyes that always gave him an otherworldly look, and a current passed between them that seemed to unlock Strider's grip, if only slightly.

Still, it allowed Cade to turn and face the man who'd been sent to take him out. "You're Courier's bitch, aren't you?"

"Nobody owns me, and I'm definitely not the bitch in this situation," Strider corrected, his tone was mild. "Tegan, I'm curious—did Cade even tell you that there was a psychopath after him?"

"Yes, he did. But I didn't realize there were two of you," Tegan shot back.

"Nice one. Have you been practicing comebacks in the mirror?"

Tegan took a step toward him, but Strider held Cade in front of him like a shield. "Now, now—let's not hurt the precious boy." Cade struggled but it was no use—Strider's hold had always been one of his strengths.

"I'm losing patience fast," Tegan warned.

"That makes two of us. I'll let go—but you should warn him not to try something stupid."

Of course, as soon as Cade was free, he turned and threw a solid left that made hard contact with Strider's jaw. It didn't take him down, which no doubt surprised Cade, who continued to try and got in several more good punches, mainly because Strider let him before he slammed him face-down to the ground, stepping on his neck while rubbing his jaw.

"Who knew Strider had a glass jaw?" Oz mused.

"Thanks for the help," Strider grumbled.

"Oh, did you need help? I didn't notice." Oz sounded bored.

Cade groaned and Vic shoved Strider off him and helped Cade up. Cade went for Strider again, but Strider rolled his eyes. "Call your boy off so the grown-ups can talk."

"I'm going to kill him the second I get the chance," Vic told the room.

"Get in line behind me," Oz answered.

"Strider, start talking. I'm assuming that if you really meant to follow through on your job, Cade would be dead and you wouldn't be here," Tegan pointed out.

Strider put his hands up in a well-you-caught-me pose. "You all act like I don't have a heart."

"It's just very small and black?" Oz offered.

"You missed me—don't deny it." Strider wagged a finger at him.

"Strider—focus. Who sent you here to kill Cade?" Tegan thundered, done with the man's bullshit antics.

"Why is *Cade* here in the first place?" Strider asked.

Oz threw his hands up "Asshole can never just answer a question."

"Cade's here for Fantasy Week," Tegan lied as calmly as he could.

"When did hanging out with all of you become a fantasy?" Strider shook his head. Oz picked up a shotgun that he kept under the desk and aimed it at Strider, who put his hands up and addressed Cade. "Why does Courier want you dead?"

"Strider, you're answering *our* questions," Tegan reminded him.

"I never agreed to that." Strider crossed his arms.

"Courier wants me dead because he's a fucking sociopath," Cade muttered from where he sat, near Oz, with Vic half in front of him.

"Now you're actually making sense." Strider smiled. "And yes, Courier's the one who hired me to kill you. He didn't give a reason—just dangled the money with a promise of more to follow once the job was done."

"And you took the money?" Oz asked, the shotgun still raised.

"Guy's gotta eat." Strider shrugged. "But I like having a reason. The reason is very important to me, and my cursory search into the big bad, dark, and ugly places on the dark web brought up zilch on the boy there. So either I can dig deeper, which I'm always happy to do—"

"Not a boy," Cade growled.

Strider gave Cade a once-over. "A night with me would make you rethink that...you'd beg me to call you boy."

Tegan stepped in front of him before Vic charged. "I need more intel. Now."

"I'm supposed to show proof of death," Strider offered. "Does that count as intel?"

"I'm going to kill you myself," Tegan promised. "Tell us what Courier said."

Strider gave a completely put-upon sigh. "Kill Cade. Money, half up front and half after proof of death—the usual hit-man dance. He didn't give a reason, but he did promise to show me the video he's got of him with Cade. He said that Cade promised him money not to show it, but you're behind on payments."

Tegan glanced at Cade, who looked nonplussed at the sex video revelation. "Do you think I've got a fucking problem starring in one man's version of a porn flick? What's he going to do—show it to my bosses? Hell, they'd probably show it as a backdrop to my fights." Cade said.

"He's not wrong," Oz admitted. "And none of this makes sense."

"Maybe the connection's not so much about you," Tegan reasoned and saw the recognition bloom behind Cade's eyes before he quickly schooled his expression. "Did Courier say anything else about..." Cade started to ask Strider, then stopped when he realized everyone had whirled around to stare at him. "Anything else?"

Strider looked around Tegan's body, which still blocked Cade. "Anyone specific?" Vic growled and Strider rolled his eyes. "Fine. Courier did advertise a second job. He outsourced it because I can't be in two places at once, and when you go after someone who's active duty and deployed—"

The crash came from Cade's chair and he was up, heading fast toward Strider. But Vic grabbed him in time, held him in place.

Strider supplied, "I believe the mark is in West Africa, if that helps."

"He's not a mark," Cade snapped.

"The mark's name is Theo Davies, aka Theo Dolentz. I don't know who got the job, but the position was filled," Strider finished. Cade sounded like he was breathing through a straw. "You sound terrible—you really should have that looked at."

"Please, Tegan—can I just wound him a little?" Oz begged.

Vic made him sit and commanded him to "Just fucking

breathe" and Cade would've laughed at the absurdity of all of it...if he could *just fucking breathe*.

But finally, he was calm enough to do so. Vic handed him water and he gulped it while realizing that Oz hadn't been allowed to wound Strider. That instead, the tall as hell, lanky, dark-haired man with the oddest amber-colored eyes Cade had ever seen had made himself comfortable.

"It's nice here, Tegan. This whole 'good works' vibe is working for me," Strider observed.

"He's not staying," Oz told Tegan before turning to Strider. "You're not staying."

"I figured you'd rather me here for a bit—at least until you figure out your do-gooder plan of attack. So, what's for dinner?" Strider clapped his hands together.

Cade stared at him, wondering how he could make jokes. But when Strider glanced back at him, for the briefest of seconds, Cade saw something deep and dark, a bottomless pit of pain emanating from him.

He didn't kill you when he could have.

"Have you met Courier before this?" Tegan was asking Strider now.

"No. I've never heard of him either, but his money is real. I think this is his first time on the big bad dark web."

"Because you know everyone on that superhighway?" Oz asked.

"Yes, I do. He's new. That doesn't mean he's not danger-ous, but this is his first time advertising for death." Strider turned to Cade. "What did you do to him?"

"Fucked him and then didn't want to anymore," Cade admitted.

Strider frowned. "When you say '*fucked him*,' does that mean..."

"Strider!" Tegan shouted.

"A man can't even be curious anymore?" Strider shook his head and turned his attention back to Cade. "So that's *all* you did to him? I mean, no offense, but are you *that* good in bed? I mean, I am, so yes, I could see something like that happen to me but..."

"Strider, please," Tegan ground out, and it almost sounded like a beg. "Do you have any idea who's going after Theo or how close they are?"

"I might, yes."

"Strider, please." Cade echoed Tegan, hated that his voice broke, but he pressed on. "I'll go with you—I just need to know that Theo's safe."

Strider leaned forward and stared at him. "You're willing to die for your friend."

"Yes," Cade told him, ignoring Vic cursing in the background. "I am."

To his surprise, Strider looked up at Vic and began reciting coordinates.

"I've got them," Oz called and Vic was over his shoulder, looking at the screen.

Strider's attention was back on Cade. "Would your friend do the same for you?"

"Definitely." Cade stood and walked toward him. Tegan didn't stop him, either.

Strider glanced up at him curiously. "Going somewhere?"

"With you, like I told you I would."

Strider shook his head. "You couldn't have made it this

easy when I had you in a good position to drag you out the door? Because now..." With a sweep of his hand, he motioned around the room at the men who stared back at them. "I'm not getting through them without some bloodshed."

But that wasn't the only reason—Cade was pretty sure of it even though Strider added, "Besides, the only reason you'd want to come with me would be to try and talk me into letting you kill Courier. Am I wrong?"

He wasn't. Cade rolled his eyes and Strider mouthed, *How much money do you have?*

"Strider, that's not happening," Tegan told him. "Oz, anything?"

"Strider, you're sure the coordinates belong to the assassin sent to Theo?" Oz asked.

"Very." Strider looked confident and far too comfortable.

Cade looked toward the monitor and Vic leaned into him. "Our man is closer."

Cade closed his eyes and sagged against the chair. "Good. That's good."

"Seems like a great opportunity for a group hug here," Strider stood.

"Over my dead body," Vic growled.

"I could definitely arrange that," Strider said pointedly. "We've still got a big problem here with Courier, not to mention that I'm giving up an awful lot of money by not killing the boy."

"Not a boy!" Cade shouted.

"You know what they say it means when you protest too much," Strider murmured.

"I'm supposed to fight in under an hour," Cade told Tegan. Andrei had been blowing up his phone.

"So, what kind of fight is Cade involved in?" Strider asked way too casually. "An illegal one?"

"They're legal," Oz told him.

"Nothing legal is all that much fun," Strider pointed out.

"God, he just gets worse over time," Oz groaned.

"Like spoiled milk," Tegan agreed.

"Can I please kill him?" Oz begged.

Tegan shook his head sadly. "Maybe later. For now, don't let him out of your sight."

"Wait, you're leaving him alone with me?" Oz called as Tegan and Vic ushered Cade out of the room.

"No way—I'm going to get a rep as someone who can't do their job!" Strider yelled louder. "You're not taking my street cred. Courier wants updates in real time."

Cade doubled back. "You made contact with Courier?"

"Maybe."

"And you didn't mention it?" Tegan demanded.

"I don't work for you," Strider said seriously.

CHAPTER 15

"AM I being chauffeured or can I take my own truck?" Cade asked as they walked out the back door of Crave, leaving behind Oz's yells of "I can't promise what I'll do if you leave me alone with him."

"We'll drive you," Tegan told him.

"Why don't you just carry me across the threshold of the fight club when we get there?" Cade muttered.

"Didn't know you needed that level of romance," Vic said seriously. "I'll keep it in mind."

Cade sighed heavily and got into the back seat with Vic, while Tegan drove. He guessed it was for protection, and arguing wouldn't change a damned thing. He needed to preserve his strength anyway.

Vic handed him a Gatorade and a PowerBar. "Eat up."

Cade muttered, "Fucking starving and this shit tastes like cardboard."

"Fight first, then I'll get you a goddamned buffet," Vic promised.

"There's a McDonald's on the corner," Cade pointed out hopefully.

"You had an entire pizza recently," Vic reminded him.

"Recently to me is the last hour." Cade bit into the PowerBar and stared at Vic. "I think this went bad."

Vic frowned. "They can't go bad."

"Worse than MREs." Cade tried to chew and ended up just washing it down with a half choke. "So, what exactly does Strider do?"

"Do you really want to know?" Tegan asked over his shoulder.

"When you put it like that? Definitely."

"Fucking reverse psychology never works around here," Tegan muttered. "He's a mercenary."

"Sounds more like an assassin." Cade shoved the unfinished PowerBar into his jacket pocket and Vic shook his head.

"He used to work with us," Tegan continued.

"You fired him?"

"We parted ways amicably. He wasn't a good fit." Tegan shrugged. "He'd get us in trouble eventually and he knew it."

"But you still watch out for him. And obviously, vice versa."

"He keeps an eye out," Tegan conceded. "He's happy doing what he does best, in corners of the world and the internet that we don't want to know about."

Worry bloomed anew in Cade's gut. He stared out the truck's window space, his mind racing a million miles an hour.

"Listen, your friend's in the middle of the jungle—and he's Delta, which means he's damned good. No one's getting the jump on him," Vic reminded him. "Whoever took the job's probably waiting for him to come out—no one's going in after him."

"But the man Tegan sent in to find him will?"

"Definitely," Tegan assured him. "You just concentrate on your fight tonight. We'll be right there."

"You're staying?"

"Is that a problem?"

No, it's a hell of a turn-on. "Nope."

Vic snorted, reading his mind, and before Cade could retort, his phone rang. He grabbed it, figuring it was Andrei. "Yeah—what's up?"

"Hi, Cade—it's Rourke." Rourke's voice was deep, husky with a hint of laughter, like he knew Cade was sitting there, surprised. Rourke was without a doubt a guy who liked getting—and keeping—the upper hand, and if he'd met Rourke earlier, there'd have been a definite attraction.

Cade swallowed and glanced at Vic. "Hi, Detective—"

"Rourke," he insisted, and then Vic was leaning in, listening to the entire conversation. "I'm wondering if you're coming home tonight?"

Cade put a hand over Vic's mouth to muffle the growl. "Do you have more questions for me?"

"Not on an official basis, but yes. I've got...questions. And I'd like to ask you them face-to-face."

"Oh." Cade's face went hot and Vic narrowed his eyes. "I'll have to get back to you on that. I'm kind of...busy."

"I figured after your fight tonight would be the perfect time. I signed up to get text message alerts about you, so I'm really looking forward to watching you. Think about it. I'll check in with you later."

"Okay, yeah, I will," he said, and Rourke chuffed a laugh

before hanging up. Cade put his phone back into his pocket and studied the PowerBar intently, not planning on going over the conversation with either Vic or Tegan.

But obviously, he was the only one with that plan.

"That's it?" Vic demanded. "That's how you're going to play this?"

"It's not a big deal."

" 'I'll have to get back to you on that'? So you're going to meet Rourke for questions? Do you know what his brand of questions entails?"

"I don't want to piss off a detective who's investigating me. And yeah, I'm kind of figuring out what his brand of questions would entail." He cut a glance to Tegan, who watched him through the rearview mirror.

"So flirting with him is better?" Vic directed his conversation to Tegan. "Rourke's trying to get in his pants."

"So are we," Tegan reminded him.

"No, we've already been in his pants," Vic corrected.

"Oh, Christ." Cade flexed his hands, warming them up. "Rourke wants intel. He thinks flirting with me's the best way to get it."

"Isn't it?" Vic asked.

"You heard me tell him I was busy."

"Which you are," Tegan growled and whoa, the men were actually jealous. "I'll make sure Rourke knows it."

"How about letting me manage it?" Cade suggested.

"No," both men said at once.

"So, do you have to get the guest room ready for me? Or is

Cade staying there? I could stay with him, no problem, because I wouldn't mind seeing what has Courier so enthralled." Strider was reclining in one of the office chairs, his feet up on the desk and looking far too comfortable for Oz's liking.

"You're not staying long enough to sleep."

"If I leave, I'm supposed to bring Cade's dead body with me. So you might want to rethink that." Strider reached across him and grabbed Oz's bag of chips. "Seriously, can we order dinner now? And for this Cade problem, I'm going to need to know more."

"Like?" Oz resisted the urge to bang his head against the desk.

"How long the three of them have been fucking, for one thing."

"And that will help you how?"

"It won't help at all. I'm just very curious," Strider said in a stage whisper. Like they were conspiring against invisible people, since they were alone in the room.

But who the hell knew—Strider might actually have imaginary friends. Because knowing him... "Don't you have anyone else to kill, Strider? I hear the FBI's still investigating you."

"They are—it's all very hush-hush undercover. I think I'm not supposed to even know about it." Strider was like a little kid with his insider information. "But I'm surprised that you're still keeping tabs on me. And here I didn't think you cared."

Oz kept his voice as bored-sounding as possible. "If it was up to me, there'd be a hit out on you."

"So why isn't there?"

"I was outvoted...although I'm guessing now they're all regretting that decision."

Strider had been one of the original members of Gray Ops until they realized just how far he went for his...reasons, as he liked to call them. He was too much on the side of vigilante justice, and Oz and the others had voted him off the island. Granted, Strider didn't really know that, and he'd ended up leaving right before they told him. Oz was never sure if he did that just so he wouldn't get fired, or if he didn't want to fuck them over.

He was pretty sure that somewhere under the sarcasm and darkness, there was a heart. It was just small. And probably black.

Maybe they'd study Strider's body for science one day.

"You're smiling. Thinking about me?" Strider asked.

"You have no idea. Can we talk about Courier now? Because you know more than you're saying."

Strider's legs slammed down to the ground and he rolled to the closest monitor. "Courier's a head case—an obsessive stalker type." He didn't bother asking permission, just started typing while Oz accessed his screen so he could see exactly what Strider was doing as he surfed the dark web more deeply than Oz ever cared to go. "Cade's not the first guy he's done this to."

"Did he hire someone to kill all of them?"

"No. Apparently, our Cade's *very* special." Strider tapped a few more keys. "I'm going to have to dig deeper into Cade's background. Much deeper."

"Fine," Oz bit out, feeling sick at the information Strider had already pulled up.

"Is this harming your delicate sensibilities?"

"Yes. But if it helps Cade..." Oz sat back, happy to rest his fingers on this one. "But I want to know why you really came here."

"I told you—I need a reason and Courier didn't provide me with a satisfactory one."

"Don't bullshit me, with all your 'you need a reason' shit."

Strider managed to look offended. "You know I do."

"You already have it, which is why Cade doesn't have a bullet in his head and his picture isn't posted like he's big game on the dark web. If you looked into Cade and saw nothing? You saw the same paperwork I did."

"The foster care thing? Please." Strider shook his head. "If I boo-hoo-ed for every foster care kid who whined about how bad his past was, I'd be broke."

"So what was it about Cade?"

"I don't know, Oz. Maybe I'm getting sentimental in my old age."

"You're not even thirty yet."

"I was actually hoping you'd throw me a dirty thirty party here—my birthday does fall during your next Fantasy Week. Perhaps Go-Go boys? I do enjoy a good Go-Go boy."

"Now there's an image I'll never be able to erase from my brain. Christ, why are you still here?" Oz groaned for what seemed like the thousandth time that hour.

Strider was strangely silent on the topic.

When Oz turned to face him, the man was watching him. Intently. "I'm here because you called me here, *poppet*. Now tell me why a man surrounded by mercenaries—and one who's a decent enough shot himself—needs to hire one from the dark web?"

Oz stilled because motherfucker, what were the chances

his outreach would pull Strider in? He pulled himself together enough to say, "Poppet? You're not even British."

"I just like the sound of it. Obviously, so do you. And you can keep changing the subject but eventually, we're going to need to discuss it."

Oz gritted his teeth. "Eventually is not now."

Vic spotted Rourke standing outside the club as they drove into the back lot. He wasn't surprised Rourke showed up there—the man would've been far more aggressive with Cade than he'd been had it not been for Vic and Tegan. In truth, what Cade didn't know was that Rourke was a regular visitor to both Crave and the back rooms, and an active participant in Fantasy Week. He was a definite Dom with a big following, and Vic was prepared to let him know that Cade was not up for subbing to him.

So he left Cade to warm up—and left Tegan with him— and walked back outside.

Rourke was waiting for him. At least it seemed that way, because he walked right up and stuck out his hand for Vic to shake. "Good to see you again, Vic."

Vic gave the handsome man's hand a firm shake. "Why are you here?"

"Last I looked, I was allowed to go anywhere. But, to answer your question, I'm here for Cade, to see if he wants some company."

"He's got *plenty* of company," Vic informed him.

Rourke shrugged. "He didn't tell me that on the phone earlier. And he hasn't given me an outright no, which you obviously know. So until then, I'm going to enjoy watching him fight."

"Don't bullshit me, Rourke. You might want to fuck him —and you would, given the opportunity, but you're not coming on all that strong."

Rourke ran a hand through his blond hair and gave Vic an innocent shrug—or tried to, anyway. He was about as innocent as Vic was. "I figured I'd spook him otherwise. He doesn't realize what it is he needs—not yet."

"You're not the one who'll help him figure that out."

Rourke studied him for a long moment and finally smiled. "So, you and Tegan are going to help him figure it out —together?"

"Yes."

Rourke dipped his head in deference. "Then I'll back off."

"I know you'd have come on to him a lot stronger if he wasn't still a suspect."

Rourke smirked but got serious again quickly. He jerked his head toward the fight club building. "Your boy there? He's in trouble."

"And that's why you've been trying to question him?"

Rourke leaned against the wall. "Whoever put out the call to investigate Cade, his friend, and the stepfather has some clout. I thought it was a bullshit investigation and I still do. But it's not just going to go away. I'm supposed to pull Cade in for questioning."

"So why haven't you?"

"Talk him into getting a lawyer, not a public defender."

"Who's behind the calls?"

"That shit's above my pay grade. I got a visit from the chief today. The case is moving up in the world."

Vic shook his head. "Dammit. I'll make sure he's covered."

"I'll hold off pulling him in as long as I can. Especially if I can't find him," Rourke called as he walked away and fuck, Vic was going to owe him one.

And Rourke? He'd definitely collect.

Before Cade fought, Andrei needed him to work the floor. It was a job Cade never minded. Most of the men who came here were chill. But sometimes, losing money caused issues like the one that cropped up tonight, right in front of the ring, where the entourages that accompanied tonight's new, young fighters were pressed in like sardines.

He shoved his way through the crowd with Ivan behind him and together they worked to separate the two men who'd come to blows. The one Cade grabbed twisted away from his grip and pulled a knife on him.

Cade cursed. "You've got to be fucking kidding me—I don't have time for this shit." He faked the guy out and got a hold on his wrist, twisting and breaking it easily. He caught the knife before it fell as the man he'd taken it from sank to his knees, howling in pain.

"You little fucker—you need to watch your back," he started, but Dobry—Cade's boss and the big boss of the entire place—aka the man no one wanted to fuck with—leaned in from behind him and dragged him to his feet.

Dobry cursed in Russian and, with his heavy accent, said

something to the effect of, "You're dead if you touch him," (meaning Cade) and "You're dead if you ever set foot in here again," and "Maybe just killing you now would be easier."

"Cade, go get ready—I've got this now," Ivan called to him with a smile and a thumbs-up.

Cade nodded and walked through the now-separated crowd to applause that had him shaking his head. He was actually surprised babysitters one and two hadn't jumped in to rescue him...and wasn't surprised to find them scowling at him as they waited by his assigned room.

"Problem?" he asked casually.

" '*Problem?*' " Tegan mimicked as he followed him inside. Vic shut the door and leaned against it. "Yes, Cade—big problem."

"Did you want to protect me from the big bad knife?" Cade asked as he changed, throwing clothes off and riffling through his bag for his shorts and tank.

"That's not fair," Vic said.

Cade straightened. "What's not fair?"

"Getting naked to win this fight," Tegan growled. "Get dressed so I can keep yelling at you."

Cade snorted but tucked that piece of information into the back of his mind, because he figured he'd need to utilize it again.

———

Cade won his fight, although it was a tough one. His side still hurt from sparring with Vic, but he was never one to make excuses. The guy he fought—Knight—was good. They'd won and lost against each other equally over the years, a good-natured rivalry, but the betting was always intense when they squared off in the ring.

Cade showered and dressed and found Vic and Tegan waiting for him outside the locker room. He rolled his eyes. "It's like having an entourage."

Vic cocked a brow at him. "Would you like your entourage to chauffeur you back to Crave?"

"Like I have a choice?" Cade asked, but in truth, he was glad as fuck he'd agreed to that earlier, because he was all worked up.

Vic steered him out the side door instead of the back, and Cade frowned as the door closed behind them and a look passed between Vic and Tegan that made his gut tighten with a nervous pleasure.

"Aren't you scared to have little unprotected me out here, without my bubble?" he asked, but his voice sounded hoarse to his own ears and hell, was this going to happen, out here, with them?

"Funny boy. We *are* your goddamned bubble," Vic growled, and Cade felt it shoot straight to his cock. Vic dipped his hand inside his sweats and palmed him, his touch like a lick of fire that had Cade gripping his biceps and panting.

"You're sure you want to come back to Crave with us?" Tegan asked innocently. "You seemed unsure—"

"Yes. Fuck, yes, please." Cade heard the pleading in his own voice. "Fuckers."

Vic laughed—and it was really good to be able to make Vic laugh, even if Cade needed to come so badly he might die if he didn't. "What do you want, Cade? Tell me."

"I want to come," he managed, but then other words were

spilling out, so fast, before he could stop them. "And I want my fantasy. In Room Four. With just you two." Both men stilled, and Cade held his breath. Did they not want that?

Finally, Vic murmured, "We can definitely do that."

"So this fantasy," Tegan started, "is up to us to plan?"

Cade looked between them and nodded. "As long as it's just you two, yes. But you really don't want me to have any say?"

Vic glanced at Tegan, who asked him, "The bigger question is, do you trust yourself—and us—enough to let go?"

"I mean...I do. I trust you guys more than me, but I'm guessing that's expected," he said, and Tegan's answer was a nod. "But I still I want to know more...just because."

"Of course you do, but I'm not spoiling the surprises." Tegan smirked.

"Okay, just tell me this—you obviously think you know me well enough to plan it. Tell me one thing you've learned about me," Cade pressed.

"You like to fuck in public but still be protected," Vic said roughly. "It's more about the possibility of humiliation that gets you off. Like the other night when I held you open. When we talk about you to each other. For you, it's up here." He touched Cade's head. "As much as here." His hand landed briefly back between Cade's legs.

Heat flooded through him, and he couldn't argue. "I mean, I get how you know that now—and I told you I fuck out here all the time—but the other stuff...*how* did you know?"

"I'm not giving away all our secrets," Tegan told him. "Trust me, you'll be grateful for them."

Relief whooshed through him. "Good. But after you find

Theo." Because then and only then could he actually relax enough to appreciate it.

"What about now—and this?" Tegan asked, a hand between Cade's legs. "We know you usually come out here after your fights. Can you handle two groupies?"

Cade closed his eyes and wondered if, when he opened them, he'd find out he'd been knocked unconscious and this was all a dream. But when he opened them, he was in the same position, and they were semi-patiently waiting for his answer.

"Yeah," he said finally. "I can handle it. If you'd waited for me that first night, I'd have let you fuck me here."

"Both of us?" Vic asked.

"Both of you," Cade confirmed.

"You're in so much trouble, little one," Tegan murmured.

"I'll probably love every goddamned minute of it," Cade shot back, ignoring the "little one" comment because fuck, everything they said made him both hot and embarrassed, which only served to make it hotter.

Tegan spun him so he faced the wall, his palms flat against the brick, and yanked his sweats down. He wore no underwear and neither man complained.

Vic's hand trailed down his spine. "Open him up, Tegan. Get him ready."

Cade heard the snap of a lube bottle and then felt as Tegan's blunt finger pressed his hole, even as he reached around to tease Cade's cock. "You wanted this last night, didn't you?"

Cade could only nod as Tegan's finger slid inside of him, teasing. Torturing. He groaned into the push of the second finger and Tegan murmured, "That's it, baby. Fuck yourself on my fingers."

Vic leaned against the brick wall next to him, watching him. "You need Tegan's cock inside of you, Cade? You need to be filled up? Taken, out here, where anybody could walk by and see you?"

"Fuck, yes," Cade moaned because yes, that was a big part of it. Didn't matter that the alleyway was cordoned off and mainly private—for this very reason, because he wasn't the only person seeking post-fight relief—but that didn't matter.

Vic ducked under his arms and ended up face-to-face with him. "You going to put him out of his misery, Teegs?"

Tegan rubbed the scruff from his cheeks along the back of Cade's neck. "I'm not sure how badly he wants it."

"Fuck—I want it. Please," Cade growled, rubbing his ass against Tegan's cock.

Tegan growled back, a deliciously possessive sound that grabbed Cade by the balls as his lubed fingers played with him. And then his fingers left, and Cade heard the snap of a condom before Tegan pushed up inside of him.

Vic kissed him, muffled Cade's cry at the invasion, and kept kissing him as Tegan's thick cock slowly worked inside of him. Vic's fingers played with his nipples as his tongue played in Cade's mouth, until all the sensations—pleasure and hurt—began to combine and roll together until he couldn't pick them apart.

As the burn began to travel outward, Cade pushed back to take Tegan more deeply inside of him. Vic took his mouth—ravaged it—as Tegan took his ass. Vic pulled his mouth off Cade's and grabbed for Tegan, moving between kissing both of them, stroking his and Cade's cocks together. It was so public and dirty, hit all his wants and needs.

It was perfect.

"Fuck—need to come," he groaned, and then he was, all over Vic's hand, and his orgasm milked Tegan's cock and triggered his shuddering orgasm, jerking his cock deep inside of him.

He sagged between them, his forehead on Vic's chest, Tegan's face buried in his hair and they were all holding each other up. Cade hadn't wanted that part to end, because reality would come crashing down as soon as his orgasm high ended.

But Tegan and Vic were both stroking rough palms over his skin...and then Tegan rolled a condom onto Vic. Vic turned Cade so his back was against the bricks, lifted his thigh, and entered him.

"God—Vic!" Cade yelled as Vic seated himself fully inside, balls touching his ass. Vic smiled but didn't stop thrusting against him, rough and so fucking good. His own dick had stayed mostly hard through his last orgasm and now, with Vic hitting his gland just the right way, he felt another one building.

Even though Vic's thrusts were deep, he was still taking his time as Tegan leaned against the wall, watching them, jerking Cade's cock, leaning into Vic, which Cade loved watching. Finally, Vic held fast to his hips and fucked him with a brutal pace as he keened, and Cade whimpered as Vic came, swore he could feel Vic pulsing into the condom.

Tegan's hand was still on his cock. Vic's joined it and both of them were stroking him.

"Fuck, wish I could come inside of you—my come and

Tegan's mixing together," Vic whispered against his ear, and that was all it took for him to come again, crying out both their names together like a chant.

Vic muttered something against his ear that wasn't English—Gaelic, maybe—and Cade fisted a hand through Vic's hair as Tegan brushed kisses against his cheek.

As they helped him pull his pants up and get into the truck, he murmured, "What the hell are you guys doing to me?"

Tegan stroked a hand down his cheek. "We keep asking ourselves the same question about you."

CHAPTER 16

THE LAST THING Cade wanted to do when he got back to Crave was talk to Strider again. But Tegan had to check in about Theo, and that was the most important thing. Cade's dick had been appeased enough—at least momentarily, because he swore he could still go another couple of rounds—but instead, he went into the war room, where Oz appeared stressed as fuck, a fact that definitely didn't go unnoticed by either Vic or Tegan, the former of whom left and came back with a sandwich that he put directly in front of Oz.

Oz sighed but didn't argue, just started eating.

Cade made a mental note to find out more about Oz—added it to his list of information to find out, because he still had plenty of questions about Tegan and Vic.

Except his dick kept getting in the way of talk time.

When Tegan's phone dinged with an incoming text, he glanced at it and showed it to Cade.

Package extracted, was all the text said.

"We'll hear more once they're safely at the compound.

But for now, Theo's with our people, and they're on the move," Tegan explained.

Which meant Theo still wasn't safe...but at least he wasn't in the dark about what was happening with Courier anymore. He was probably also pissed as hell. "Where are they taking him?"

"A safe house in East Africa. Theo will stay there, protected, until we figure this out. The military will be contacted as well." Tegan assured him.

"Does that mean he won't get into trouble?" Cade asked.

"We hope so."

Cade turned to Strider. "How do you feel about taking me to Courier instead of trying to save me once Theo's safe?"

Strider put a finger to his lips. "Interesting. I'm assuming you'd rather me take you alive than dead."

"Very much so, yes," Cade said with a roll of his eyes. "Is he for real?" he asked Oz.

"Very much so, I'm afraid," Oz told him.

"How much money do you have?" Strider pressed on. "I'm already out half the fee if I don't kill you and show Courier your body, but I'd let you make that up to me."

"Strider," Tegan growled and Vic said, "Cade, are you fucking kidding me?"

"Are you planning on hunting him down and killing him yourself?" Strider asked and without waiting for an answer, added, "Because you're not ready for that. But I could teach you—"

"You're not teaching him anything." Tegan backed Strider fiercely against the wall, hands on the man's throat.

Strider grinned, pointed to Tegan and told Oz, "See? Werewolves. Told you."

"Honestly, killing him is the only answer. To any question," Oz said, more to himself than to anyone else.

"Cade, get that plan out of your mind, once and for all," Vic instructed.

"As plans go, it's not a bad one. It's stupid, of course, but..." Strider mused.

Cade knew his plan wouldn't work, but trying to get Strider to talk would require jumping through hoops and right now, he was having trouble summoning up the strength.

Thankfully, the knock on the door turned out to be Colin, with the pizza Cade had ordered from the truck on the way home from the fight...because he was at starvation levels of hunger.

"I think we have to keep the pizza handy, since that stops Cade from making stupid decisions," Vic told Tegan.

"Dude, I'm right here," Cade said around a mouthful of pizza.

"Are you going to tell him about the problem with the c-o-p?" Strider spelled out the word.

"Do you think I can't fucking s-p-e-l-l, you asshole?" Cade asked, rising from his seat but refusing to let go of the pizza.

Oz turned, sandwich in hand, watching all the action like it was dinner and a show.

Strider didn't bother to get out of his seat. "Have you learned nothing from our earlier encounter?"

Vic caught Cade by the shoulder. "Don't bother—I can't let you kill him, and anything else is just going to be unsatisfying."

"It's true," Oz agreed glumly.

Cade turned to Vic. "Can you tell me about the c-o-p?"

"Don't worry about the c-o-p. Rigs is on the way," Oz confirmed. "Strider, we're out. Let's go."

"Are we sharing a room?" Strider asked.

"Over my dead body," and "That can be arranged," were the last things Cade heard before the door closed behind them.

"Should make for an interesting night. And who's Rigs?" Cade asked around the bite of pizza.

"Are you finishing that whole pie?" Tegan asked, then turned to Vic. "He's almost done with this entire pie."

"Yes. And I'm going to finish this second one too." Cade shrugged. "S'good. I'm starving. So who's Rigs? Another guy who works here? Or a c-o-p?"

"For fuck's sake with the spelling," Vic muttered.

"Rigs consults for us when we need him. Former JAG," Tegan explained.

"Lawyer?" Cade paused in his pizza path of destruction to gulp some soda. "Who needs a lawyer?" Tegan and Vic stared at him until the realization dawned. "I need a lawyer?"

"I'm really glad you agree with that," Tegan said smoothly.

Before Cade could protest, Vic handed him another slice of pizza. "Rourke's suggestion. He's looking out for you."

"Why don't I feel comforted by that?" Cade mumbled. But the news didn't stop him from eating half the slice in two bites.

"Christ," Vic muttered. "He's going to eat us out of house and home."

"You wanted me here," Cade reminded him...with a smile.

Vic shook his head and opened the door for the man Cade guessed was Rigs. He was a ginger, and hot, in a buttoned-up way. Hot combo in a suit and tie.

He hugged Tegan, then turned and asked, "Vic, good to see you. How're you doing?" with a hand on Vic's shoulder.

"Depends on the day," Vic told him.

"I hear you." Rigs glanced over at the pizza, then at Cade. "Feeding an army?"

"Feels like it. Rigs, this is Cade."

Cade held out his non-pizza hand but didn't get up. Rigs shook it and took a seat across from him. "Guys, I hate to do this, but you'll need—"

"Plausible deniability. I know," Tegan said. "Come on, Vic. Strider needs to talk to us."

"Christ, just kill me now," Vic muttered on the way out.

When the door shut behind them, Rigs settled into the chair across the table from him. "Do you know why I'm here?"

"Something about Rourke." Cade put the rest of his slice down.

"Anything you say to me is confidential. So you need to be as truthful as you can when I ask you a question. And if I don't ask about it, don't volunteer anything. Because I need plausible deniability too."

Cade nodded, his throat tightening. "Am I in trouble?"

"It sounds like someone's steering this inquiry. I'm guessing it's the same man who's been threatening you?" Rigs took out a legal pad and began taking notes. "I don't like recording sessions. Call me old fashioned, but after hanging around with the men who run this place, I realized that nothing about technology is safe. But none of them can read my writing." He glanced up. "You're suddenly pale. It's going to be all right—you've got me on your side."

"And you never lose?"

"We're going to get rid of this long before it gets to win or lose—that's the goal," Rigs assured him. "Let me lay out what happens next. We're going to talk. And then, we could go into the police department and give a voluntary statement, based on what you're going to tell me, and what you've already told Rourke."

"Didn't I already do that when I talked to Rourke?"

"This would be more formal. And, in lieu of questioning Theo, who they can't find—and don't tell me a goddamned thing, because the less I know on that the better. So, tell me about your conversation with Detective Rourke. Did you know he was looking for you?"

"No, that was a surprise. He asked me about Theo's stepfather, and I haven't seen the guy in forever." Because that was the truth.

"But you lived in his apartment. So did Theo."

"I stayed there sometimes. I was in foster care at the time."

"With the Nelsons. They said you rarely slept home."

Cade hated that Rigs knew about his past. *But he's on your side.* "Didn't stop them from cashing the state's checks, right?"

Rigs sighed. "They're not the ones on the hot seat here. You are."

"Courier's not going to let this go."

"I suspect not." Rigs leaned back. "But I'm not in the

business of letting my clients get in trouble. So we're going to have to go over everything again—remember, answer only what I ask you."

"I'm definitely going to need more pizza."

CHAPTER 17

TEGAN AND VIC settled into the media room across the hall from the war room to wait for Cade's meeting to be over. Tegan had been particularly concerned with Rourke's news, and he'd put in a call to Paulo to see what more, if anything, he could find out.

He'd been staring at his phone, willing for some goddamned good news to come in ever since.

"Tense, Teegs?"

"Like you're not?"

Vic shrugged. "Should've heard something by now. Maybe Deran's not up to the job."

"I want to see you say that to his face," he started and his phone beeped. "Speak of the devil and he will appear."

"And?"

"He's got Theo—they're at a safe house."

Vic's relief was palpable, albeit short-lived, and he voiced both their concerns immediately. "Think Cade's going to take off now?"

"No fucking clue. Maybe we should get more pizza."

Tegan shook his head. "I know he's not serious about going with Strider..."

"But he's more than a little serious about his grab for intel," Vic finished. "I can't blame him. But I can blame Strider. Speaking of, is Strider *really* staying here? Because I want to lay bets on how long it takes before Oz does kill him."

"I'm actually afraid of that." Tegan ran his hands through his hair and noticed Vic's eyes watching his every move. His lips went dry...and why the hell was he nervous? He was the one who made men nervous, not the other way around. "We've got to keep Strider underground or else Courier's going to get suspicious."

"Like Courier won't be when Cade is still alive and fighting every other night?" Vic reminded him. "We need to do some major convincing."

"Yeah, convincing," Tegan echoed, biting his bottom lip and shoving his hands into his pockets to stop himself from walking over to Vic and kissing the shit out of his full lips. Not that Vic would mind at all...

Just then, the door to the war room opened and Rigs came out. Cade was still sitting at the table, surrounded by empty pizza boxes.

"I'm just going to let what he and I talked about settle in," Rigs told them. "I'll check in with him in the morning. In any case...I wouldn't give Rourke access to him, if you can help it. Which means, keep him here."

"Did you tell him that?" Vic asked.

"I did. But he's more stubborn than you two."

"Fuck you, Rigs." But Vic smiled as he said it.

"I won't let this touch him—you know that," Rigs assured them. "But Courier's got reach. I can't deny that."

Tegan nodded, feeling the familiar sweep of dread he always did when dealing with a deranged spook. Shit never ended well.

"You talk to him first. Last time I tried..." Vic let that hang in the air.

"I'm not altogether certain it wasn't exactly what worked." But Tegan pressed forward into the war room as Vic walked Rigs out.

Cade looked serious, but not angry. "I'm still thinking over my options."

"And you're clear about what they are?"

"Very. It's more about me. If I can hold my temper." Cade stretched out, hands overhead, shirt riding up to reveal flat, ripped abs. "I mean, I think I can, but Rigs wants me to be really fucking sure."

"Well, maybe this news will help—Theo's at a safe house."

"That's good." Cade actually covered his eyes for several long seconds with his forearms as he finished stretching, and Tegan wasn't surprised to see his eyes slightly red-rimmed when he pulled his arms away from his face completely. "Really good."

"It is."

"So this team who rescued him..."

"It's run by my brother."

Cade frowned. "Your brother works for you?"

"No, he doesn't. He's mainly based out of Africa and he runs his own team. We help each other out when the need arises."

"And he's not military?"

"Not anymore. He was a SEAL, like I was," Tegan told

him. "And apparently, Theo and my brother are already acquainted."

Cade put his elbows on the table and frowned. "What's his name?"

"Deran."

His mouth fell open, but he shut it quickly and muttered, "That is *not* good," more to himself than to Tegan.

"That's pretty much what Deran said."

"Fuck, this just keeps imploding. And I've stuck them together for who knows how long." Cade ran his hands through his hair. "Is Theo really safe?"

"*Safe* and *Deran* aren't words I usually use in the same sentence, and if Theo knows Deran, he knows that already too. But, Deran *will* protect him from Courier's bullshit —*that*, you can count on," Tegan assured him, but Cade didn't seem reassured at all.

Cade should've known that getting Theo to safety would only be a minor relief in this entire Courier debacle. It was a good step, yes, but it was just a step. And screwing with his best friend's career wasn't the best choice he could've made, but for the moment, it had been the only choice.

Add Deran into the mix, and he could hear Theo cursing all the way from the dark continent. "I need to talk to Theo. I normally talk to him almost every day, even though that's technically against the rules but..."

"Fuck the rules?" Tegan asked as he pulled his phone out and started typing. A few seconds later, one of the SAT phones started ringing, and Tegan pointed to Cade and then the phone.

"Thanks, Tegan." Cade went to it and picked up, relief coursing through him at the sound of Theo's air-siren-like demand (aka his normal voice) of "Goddammit, Cade—are you okay?"

He looked up and saw that Tegan had left him alone, closed the door, and that bit of trust? Felt nice. "I'm fine, Theo."

"Christ, whenever you say that you're so far from it." Theo blew out a frustrated breath. "Is this what's been bothering you? You think someone's after me."

"Kind of."

"Cade—"

"Okay, yes. I wasn't going to bother you with it."

"But sending in Deran, of all fucking people, to literally drag me out of the jungle—because that's what he did, you know—he threw me over his goddamned shoulder, caveman style...and that was the best way you could think of?" Theo asked and Cade tried to picture it without it being hot. And failed. But Theo was still bitching. "You do realize I can take care of myself."

"Not against this guy."

"Oh, okay—so how are you protecting yourself then? Is anyone carrying you around against your will?" Theo asked and again with the mental images.

"So you and Deran still aren't getting along?"

"Cade—are you listening? Can you fucking focus? Because last I heard, you were only worried about me...so *exactly* what are you planning?"

Fuck. He closed his eyes, knowing his best friend could see right through him. "I'm sorry."

"The only thing you should be sorry about is not telling me. I'm not mad at you for trying to protect me, Cade. How could I be?"

He could picture his best friend, still in his jungle BDUs, looking serious but fierce. "I'll make sure this is over soon."

"Are you planning on killing him? Putting yourself in complete danger against an assassin? Because you just told me that I couldn't take care of myself against him."

"I think he's overrated. He's just a man, Theo," Cade lied softly as if that would calm Theo down.

"Ah, Cade. Fuck." There was silence for a long moment after Theo bit the words out. "You've got to let Deran's brother and his friends help you. Please. For me."

"Dirty pool."

"And I'm not ashamed of it." Theo lowered his voice. "If this guy is dangerous enough for you to drag me away unauthorized from a mission, do you really think you can just walk right up to him and take him?"

"Sometimes the simplest plans work."

"Fuck, Cade." Theo drew a deep breath. "Let's talk about something else. Deran's brother? Is he nicer than Deran? Because honestly, I can't be responsible if I commit a murder of my own here."

"I've never met Deran, remember? I've just been listening to you bitch about him since you met him."

"Well, Deran's a royal prick," Theo announced bluntly, and Cade had a strong feeling that Deran had been standing right over Theo's shoulder since he'd mentioned "murder"... and that Theo knew it.

"Tegan can be. But I like him...and his friend."

"*Like* as in..."

"I slept with them."

Theo snorted. "Are you planning on working your way through the entire team?"

"Funny." Cade smiled, in spite of himself. "I slept with the two of them together."

"First threesome? Moving up in the world, are we?"

"I want to do it again."

"And they want to as well?"

"I think...they like me."

"You sound surprised."

"Yeah, well..." Cade stared at the ceiling. "I'm scared, Theo. More scared of them—of that—then I am of going up against Courier."

Theo sighed. "If I could get away from Deran, I would in a heartbeat and come to you. And no, Deran—you fucking spy—I'm not threatening to escape. I'm giving empathy. Something you know shit about," Theo yelled, Cade assumed, to Deran, before turning his attention back to the conversation at hand. "Sorry about that. Asshole keeps listening in."

Cade decided not to mention that Theo had threatened Deran with murder as well. "So you and Deran *are* getting along then?"

"Swimmingly." Theo went serious. "Please, Cade—let them help you—with Courier...and with the other stuff."

"I'm supposed to do that to make you feel better?"

"You're supposed to do it for you, but if the only way I can get you to do it is to guilt you into it, I'm down for that. You've got to let people in."

"Because you've set such a good example."

"Okay, fine—I'll let more people in too—but you first."

"Such an asshole."

"Swear to it, Cade."

"Theo—"

"For me."

For the friend who'd never steered him wrong. "Okay, fine. I'll give them a chance. I'll let them in—a little. On my terms."

"You're such a romantic."

"Shut up." Cade smiled. "Love you, man. And I'll be careful with Courier."

"You have to be—or I'll kick your ass when I get there. And no, that's not a threat to escape, Deran. *Christ*. Cade— I've got to go before I hurt this motherfucker. Love you, Cade."

The line went dead and Cade smiled to himself. Theo was okay. Deran might not be once it was all over, but hell, nothing in life was perfect.

CHAPTER 18

VIC HADN'T MOVED Cade last night from the couch in the war room, SAT phone in hand. He'd no doubt talked to Theo until he'd fallen asleep, which he'd mentioned they often did, and he'd looked too peaceful to wake up and move. And Oz had a particularly bad night, so both Vic and Tegan slept around him, all of them waking every couple of hours.

Now, it was still dark out when Vic headed down to the gym, wrapping the narrow blue strips of cloth around his hands as he went. He was usually the only one in here at this time. Oz preferred to work out before the club opened so he could be mellow for the crowds, and Tegan usually joined him.

Vic was used to the solitude. He warmed up with a light jog around the perimeter, stretched, and then faced the bag.

This was rote. Perfect. Exactly what he'd been trained for from the age of five, when his uncle put the gloves on his hands and made him punch the bag. He'd been eight when they'd started him toughening his hands up, alternating rounds of punching the bag with the gloves on and off. His knuckles had been broken countless times, in countless fights and in combat as well. They ached before it snowed or rained, a constant reminder of his past. But fighting was a habit he couldn't break—not that he'd wanted to.

He got into the zone, moving his feet to the familiar *thwack, thwack*, the rhythm of his fists hitting the bag, echoing in this nearly empty portion of the gym. Beyond the next wall held the other equipment—treadmills and weight machines—but they'd kept this all mats and hanging bags, perfect for recreating battle plans, general fighting...and sex, as he and Tegan had realized the other day.

Things had gone too quiet on the Courier front, and shit like that always made Vic nervous. It meant that Courier was a true predator, watching patiently, waiting in the wings before he made his next move. Vic figured that they'd done exactly what Courier had hoped—and while he knew that Strider was their wild card in this situation, it took everything he had not to take off and start poking around the dark corners of this world that he knew existed.

He finished a set with a roundhouse kick to the bag...and found himself facing Cade. Cade was dressed and ready for sparring, his hands taped. "How long have you been watching?"

"Long enough. You were in the zone."

"Are you?" Vic smiled and then lunged at Cade, who backed up out of reach fast. But Vic kept moving forward, all predator, and Cade's fight instincts kicked in. Soon, they were in an all-out brawl on the mat.

Cade's motions were those of a self-taught fighter and in Vic's opinion, there was nothing more perfect. His moves held that raw edge, which was why Vic preferred to watch underground fight clubs, because those moves weren't trained out of them into a more precise, efficient motion. The energy emanating from Cade was palpable when he hit out, and Vic easily evaded his moves.

"Army's not teaching you boys anything these days?" he asked after he'd taken Cade down to the floor, because shit-talking was a sport unto itself.

But Cade didn't get involved in that—if anything, it just focused him more, made him hit harder.

He took all of this seriously. He studied. He watched. He got up off the floor and hit Vic back twice as hard. And when he half pinned Vic, he leaned down and bit his earlobe, then licked a spot behind Vic's neck that made him shiver.

He threw Cade off and then grabbed him and pulled him close. "Are you teasing, or are you prepared to put out?"

Cade bit his bottom lip and that was it. Vic's hands went to either side of his head and yanked him close for a kiss.

"You're thinking about your fantasy," Vic said.

"Stop reading my mind. But yes," Cade bit out.

"You're not ready."

"But I was ready to be fucked in the alley?"

"Yes." Vic motioned for Cade to follow him, out of the gym and upstairs.

Cade let him lead, ended up in Tegan's bedroom, where Tegan was lying on the bed, reading. If he'd heard the conversation, he didn't let on, but now that they were right near him, he put the book down and listened. "Everything okay?"

"I told Cade he's not ready for his fantasy—yet. But he's

close." Vic directed his next words at Cade. "You don't like people knowing things about you that you don't tell them, but you read cues. You'd be a shitty fighter if you didn't."

"Okay, yeah, maybe," Cade conceded.

"You need it rougher. And I'm not just talking a hard fuck, although that's part of it." Vic's accent rumbled through him.

"Like what happened in Room Four?"

"Like that...but you only got a small taste of it."

Cade's mind flashed by the cuffs, the paddles. "What would've happened?"

"At some point, I would've turned you over my lap and you would've fought me—at first. And then you'd realize how much you needed it."

Cade wanted to tell him that he was wrong, that there was nothing about being spanked that got him hot, except he heard his heartbeat in his ears, and he was breathing fast just picturing it. "I..."

"Yeah, you'd definitely have loved it." Vic's palm slid down over the curve of his ass. "Tegan would've tied you up and fucked you, and you wouldn't have been able to move. You'd have to lie there and take it, your ass red and stinging from my hand, your hole filled with Tegan's cock. Maybe he'd put a vibrating plug inside of you, and then he'd make you come until you were milked dry. Or maybe we wouldn't have let you come at all, so you'd be frantic. Begging for it."

"Jesus, Vic." His voice sounded thick to his own ears, his throat dry, his dick leaking. Vic smiled and looked behind him, and Cade turned to see Tegan, sweat pants pulled down, cock out, jerking himself. No doubt he'd been doing it in time to Vic's storytelling, and Cade watched, fascinated.

"I'd start with you after Cade was wrung out," Vic told Tegan. "Definitely the vibrator, because you'd hate that loss of control. I wouldn't let you up, no matter how hard you begged."

"Vic!" Tegan's orgasm hit him hard; thick, white ropes striped his belly, chest, hit his chin, and spilled over his hand. He lay there, still stroking, half-hard, eyes closed.

Vic turned his attention back to Cade. "Go make your own mess on him. Mark him up."

It sounded like a mild request—a suggestion—but Cade followed it like the order he had no doubt it was.

He stripped quickly, straddled Tegan's thighs and stroked himself with both men watching. Tegan sat up and surprised Cade, pulling him closer, locking his mouth around Cade's nipple and suckling.

"Shit." Cade let go of his cock and grabbed Tegan's shoulders, scrabbling to find quarter but realizing all he could do was snap his hips and go along for the ride. His cock rubbed against Tegan's stomach, sliding against the wet of his come and it was messy and hot.

"He's going to come just from that, Tegan," Vic murmured. "Cade, come now, or you're not coming tonight."

Cade waited to tell him to fuck off, but he couldn't because his dick was too busy following Vic's commands. He cried out, spilling against Tegan and holding him tight, his body bucking with aftershocks from his climax.

Still jerking from the aftershocks, he half collapsed against Tegan, who finally had mercy on him and released his nipple.

Vic was kneeling next to them, a hand on Cade's shoulder. "Tegan, you're not done yet."

That intrigued Cade enough to pull back. He watched Tegan lean against the headboard and smile lazily at Vic, who said, "Open up, baby."

Tegan—big, strong Tegan—complied easily, opening his mouth and Cade panted, watching Vic feed Tegan his cock.

That could be you. And that made his dick half-hard again instantly. He groaned, "Fuck," as he found himself moving closer to Vic, grabbing his hair to pull him in for a long kiss. His hand carded through Tegan's hair as well, connecting them as Vic pulled out and added his cum to Tegan's chest and belly.

"Jesus Christ, Vic." Tegan's voice was rough from Vic's cock.

"I'll take that as a compliment." Vic bent down to lick the mixed cum, and he kissed Tegan and then did the same to Cade, all their flavors mingling together.

And they were all still touching one another. Connected.

"Sex—and BDSM—are both as much here," Vic pointed to Cade's forehead, "as it is here." He cupped Cade's dick. "It doesn't have to be about pain. It doesn't have to be about power. It doesn't always have to be about the same thing each time. It's about trusting someone to give you the experience you need. Trusting them to tell you what you need, and trusting yourself enough to tell them if they don't get it right."

Cade swallowed. "You, ah, got it right."

Tegan laughed weakly. "I'd have to agree. Maybe we can have a Vic's storytelling night at Crave."

It had been hot and oddly intimate all at once, and Cade had never been a part of something like that. It left him vulnerable, so much so that he had to fight the urge to escape to the roof, an urge that came on so suddenly, he panicked.

Instead of leaving up the fire escape, he went into the bathroom under the guise of cleaning up, and Vic followed him in and immediately manhandled him back to the bed.

"Aftercare helps," Vic explained as he placed Cade between them on the bed.

"Not leaving you hanging," Tegan murmured as he and Vic half wrapped around him, solid and strong and that floating, discounted feeling gradually dissipated, replaced by contentment.

"How did you know?" Cade asked.

"Your reactions. The way your body responds. The way your expression doesn't." Vic stroked the side of his face. "You want me to spank you, but you're not ready yet."

"Christ. No one's ever been able to make me blush," he admitted hoarsely.

"Then you weren't with the right men."

CHAPTER 19

AT ONE IN THE MORNING, Crave was still crowded with a line at the door. Tegan stood in his usual spot, behind two-way glass, so he could survey the entire floor in one sweep.

"Checking out your kingdom?" Cade came up from behind him.

"Basically, yes," Tegan admitted. "I didn't get a chance to ask you earlier...is everything okay with Theo?"

"I'm not sure Theo and Deran are going to survive this. Things sound a little...tense."

"Deran's not an easy man."

"Think it runs in the family?" Cade asked with a smirk. "That's rhetorical, by the way."

"For the record, Deran's way worse than me."

"I'm betting he'd say the same thing," Cade said and Tegan dipped his head slightly in acknowledgment. "Theo doesn't want me to take Courier on myself."

"You don't say," Tegan mused sarcastically, and Cade rolled his eyes. "I really like Theo a lot."

"Yeah, me too."

Tegan put a hand under Cade's chin, forcing Cade to look at him. "I understand vengeance, Cade. More than you know. So does Vic. And Oz. But we also understand the value of teamwork. I thought you knew that too."

Cade considered that as Tegan released his chin and let a finger play along his jaw. "I always worked with Theo."

"And the men from fight club too."

"Okay, yeah."

"So, you've worked in team situations beyond the Army. So how about letting us find Courier, like Theo wants? You're not being excluded from helping us get him. But having you running off alone, looking to take him down? That puts all of us at a tactical disadvantage. Just think about that." He didn't want to broach the subject of Cade staying close, since he wasn't fighting it at the moment. Why give him other ideas?

"I will."

"Good." Tegan turned back to the glass. "So what's the deal with Theo and my brother anyway?"

"It's complicated."

"The good stuff always is."

Cade didn't disagree. "They always fight—whenever they're together. Which means they don't stay together very long."

"Sometimes fighting's just foreplay."

Cade's eyes drifted up to his. "Fuck or fight—same thing, right?"

Tegan snorted softly, and he'd like nothing more than to test that theory—immediately—here, in the hallway, but he and Vic had adult responsibilities. And Oz was already taking on too much. He could see both men at the bar for the moment, prepping to take a walk around the floor to survey the crowd, and their employees. "Do you want to go down and hang out?"

"I could use a drink," Cade admitted.

"Go ahead. It's going to be a while before Vic and I get any sleep."

Cade glanced at him with a look Tegan couldn't quite place...at first. "So that fantasy stuff...it doesn't happen outside of that week?"

"Twice a year, actually. And people do sign up for the rooms and explore their fantasies all year round, but Vic and I don't help out with any of those."

"Ever?"

"Not if we're with someone else."

"Have you ever been...during Fantasy Week, I mean?" Cade asked casually, and Tegan liked that he was actually interested. Or maybe jealous.

"No, I haven't ever been with anyone during Fantasy Week," Tegan told him.

"I can't decide if that's good or bad."

"How many relationships have you had?" Tegan pressed.

"Let's see..." Cade pretended to count on his fingers, then turned to Tegan. "Exactly none. And you?"

Tegan snorted. "None for a long time. Maybe some when I was in the military—some the first couple of years I was out, but nothing that lasted. Obviously."

"Your fault or theirs?"

"Probably mine."

Cade nodded. "When did you start the...Dom thing?"

"The Dom thing?" Tegan smiled. "Seemed like a natural

fit. Deran and I messed around with it during the Navy—met a lot of guys who were into the scene. And that was enough for a really long time."

Cade's unspoken, "Is it still?" question was palpable to Tegan, but Cade only voiced, "But you don't dom Vic. If anything...he's in charge when we're together."

Tegan's gaze snapped to his, nearly flattened him. "He's a Dom too, but he's not ready for anything more. Might never be and that's fine. I can give him what he needs."

"Sexually?"

"Yes, sexually," Tegan agreed. "Vic's not ready for more, and I'm not trying to be ready for more."

"Where do I fit in?"

"Where do you want to fit in?" Tegan challenged and watched Cade fight what he was feeling...again. He let Cade off the hook, the way he'd been doing. "You're healing, Cade. Just like we are."

Cade nodded like what Tegan had said was no big deal, but Tegan knew better. Still, all Cade said was, "I'm going to go get that drink now." He stared out into the crowd. "You know Strider's down there, right?"

"That's why Oz is there. He's kind of like Strider's keeper."

"Sucks for him," Cade muttered.

"Yes, it does. Come to think of it, a drink's not a bad idea." Tegan led Cade through the crowds and over to the bar. He often forgot how much fun this place actually was— he tended to lose himself in it when he allowed himself to come down here and not act like the owner.

While Tegan went behind the bar to grab a couple of beers, Cade started talking to Josie. They'd been briefly introduced, but Cade was sitting, taking an interest in her, which made Tegan happy. Josie was someone they watched over very carefully, and even though she could hold her own, she still had a shit-ton of backup if they thought anyone even breathed wrong in her direction.

Tegan heard the breaking of glass, the cursing, the battle cry of "Fuck you, asshole!" before he saw the surge of bodies by the dance floor.

"Shit."

He headed that way, and Colin was already in the mix, as were Vic and Oz. None of them minded a good bar fight to get the blood flowing, but they preferred to be the ones doing it. Otherwise, innocent patrons might get hurt—or start a riot.

He dodged a few swings, put a guy in a headlock, and hauled him outside. The others also had their hands full—Vic talked to the guys who started the fight, and Oz talked to the group that claimed they were innocent, and all of them would be welcomed back in, just not tonight.

The music never stopped—there was no reason to let people watch the fight, because it just encouraged a pile-on. He took a shot that Colin handed him in honor of a job well done and glanced around...

And realized he'd lost track of Cade. "Have you seen Cade?" he asked Vic, who came over for a shot of his own.

Vic swung around to where Cade had been talking with Josie before the fight. "I'm surprised he didn't jump in to separate the guys."

"Yeah, me too." He went over to where Josie stood with Oz. "Hey Josie—did you see where Cade went?"

She nodded. "He got a call right before the fight broke out. He took it outside—he couldn't hear."

It had gotten loud during the fight, but Tegan and Vic had escorted the fighting men outside, and there hadn't been any sign of Cade.

"I'll look outside again," Vic offered. "Maybe he's in the alley."

"I put a tracker in his phone. He took it but he turned it off—he's smart." Oz stared at his own phone. "But he's going to need to use it. Even if he turns it on for a second, I'll have his location."

"When did you...never mind." Tegan watched Vic come in with a shake of his head.

"No luck. And he's not answering his phone," Vic said.

"It's off." Oz showed him the tracker, which showed Cade's last location, just outside the bar.

Vic snapped his fingers suddenly. "Can you pull up the video feeds?"

"Yeah—so can you, remember?" But Oz was showing him the screen. "Here

he is."

Vic took the phone and stared at it, then used his fingers to zoom in.

"What are you looking for?" Tegan asked.

"Reading his lips," Vic said and Tegan and Oz both crowded around him to look.

Calm down. Do nothing and get out of there. I'm coming to you—I'll take care of everything...I'll get you to Pat's.

"What's Pat's and where is it?" Tegan asked.

"I think it's a bar—next town over. Maybe fifteen minutes away."

"We could head that way and see if we pick up his phone signal," Vic suggested.

"Pat's is about two blocks from where Cade was in his first foster home. It's close to the school he and Theo went to," Oz confirmed. "It's a toss-up whether it's about Courier or not."

"He fucking promised to stick close," Tegan fumed.

"Then it must be something important...and something not related to Courier," Vic told him. "And we can't body-guard him forever."

"Why not?" Tegan demanded.

Vic put a hand on his shoulder. "He's going to resist it."

"Ask me if I give a shit."

"Teegs, I didn't say not to tail him. Just don't let him know," Vic advised. "Which is what I'm going to do right now."

"I'm coming with you."

"Wouldn't bother trying to stop you." Vic opened the door. "After you, princess."

"Princess, my ass."

Vic patted his shoulder. "We can work on that later."

Cade caught a cab to the apartment complex that wasn't too far from where he'd grown up. Nothing much had changed—this part of town was still a mix of good and bad, rich and poor, but these buildings were mostly for fixed-income families. They were also farther away from the fight club and most other places that a kid might find solace or self-esteem... or any kind of real help.

He hated not having his truck but there hadn't been time —not with the major fight that broke out inside of Crave. He couldn't bother Tegan or Vic, because they needed all the help they could get, and waiting wasn't an option.

He stared at his phone. He knew Oz had put a tracker in it at some point, although he couldn't quite figure out when, and so he'd turned it off purposely. Instinctively.

Now, he turned it back on and shoved it into his pocket. They'd find him soon enough, and he needed to get to Max. He shoved cash at the cabdriver and then took off at a light jog around the buildings. If Max had stayed upstairs, there would be major trouble because his foster father was big and mean, and shit got ugly fast.

But Max wasn't where he was supposed to meet Cade, and Cade wasn't in the mood to wait. Gaining entrance into the building's main doors wasn't hard—they were supposed to be locked, but the door was propped open for convenience —and for those who allowed trouble into where they lived. He dashed up the three flights and was rounding the fourth carefully when he spotted Max, half sitting on the top step, trying to navigate his way down.

Once Cade got close, he could see why the kid was having so much trouble. He'd taken what was no doubt the worst beating of his life, and Cade would make sure it would be the last, especially at the hands of that monster of a foster father.

Max grabbed for his wrist. "He wouldn't stop. I tried to get away—"

"Shhhhh—it's okay. You did great," Cade assured Max as he heard a clatter coming down the stairs.

"He's coming."

"I know. He's not touching you. Come on." Cade picked him up and carried him down, trying to be gentle but needing to stay ahead of the man stalking them. Cade was going to beat the shit out of him, but he needed Max on stable ground and not in a place where the asshole could throw him down the stairs.

Finally, they reached the landing. He put Max in the small hallway between the inside and outside doors. "Stay here. Two men will come in—both tall, one's blond and one's dark haired. Tegan and Vic. Tell them you're with me." He handed Max his phone. "If no one comes for you in five minutes, call 911."

Max nodded seriously. "Be careful—he's—"

"I know what he is." Cade closed the door between them and faced off with the large, angry man charging toward him.

Vic was watching his phone, with the newly installed tracker, and the streets as they drove around Pat's. A beep signaled that Cade's phone had been turned on, and Vic breathed a sigh of relief for that.

He guided Tegan along, then pointed. "Here. The tracker points to that building."

Tegan pulled in front of it and stared out.

"There's someone in the doorway." Vic was halfway out of the truck by the time he finished his sentence, and Tegan was on his heels. He slowed when he got to the doorway, because he heard shouts, and when he pushed in he saw the half-terrified, half-angry face of a badly beaten teenage boy who stared between him and Tegan.

"I'm Max. You're Vic and Tegan. Cade's inside." He jerked his head to where the shouts were coming from.

"He's with the man who did this?" Vic asked, and Max nodded.

"Come on, Max—come with me to the truck," Tegan reached out to help him.

"Not without Cade," Max told him.

"Trust me, we're not going anywhere without Cade. But if this gets uglier, I don't want you close. Come on." Tegan helped Max walk out of the building, glancing over his shoulder at Vic.

Vic could see the figures through the darkened-for-privacy Plexiglas. He wanted to give Cade a chance to fuck up the man he was fighting, but he wasn't about to let Cade get into trouble for it. When the shouts lessened, he cracked the door and saw Cade, half-crouched onto a larger man's back, whispering into his ear.

Which meant the man was alive...but he'd been as badly beaten as Max had been. Finally, Cade pushed up and stood. His cheek was bruised and there was a cut above his eyebrow, and he nodded at Vic and followed him out.

"We good here?" Vic asked.

"He's not going to say a word. Max—"

"Needs a doctor."

"I can't take him to a hospital. But I know someone—he's close." Cade's expression was stony, but he grabbed Vic's hand. "Please."

CHAPTER 20

PAT'S WAS on the corner across from the elementary school Cade and Theo had both attended. The neighborhood hadn't changed much from when Cade had lived here, and thankfully, Pat's hadn't either. It was still a refuge for the young boys who needed an escape from their lives.

Pat had been in his midtwenties when Cade met him. He was the first openly gay man he and Theo had been exposed to, and he and his partner were the first ones to note Cade's bruises and Theo's broken wrist. They hadn't asked too many questions, but they fed the boys and showed them to a room in the back with a bed and a TV. And they gave both boys a key.

There was never anything creepy about what Pat and Lee had done. They'd been aboveboard, but still, neither boy told anyone, because kindness could be easily misinterpreted. Still, it always amazed Cade how the predators were the ones who got away with murder and the nice guys always endured the most scrutiny.

Pat and Lee had gotten married; they still lived above the

bar, and they still gave out keys to select boys, the way they once had to Cade and Theo.

Now, the look of relief on Pat's face when he saw Cade in one piece was palpable, but it didn't stop him from doing a quick check-over for broken bones and the like.

Pat was an ER nurse and Lee, a former medic in the Army, now worked part-time as an EMT. Pat was Irish-American pale and Lee was African-American, dark-skinned with a deep Georgia drawl. Cade had always thought they looked perfect together.

"I'm okay, Pat," Cade assured him.

"You don't look all right."

"But Max is worse," Cade said quietly. "My friends are helping him in."

Pat stared at him for a long moment before moving toward the back door, and Lee came out from the same door, not stopping until he'd gathered Cade carefully in his arms. "Baby boy, you're still scaring the shit out of us, more than any other child we've had."

"Thanks, I think."

Lee snorted and pulled back, going over him in much the same way Pat had. "Ribs?"

"A little sore, but nothing terrible. Max needs more help than I do."

Lee glanced over Cade's shoulder. "Max first, then you. Sit."

Cade didn't bother arguing. He took a seat in the same familiar booth he used to sit in with Theo, whether out of habit or nostalgia, it didn't matter. It was comforting just the same. And in between helping Max, Pat was bringing Cade and Vic and Tegan food. By the time Lee got to Cade, it was just before dawn. Now Max was sleeping peacefully, and Tegan, Pat, and Lee were talking by the bar.

"That's never good," Cade grumbled. He was half sleeping on Vic, crushing him into the booth, but Vic wasn't complaining. Instead, his arm was banded around Cade's chest, holding him lightly in deference to his injuries. He'd also just fed Cade a pain pill and its effects, mixed with exhaustion, were kicking in. "You know they're talking about me, right?"

"I'd expect so." Vic's brogue was heavy, got that way when he was really tired, Cade realized.

"And that's never good."

"You said that already."

"I know." Cade waved a hand. "Tegan's probably going to lock me to the bed, like Deran wants to do to Theo. Or Theo said he'd do to me. But not in that way—said it would help you and Tegan handle me. *Pffffft*. Like that would do it."

Vic's chuckle rumbled against his back. "What would help us?"

Cade considered that. "I guess the bed tying might work for a while. Maybe. Not sure I'd like it."

Vic leaned in to murmur, "I'd make sure you liked it. You'd be too preoccupied not to."

"Why?" Vic sighed and reached a hand around to surreptitiously tug on one of his nipples. "*Ohhhh*. That would definitely work."

"You're cute when you're high."

"Not high." Cade stared at his hand and wiggled his fingers. "Maybe a little bit. My fingers are moving slow, right? Why are you laughing? And cute? I probably should be offended."

Suddenly, all three men by the bar turned to face him.

"Uh oh," Cade murmured in a singsongy voice. "Someone's in trouble."

"Cade, babe? I think it's you."

"Oh. *Ohhh.* Shit. Cover for me. Why are you laughing?" Cade demanded, then stared up at the three men looking down at him. "Hey, guys—how's it going?"

"It's going," Lee said with a smile that was pure affection. "How're you feeling?"

"I'm fine. It's fine," Cade repeated his mantra, and it was good to know he used that line on everyone. "How are Jack and Timmy?"

Lee sighed. "They're definitely not fine, but I've seen them worse. Most nights they stay here, but that's not always reliable."

Cade sobered up a little with that. "Foster application didn't come through?"

"Bottom of the pile."

"Why's that?" Tegan asked.

"I guess two gay men are considered a bad influence." Pat rolled his eyes. "We'll figure it out. We always do. And Cade, Tegan told us that you're in some trouble. You've got to promise us you'll stay with them until it's figured out. Okay?"

"Not fair to use them against me," Cade told Tegan.

"I don't care, as long as it works."

After dragging a heavily medicated Cade out of Pat's and driving him home—during the entirety of which he sang "Paradise by the Dashboard Light" like he was part of some reality show karaoke club—Vic maneuvered him into the back door of Crave and announced, "Bed."

"What about the tying-up part?" Cade stage-whispered.

Tegan shot Vic a look.

"I'll tell you about it later," Vic promised as he carried Cade up the stairs. By the time he tucked him into bed, Cade was sleeping. He and Tegan curled around him, propped on their elbows on the pillows above him.

"He looks so fucking peaceful when he sleeps." Tegan was watching him with such tenderness that it tightened Vic's throat.

"We're really doing this, aren't we?"

"Yeah, we are." Tegan smiled tiredly at him.

"Oh, we're supposed to tie him to the bed. Theo said he'd do it in order to make Cade stay put. I think Deran threatened to do it to him."

Tegan laughed softly. "Sounds like my brother."

Tegan felt Cade stirring a couple of hours later. He got up and preemptively brought him soda, some crackers, and ice packs that Vic helped him place gently around Cade's ribs.

When Cade opened his eyes, he sighed. "No more drugs."

"You need them," Tegan told him.

"Too soon. Everything's still all foggy. I'd rather feel the pain."

"I know what he means." Vic brushed some hair from his face and frowned. "Your cheek's swollen."

Cade shrugged. "I've had worse."

Tegan hated hearing that. He threaded his fingers with Cade's, and Cade stared between the hand and Tegan. And then he smiled, a loopy, sweet smile and said, "I worried you guys. I didn't—"

"I know," Tegan told him. "You're an adult. Grown man. Former soldier. I wouldn't let anyone keep me under house arrest."

"Is that supposed to be helpful, Teegs?" Vic muttered. "Because the boy likes to try to e-s-c-a-p-e."

Cade frowned. "Seriously? I'm not that high," and Vic gave him an it's-questionable look.

"How about we make a deal? I'll get Pat and Lee approved as foster parents and you do what we say...within reason," Tegan offered.

"How are you going to do that? Oh, Oz. Great and powerful," he murmured.

Vic laughed. "That will definitely go to Oz's head."

"I still need to fight. I give the money to Pat and Lee," Cade said now. "Shit, did I say that out loud?"

"Yes." Tegan paused. "I gave Pat the money you gave us— told him to use it for Max."

Cade drew in a stuttered breath. "Fuckers. Gotta stop doing that."

"Doing what?" Vic asked.

Cade closed his eyes and murmured, "Taking my breath away," like it was the most obvious thing in the world.

Once Tegan was assured that Cade was back to sleep, with Vic's arm around him, he moved out into the hallway to call

Law. He and Pat and Lee had discussed making contact with him, and Tegan was going to make the introductions.

No better time than the present.

"Christ, you're out of the military—what's with the oh-dark-hundred shit?" Law mumbled.

"You're getting old."

"Did Paulo tell you to say that?" Law sounded like he was moving around. "I'm just finishing up a run, if you must know."

"So much for no oh-dark-hundred."

"So, is this call about your Delta boy or your Ranger boy?" Law asked.

Perceptive bastard. Of course, Paulo had talked. "The Delta boy's with Deran," Tegan told him and Law whistled. "It's going about that well."

"So, the Ranger boy's still with you and Vic?"

"Paulo likes to gossip."

"Are you kidding? We live for that shit. I even called Oz to see if he had a recording, but he gave me some bullshit about not using surveillance recordings in the apartments."

"Such an asshole. Why are all my friends assholes?" Tegan asked out loud.

Law laughed. "Maybe look to yourself for the answer? But seriously, what's going on?"

"I've got a kid in trouble. He's at Pat's, who's a friend of Cade's." He told Law the story, including the fact that Cade beat the shit out of the foster father. "He says the guy's not going to report it."

"Likely won't. He's going to want to keep collecting the checks for as long as he can."

"And how long will that be?"

"If Max isn't reported missing? Until a CPS worker shows up for a random visit. They're spread thin so without a report, it might not happen for years. Even if it is reported, it might not happen fast." Law said it matter-of-factly, but Tegan knew it was anything but to him. "I've got a spot for him, if he's willing."

Law ran a shelter—it only had ten beds, so they could keep track of the older foster kids. The younger ones were placed with trusted families and people that Law and his friends knew. "I'll have Cade bring him down, if that's okay. I'm sure he'll insist on it."

"Cade sounds like someone I need to meet. I've been hearing his name an awful lot."

"Because he's an awful lot of trouble," Tegan told him.

"Best ones usually are, Teegs."

Cade woke, less groggy, the pain a familiar friend. He slid out of bed, sure one of the men would wake, and when they didn't, he went out the window and up onto the roof for some air. It was fast becoming his spot, his place to go when he needed to think.

The claustrophobia was setting in, and the cool air helped alleviate it somewhat. He'd spent thirty days locked in a fucking closet—"for his own good," according to the Nelsons, and ever since then, anything done for his own good freaked him the fuck out.

At least he was outside, and if there was a sniper after him, sitting behind the chimney should shield him from the shot. Just because Courier hadn't made any recent moves didn't mean shit.

Cade could feel it in his bones—he was winding up for another move. Something bigger. He had the means, motive, and opportunity, and he wasn't going to fade away.

The urge to leave and track him was strong. His connection to the men who'd helped him tonight?

Stronger. Which scared the fuck out of him.

Speaking of scary...Strider appeared out of nowhere. "What are you doing in my spot?" he demanded.

"Didn't see your name here."

Strider hrrrmpphed, sat next to him, and lit a cigarette. He offered Cade one but breathing correctly was on his list of things to do tonight, so he declined. "You sure? You seem irritable."

"And a cigarette will fix that?"

"Helps me." Strider blew smoke in a perfect arc into the night air. "Why are you wasting so much time thinking about Courier?"

"Sorry, you're right—I should just push that psychopath from my mind."

"You have to—otherwise you give him all the power."

"How Zen of you."

"Thank you," Strider said modestly. "He wants into your mind. Psychological warfare will kill you every time."

"So just don't think about him and things will be better?"

"No, he can still kill you. But worrying about it isn't going to change anything. Have a plan, several contingencies."

"My only contingency is keeping Theo away. That way, the only person who can get hurt is me—and I can handle myself."

Strider frowned. "And Theo can't? Because hi, Delta Force. Or do you still see him as helpless?"

"Are you a shrink in your spare time?"

Strider side-eyed him. "Sidestepping the question. Interesting."

"Cut that shit out."

"Fine. Have you and Theo ever slept together?"

"No. He's my best friend."

"Best friends sleep together all the time, especially in the books I read."

Cade sighed. "He's like my brother. He *is* my brother."

"People sleep with their brothers all the time in the books I read too. Well, technically stepbrothers, so no relation, like you and Theo. So I could recommend some of them to get you thinking..."

"I'm not sleeping with Theo."

"You're very defensive about it." Strider shook his head and Cade felt his head start to ache.

"Are you always..."

"Like this? Yes. I'm not killing you when I'm supposed to. I'm losing a lot of money—the least you can do is answer a simple question."

"Fine." At least this took his mind off the shit with Courier.

"How are things with you and Vic and Tegan?"

"Jesus Christ."

"Did I mention the amount of money I'm out?"

"It's not a simple answer, okay? It's just...I can't believe it's real. I feel like, whatever's happening between us is going to disappear between my fingers, no matter how hard I try to catch it," he tried to explain, and for once, Strider didn't have any smart answers. He was just listening. "It's going to go away, and now I know it exists, and it's going to hurt way more than if I just wanted it to exist. Now I know. And I'm not sure I'll ever get over it."

Strider watched him quietly, and Cade couldn't quite place the emotion behind his odd-colored eyes. "You're quite taken with them."

"Maybe." Because admitting it full-out would make it that much worse. "I don't want to talk about this anymore."

Strider seemed to respect that boundary, which should've made Cade suspicious. "Cade?"

"Yes?"

"What's the worst that could happen with it?" he asked and Cade frowned. "You said you already know it exists. And I don't think Tegan would be this angry if he wanted you to really go away. If it's going to hurt anyway...what's the point of not trying?" He paused while Cade tried to control his breaths. "We're all so broken. You have to know that, don't you? You're not the only one. We're all broken, and it's okay."

After a long moment of silence, Strider added, "I feel like you owe me money for that session. I accept money orders or cash."

"Really?"

Strider stood and walked away, calling over his shoulder, "My services don't come cheap."

Cade laughed into the night...mainly because he knew Strider meant it about the money.

CHAPTER 21

TEGAN WOKE to only Vic in his bed, and while that was definitely a good thing, the missing middleman was a definite problem. He glanced over to the bathroom and checked the living room—nothing.

He grabbed his phone and checked the cameras...and was relieved to see Cade sitting on the roof. How the hell he climbed up there after the hits his ribs had sustained was beyond Tegan, so he shoved on clothes and hurried out there, leaving Vic to sleep.

"Cade, I'm coming up." He didn't yell it, but he didn't want Cade to worry that someone was sneaking up on him.

"Hey." Cade was wrapped in a blanket, leaning against the chimney. "I should've left a note."

"How the hell did you climb up here?" Tegan sat next to him.

"I told you—I've had worse." He said it so matter-of-factly that Tegan decided to drop it.

"I just wanted to check on you—stay as long as you want."

He went to stand but Cade said, "I didn't mean to leave Crave without help. I just—"

"Reacted," Tegan finished for him.

Cade turned to face him. "It wasn't Courier, but it could've been him using Max to get to me. I didn't think of that until..." The unfinished thought of "it was too late" hung between them. "I'm sorry. Okay?"

Tegan knew Cade didn't apologize easily. The bruising on his face was more purple than it had been earlier, now under the floodlights from the building, and he looked tired. For the first time that night, everything seemed to sink in, and Tegan let Cade sink against him, folded him in.

Cade accepted the embrace, the comfort, resting his head against Tegan's shoulder before admitting, "You asked earlier...where I wanted to fit in. All I know is that I'm getting attached."

"To Max?"

"To you and Vic," he bit out. "I didn't mean to—it just happened."

Tegan nodded. "Is that a bad thing?"

"It might be, Tegan. I know you and Vic have history. I know...you two belong together, no matter how you try to play it off, and if I wasn't here..."

"Are you trying to say you'll step aside?" Tegan asked and Cade nodded, hands stuffed into his pockets.

"If it means your happiness—yours and Vic's—then yes."

Tegan growled, low under his breath. "Are you trying to get rid of us?"

"What? No," Cade protested. "But you said...fuck, Tegan, you said you were healing and protecting me...and then what? I've been surrendering to you, and then you're going to let me go because 'you aren't trying to be ready for more'?"

"I'm not fighting it, Cade. And it's happening, whether I wanted it to or not. So I don't need you to step aside—I need you to step in."

"I'm trying, Tegan. But I don't know what the fuck I'm doing. When you said that...fuck." Cade looked miserable.

"I told you that none of my relationships ever worked out. And it definitely was my fault." Tegan never wanted to get into his past—less now than ever. But he'd asked Cade to step in, and now, Cade was. He couldn't pick and choose. "Deran and I...we're a year apart. We were always close—and he was always bossy as fuck. My big brother. My protector." He felt Cade settle in beside him for the story. "Growing up, things were always rocky. Our mom was a drinker back then, blew up to a full-fledged alcoholic by the time we were in middle school. Our dad wasn't much better. They got divorced early, and both of them had a string of shit relationships. No one we knew stayed together—ever. After Mom moved us away from Texas when Deran and I were eleven and ten, respectively, things went from bad to worse. Deran and I protected each other, and he pulled me into the Navy with him when he turned seventeen."

Cade frowned. "They take you as a special case?"

"As far as the Navy's concerned, Deran and I are twins."

"Got it."

"So, you asked about relationships. Simple enough—Deran and I...after what we saw, we decided we were from bad stock. Not that we were bad, just that, relationships on both sides of the family were bad. Really bad. So, we decided we were better off without permanent attachments." He shrugged like it was no big deal, an everyday, run-of-the-mill decision. And at the time, it had been.

"And now?"

"And now..." Tegan sighed. "I'm beginning to think I might be ready for more. Vic's ready too. We've never been ready for each other before...so this is all new. Add in what's happening with you and..."

Cade was staring at him. "I'm so damaged, Tegan. You have no fucking clue, okay?"

"Then clue me in," Tegan told him.

"I've never...fuck, I've never gotten attached to guys I fuck. Ever." Cade drew in a stuttered breath and leaned his forehead against Tegan's chest. Tegan's hand went to the back of his neck. "I don't know what either of you sees in me. The healing and protection thing—I understand that. By why would you want anything more with me? I've been nothing but trouble. I don't know how to have a relationship at all. I don't know if I'm even capable of it with one guy, let alone two of you."

"Do you want to try?"

"Yeah, Tegan—I want to try."

Tegan turned to him, cupped his face in his hands. "When I look at you, I see someone brave as fuck. Someone who puts himself on the line, for people he loves and boys he barely knows." And as he said it, realization suddenly dawned on him. "This—what you did for Max—is why you left the Army." It was more of a statement than a question, but Cade nodded anyway.

"I didn't need Delta Force—not the way Theo did," Cade admitted.

"You were chosen for training, but you decided to come

out instead...and do this." Tegan spoke like he was talking to himself and coming to a realization all at once.

"I had to."

"Not an easy decision."

But choosing to never leave a man behind never was. And every time he thought he knew Cade, he ended up surprised. Tegan stroked his hair. "So beautiful, Cade. You're so fucking beautiful, and you don't even know what it is you need."

"But you do?" Cade asked.

"From the second I saw you, yes." Tegan ran a palm along the back of Cade's neck and felt him shiver. "I know exactly what you crave. I know you don't understand it—not yet, anyway. I can show you, with Vic, but you've got to trust yourself first."

"What is it that you think I need? Because I don't understand it at all."

"You need someone who'll take control from you. Someone who'll relieve the pressure that builds up inside of you, that clawing need you feel, especially after you fight. You fuck and fuck and it's not enough. I can make it be enough. *We* can make it be enough."

Cade was breathing hard. "Is what I need...bad?"

Tegan shook his head slowly. "There's not a bad thing about it, baby. Nothing wrong with it—or you. It's just a need. And it deserves to be filled."

"And you and Vic...you'll do that for me?"

"If you're willing to step in."

CHAPTER 22

ANDREI HAD LEFT him a message about an illegal fight happening soon, asked if he wanted in. The money was at least triple what he made during the legal ones, and he wondered if he could get away to do it. He wouldn't sneak away, though—he'd ask for Vic and Tegan to at least take him, and if they didn't want to wait with him, they didn't have to.

Fuck, when had this gotten so complicated?

He was still smarting from his discussion with Tegan on the roof last night, still unsure of where he stood, with Tegan especially.

He took out his phone and went to call Theo, more habit than anything, and remembered that he wasn't supposed to use his own phone.

He wasn't surprised when it rang, five minutes later. "Theo?"

"Yeah, it's me. Everything's fine," Theo added quickly. Fine was their standard "I can get through anything" motto. If they could live through what they already had, the rest should be easy. "I'm just going stir crazy. Too much in my head."

Cade sighed. "Join the club."

"Everything okay there?"

"Beyond the psychopath hiring assassins on the dark web to kill us and forcing us on house arrest?" he asked, and Theo snorted. "Things with Deran going...okay?"

"Not the word I'd use. Confusing, maybe."

"Yeah, I know the feeling. I keep waiting to fuck it all up."

"I've already done enough of that for both of us."

"I guess pushing people away from us is our specialty."

"Maybe we should make T-shirts. Or at least get a reality show deal out of it."

Cade laughed. "Glad you're keeping your sense of humor."

"So...are you still screwing around with both of them?"

"Definitely."

It was Theo's turn to laugh, but then he turned oddly serious. "Is that all you want from them? Just the sex? I mean, if that's all, that's cool, but..."

"But what?"

"I don't think you'd be all that twisted up over it if it was just sex."

He wanted to say something like "Who the fuck's twisted?" but lying to Theo would be far less successful than lying to himself. "Shit."

"Listen, I'm just saying that things sound promising. So don't fuck it up."

"I'm trying not to. But Tegan told me that I needed to step in. What the fuck?"

"Are you...friends with them?"

Cade considered that, maybe for the first time. He'd been so busy worrying about everything that he hadn't thought about the fact that he liked these men—a lot. That if there wasn't an attraction there, he'd still want to hang around them. "I would be. I don't think I've been a good friend to them at all."

"Maybe you should start," Theo offered. "I mean, it sounds like Tegan and Vic had a rough year, losing Brian and yes, Deran—I clocked you ten minutes ago. You're about as subtle as a fucking moose."

Cade bit back a laugh. "Speaking of friends..."

"Don't even go there," Theo said seriously. "Do what I said. I'll call to check in later. And yes, Deran, I will and no, you can't stop—"

The phone cut off, so apparently, Deran could stop him and did. Cade smiled at that, because Deran seemed tough enough to handle Theo.

And that was when lightning struck. Tegan was tough on him...

Tough enough to handle you at your worst.

But it sounded like Tegan was also going through hell—because who was Brian? Cade had been so wrapped up in himself, in Theo and his past, that he'd lost sight of his present—and possibly his future.

He hadn't realized, until now, how the men helping him were slowly falling apart.

You can help them. You already are. By helping him, they were helping themselves. Moving forward...trying to, at least, and all he'd done was push back and push them away, which was the last thing he'd actually wanted to do.

He opened the door of the media room and saw the door to the war room was cracked open, light spilling out. He padded over to it silently and looked in to see Vic, sitting at the monitor, staring at a screen that had two blinking white dots on it.

He took a breath. "Vic?"

Vic didn't even turn around to look at him, just raised a finger and continued to stare at the screen. Cade moved in closer, eyes on the two stationary dots while he took a seat next to Vic, who didn't protest, just pointed and said, "That's Axel and Trevor."

The other owners of Crave—and Gray Ops. "Are they all right?"

"I'm waiting for them to move. They will move." Vic's tone of voice implied that if sheer will couldn't make something so, it would.

"Were they SAS?"

"No. SEALs. Swim buddies through BUD/S and beyond."

"SEALs like Tegan and Deran."

"Yes—they were a couple of classes behind Teegs and Deran."

Cade nodded. "Tegan told me about the way they went into the Navy together. The twin thing."

"Did he?"

"It sounded like Deran didn't want to leave Tegan alone."

Vic smiled but didn't stop his staring contest with the blinking dots. "He didn't."

"That makes me feel better...about Deran and Theo." Cade turned his attention back to the screen. "How long have Axel and Trevor been gone?"

"Two weeks—they left before Fantasy Week started. They weren't happy about that at all. It's their favorite time of year. Better than Christmas, they'll tell you."

"So if they were here, they might've been..."

Vic finally turned to him. "Yeah, actually, they're exactly who would've been placed with you."

"I've always heard there were no coincidences," he murmured. "And they're moving now."

Vic's relief was palpable. "Phase two begins."

"For them—or for us?"

Vic's hand went to his thigh. "I don't give up that easily."

Cade leaned his head against Vic's shoulder. "I'm sorry I've been a selfish prick."

"You've had a right to be."

"Maybe. But it's time to stop now."

"Being selfish sometimes brings us protection."

"And sometimes it just makes you a prick," he admitted. "Who was Brian?"

Vic's eyes went haunted again. "He was a part owner of this place. Best friends with Tegan. Oz's lover and partner for six years." The pain in his voice filled the spaces in the room. "He was my brother. My twin."

The pieces clicked tighter. They were all in mourning, trying to start over, and Cade had come busting in with his anger and his pain and ignored all of it. "Fuck. I'm sorry."

"Me too." Vic glanced back to the screen. "They're good. This? Is a transmission. Means they're right on schedule."

"How long will you sit here and watch them?"

"As long as it takes."

"How about I order pizza and keep you company?"

Vic smiled. "I'd like that."

"So would I."

———————

An hour later, the pizza was eaten, mostly by Cade, and Axel and Trevor were safely ensconced in their new safe house. Cade still ate a lot of pizza, but slightly less than he normally consumed.

"You okay?" he asked and Cade shrugged. "Talk to me."

"Is that an order?"

"Do you want it to be?" Vic shot back, and from the flash in Cade's eyes, he could easily see that the answer to that was yes. "Tell me, Cade."

"Fine," he huffed, like Vic was asking him to move mountains. "You—and Tegan—you both...made me feel."

It came out like an accusation.

"You want me to take it back?" Vic asked quietly, without a touch of irony.

"It's too fucking late and you know it." He sounded so miserable that Vic tried his best not to laugh...and failed.

Vic leaned in and caught Cade's chin in his hand. "It's never too late. Not when you really want something. You could walk away from this after Courier's gone."

Cade's eyes bore into his. "I could, yes. But I don't want to. And that's a problem."

Vic moved back, but not before tracing Cade's lower lip with his thumb. "We all know about losses and sacrifices. Sometimes you spend so much time surviving and protecting yourself, you forget that there's more to life."

"Easy to say, hard to do."

"When you asked if I trusted the man who did this..." He

pointed to his scars. "I trusted him the way I trusted myself. It was a mistake and it cost me. But if I let him take trust away from me for anyone new? Then I let him win. And I won't let him win."

"Who was he?"

"My best friend. The man I loved. We grew up together. We were lovers for what seemed like forever. He was tight with Brian too."

Cade tried to process that. Because he couldn't imagine Theo ever turning on him. "I'm sorry."

"Me too. I'm sorry that I didn't see what he was doing. I'm sorry my team almost died and I'm sorry that, in their eyes and the eyes of the SAS, I'm a traitor. I'm sorry that he held me down and laughed when I struggled while he inflicted these wounds. But I'm not sorry I killed him, because he was the real traitor, or that I saved my team. Whether any of them believe me or not doesn't matter. It might hurt, but in the end, I know what's right."

Cade fisted his hands. "I'm sorry I made things harder."

"You've made things lighter too. And I've never minded a good challenge."

"Tegan's pissed."

"Yeah, he is. But it's not a terminal state."

"I talked to Theo tonight—he called me," Cade added that last part quickly.

"I'm not your father or your keeper," Vic told him gently, realizing that sometimes, he and Tegan acted like a cross between both. "It's okay to talk to your best friend."

Cade nodded. "I don't want his career to be fucked up. He fought so hard to get through Delta Training."

"I'd imagine it's a lot like what I went through—weeks of

fucking misery. There were times I was pretty sure I should just walk away and never look back, but Brian was there, and whenever one of us wanted to quit, the other one stepped in and put a stop to the pity party."

Cade was staring at his hands. "At one point, my palms were so fucking blistered...I put paper towels under duct tape and walked around like that for the final week. Theo did that to his feet. It was ridiculous and the docs almost killed us when they realized it wasn't coming off without taking skin, because the paper towels kind of disintegrated." Vic stared at Cade, who frowned. "What?"

"You're not talking about basic." Cade opened his mouth and then closed it, like he'd realized what he'd just admitted. "Cade, you went through Delta Training?"

"I did, yeah. The endurance training."

He said it like that was a walk in the goddamned park. "Did you pass?"

Cade looked offended. "Of course I passed. I was in...if I wanted to be."

"When did you realize that you didn't want to be in?"

"Before I started Delta school," he admitted. "But Theo wanted in—it was all he'd wanted to do since we enlisted. I knew he'd pass endurance and get accepted to formal training. I figured, the least I could do was make sure he was okay up until then. I mean, that's the shit you do for people you love. You do anything you have to do, right?"

"Right." Vic looked up and saw Tegan in the doorway, wondered how much he'd heard, but judging by the look on his face? It was more than enough.

CHAPTER 23

THE MUSIC POUNDED through his body as the strobe lights flashed all around him, and Cade figured that as long as he was on lockdown at Crave, he might as well take advantage of it...the way he'd tried to the other night before disaster struck. After two days of healing, he was feeling better. He'd been steadily refusing pain pills. He'd much rather deal with the ache in his ribs than the grogginess, and he was already feeling better. Thankfully, his ribs were just bruised, not fractured or broken, and the bruises everywhere were on their way to fading.

Strider had disappeared after the night he tried to shake Cade down for money, but Cade knew he'd be back.

Fortunately, Courier hadn't made contact. And Theo was okay—he and Deran hadn't killed each other—and Max was now with the guy named Law. He found out that Law used to co-own this place, and that Law now ran a PI service along with the two men he was with. As in, living with, partners with, all in.

Tegan didn't elaborate beyond that, but Cade wanted to know more about it. How it all worked.

Why it worked.

Could it work?

His feelings for both Tegan and Vic hadn't exactly been lessening. Instead, everything kept intensifying, and he guessed that was what stepping in did. He was invested in these men now, this bar, their friends...

And they're invested in you.

Maybe because of that, things had turned oddly domestic at Crave, for lack of a better word. Vic and Tegan were still babying him, cooking meals for him, and all of that was great but...

He wanted them to *touch* him. Fuck him. He got why they were circling him slowly again, thanks to his injuries, plus, it wasn't like they hadn't been busy with the club, dealing with him and Max and all the Strider drama. But that didn't stop his frustration.

So he danced—and generally enjoyed the fuck out of himself. He hadn't seen Tegan or Vic since they'd had dinner together earlier—and then after that, he'd helped Oz track Axel and Trevor for a bit so he could take a break.

Fantasy Week might be over, but according to Oz, the club was still busy with their regulars and newcomers who wanted to employ the services of a Dom or who wanted to play in their back rooms with their own Doms or subs. There wasn't a place for public play here, the way there was at The WHIP and North Street—everything that happened here was behind closed doors, save for Room 4, with its option to reveal the scene to the waiting public below. Since Cade had been here, he'd never seen or heard of it happening, so he figured it was a pretty rare occurrence, but he'd refused to ask about it.

Tegan and Vic hadn't mentioned his fantasy again, not since he had in the alley behind the fight club.

He tried not to think too hard on it, getting lost in dancing with Ash and Josie, and when he went to the bar and ordered a beer and a shot, Rom shook his head and pushed a water at him instead. "I've got my orders."

Cade frowned, but before he could ask any questions, Josie tapped him on the shoulder and said, "Oz needs to see you."

He didn't ask questions, just grabbed his water and followed her...over to the VIP section where he'd been seated that very first night he'd entered here. That seemed like a life-time ago, and still, his heart began to pound.

He sat next to Oz, who had the familiar clipboard and gulped his water as realization began to dawn of what this was really about. "Shit. This is happening, isn't it?"

Oz smiled. "Now these are the kind of nerves I expect to see."

"I feel like I'm going to die, Oz. That's not normal."

"Yes, it is, for your first time. And that's what this is." Oz pushed the now-familiar forms in front of him and Cade signed without reading. Oz went over them anyway, but all Cade heard was *"Blah-blah-red-blah-blah-yellow."*

Finally, Oz handed him his card. "It's a little different from the last one. You can look, or you can let it be a surprise."

"I'll go with surprise. I'm pretty sure I can't even read right now." His hands actually trembled as he took the card. "I'm not a fucking virgin."

"At this, you still are. So fucking enjoy it. Let's go." Oz stood and Cade followed him, watching as the crowd seemed to part around them, like they knew. Which was ridiculous.

When they got to Room 4, Cade grabbed Oz's arm. "It's just going to be them, right? No one else?"

"If anyone else tries to touch you, those two would kill them."

"Like Strider's werewolf books," Cade murmured.

Oz rolled his eyes but confessed, "He left me a few. They are good. Now go. Have fun. Remember—"

"Red and yellow." Cade walked inside and Oz shut the door behind him, and everything was exactly the same...but all so different at the same time.

He knew these men but still had no idea what to expect.

Tegan was in the same position he'd been the first night Cade had walked into Room 4. Everything had changed since then, and the one thing that hadn't? Would change tonight.

Cade hesitated as the door closed behind him, looking handsome and a little shy, which made Tegan fall for him a little harder.

More so when Cade reached into his pocket, pulled out a paper, and unfolded it. "I've been tested a couple of times since Courier—through the fight club—and I haven't been able to...not until you guys. If you still want to use condoms, that's okay, but—"

Tegan shook his head as he strode toward Cade. He took the paper and slid it back into Cade's pocket, trusting his word. He cupped a hand against Cade's cheek. He was going to make sure Cade loved every goddamned minute of what happened in here tonight. He and Vic would erase the bad, remake the memory, because all three of them needed that. They'd reclaim what Courier tried to ruin. "You know what's going to happen in here tonight?"

"I hope you're both going to tie me down and fuck me," Cade offered.

Tegan stared into his eyes and decided to make the man blush. "So eager to be held down, fucked, made to come over and over, until you're begging and you're not sure what you're begging for. Is that what you're hoping for?"

Cade's mouth opened slightly, his breathing quickened, his face flushed.

"Yes, baby? I think that's what you want," Tegan continued. "We're going to take you and you'll come again and again until you stop fucking thinking so much and just feel."

He ran a finger along Cade's jawline, enjoying making him speechless—and hard. Behind him, he heard Vic's low chuckle, and so did Cade, because his eyes widened and he turned his head slightly.

When Vic spoke, there was no mistaking the want in his tone. "So much to do tonight, baby. We should get started—since you're so ready."

Cade's dick was definitely ready, for all of it, and he swayed slightly at Tegan's touch. He leaned into it, actually, and Tegan's smile made his stomach flip.

"Need to hear you say it." Vic had moved closer, his palm on the back of Cade's neck and with both men touching him, just that was enough to erase any bad memories of this room.

"I want this. I want both of you. I want my fantasy," Cade told them.

"Good boy," Vic practically crooned.

"You're wearing way too many clothes," Tegan told him, and Cade flushed more deeply. He stripped off his shirt first, aware of the men's eyes on him. When Tegan reached out to play with a piercing, he lost his train of thought...until Tegan reminded him, "You're still wearing clothes."

"Oh. Hmmm." Cade tried to get his jeans off, but Tegan's mouth was on one of his nipples, distracting the hell out of him.

"Already not following orders," Vic said. "Someone needs a lesson in discipline."

"But..." Cade protested as he still tried to take his jeans off, but Tegan wasn't stopping with the nipple play, so it was pretty impossible. Purposely impossible. "S'not my fault."

But Vic was taking Cade's jeans down, socks and shoes too, just like that first night. Stripping him, assessing him, spreading his legs. He kicked Cade's legs apart and held his ass cheeks open. "Pretty little hole back here."

"He tastes good, too," Tegan murmured against his nipples.

"Fuck." He shuddered at the casual way they discussed him as he stood there, displayed and spread for their enjoyment.

Vic's finger pressed against his entrance; then he put his mouth there and licked. Kissed. Laved. Cade groaned loudly, eyes closed, reeling with the pleasure he received.

"How's that feel, Cade?" Tegan asked, still playing with

Cade's nipples, pinching and stroking and kissing. Cade tried to respond but only moans fell out when he opened his mouth.

Finally, Vic pulled his mouth and fingers away. "I think he's ready to start coming."

Tegan moved his mouth away from Cade's nipple but held on to one between his thumb and forefinger and used it to walk Cade over to the black leather bench that was close to the wall.

"Fuck," Cade muttered as he let himself be led that way.

Tegan grinned wickedly, because he knew, of course. "Kneel down," he instructed and held on to Cade's nipple the whole time, only letting go when he eased Cade's chest down flush to the leather. Vic was easing his arms up, cuffing them to the hooks on either side of the bench while Tegan pushed his legs apart. "I'm going to use a spreader bar," he said casually as Cade's ankles were wrapped. He tried to close his legs and realized that there was no way to do so.

He huffed a breath and looked up at Vic, who watched him carefully and then took a remote out of his pocket. With a click, the walls began to move, exposing the windows. Another click and Cade heard all the sounds from the club below—the cheers, because everyone knew that someone was in this room.

They couldn't see or hear him—not yet, anyway, and if Vic decided to let them, Cade knew there was nothing he could really do, beyond saying red. And really, he wasn't sure he'd want to do that, so he decided to play it by ear.

His dick? Totally agreed. More so when Vic picked up what looked like a vibrator. It wasn't very big, but that didn't mean anything, judging by the look in Vic's eyes as he showed it to him. "This is a prostate massager—and I can control the vibrations with a remote. So, while you're not allowed to come, you can let your prostate orgasm. In fact, I'm going to need you to."

Behind him, Tegan began to lick his hole, spearing his tongue inside, causing Cade to press back into it.

"He loves that, Teegs. You should see his face. I know you can hear him," Vic said. "He's getting you ready so we can put this inside. I'll help make sure you don't come too soon."

Vic picked up a cock ring and showed it to Cade before moving closer, leaning over and grabbing Cade's dick. He gave his shaft several strong tugs, and between that and Tegan's tongue? He put his forehead down on the bench and heard himself pleading. "Please...need to come. Please...don't stop."

Vic laughed and snapped the cock ring on. Cade looked up in time to see Vic pass the vibrating massager to Tegan.

"You ready, baby?" Vic asked.

"I don't...I mean...shit," Cade barely managed because Tegan had already inserted it and turned it on so it pulsed deep inside of him—and the spot it hit? Cade couldn't hold back his groan of pleasure as it massaged his gland, over and over.

His hips bucked and he was on display, but not really, as Vic talked. "They all want to see it, baby. Want to watch you have your first. I'll let them listen instead. Give it to them—go ahead."

He saw Vic press a button, felt the eyes of the crowd on him, the burn of humiliation on his cheeks as his body seemed to move without help from his brain. He was an animal, humping, needing. Rutting.

When the first orgasm hit, he heard himself practically howl—there was no cum, except some leaking from his dick, but his gland's contractions spread through his entire body. They were the longest, most drawn-out moments of pleasure he'd ever had. So different from an orgasm, but hell...

The cheering got louder. His moans filled the room—and was the bar below hearing that?

"Yes, baby, they heard that. Couldn't help but share how beautiful you sounded. Just for a few seconds. It's off now," Vic told him.

Fuck, that was hot, with the crowd extra riled up now—because of him—but he still retained his privacy; it was the perfect balance.

"You enjoying yourself?" Tegan asked.

"Fuck, yes. No. Yes. Fuck—just fuck me for real," Cade demanded, even as another wave of contractions hit him and rendered him incapable of words beyond unintelligible sounds for several moments.

"He's asking so nicely," Tegan said sarcastically once Cade could semi-focus again. "Maybe we should just leave him like this. Take bets on how many times he'll come. Open it up to the floor."

"The record is five. Think you can beat that?" Vic asked.

Fuck, no. "Please—I'll be good. I'll listen."

"He lies so pretty," Tegan commented. "I'm almost starting to feel sorry for him."

"Then you should fuck him, Tegan," Vic instructed, and the vibrator was taken out, leaving him so open and empty. He was unhooked, walked over to a higher bench, then repositioned onto his back, and his wrist restraints locked to his ankle restraints, so his legs were held open. Tegan was using his lubed fingers to open him farther, even as Vic stood over him, watching.

After keeping Cade on edge for what seemed like forever, Tegan stood, stripped himself completely, and then finally pressed the flared head of his cock inside of Cade, his eyes never leaving Cade's.

"Feels good, Tegan. Please," he begged as Tegan pushed forward.

"So tight," Tegan murmured. "Hot and tight and perfect."

His breath came in hard pants as Tegan's hips rocked, keeping constant pressure on his gland and fuck, he was so sensitive. And there was nothing he could do to stop the thrusts and that? Was the biggest turn on—besides the man currently in charge of his ass. "Tegan..."

"Yes, baby."

"I think I...fuck." Coherent thought was too difficult, especially when he saw Vic come up behind Tegan and nip his shoulder. From the sudden shudder Tegan gave, Cade guessed Vic was playing with his ass. Which translated into Tegan jerking into Cade's ass, which made him cry out since Tegan hit the right spot every damned time.

"Someone needs to take this cock ring off," he insisted.

"You can come with it on," Vic told him. "It just makes it harder."

"Vic," he groaned, and then Tegan groaned, his head bowing, and Cade realized that Vic was pushing inside of Tegan.

"Take me," Vic murmured against his cheek. "Open up and take me in."

Tegan nodded. "Fuck, Vic."

Cade loved watching these men together. Seeing them kiss was one thing, but watching them fuck was like watching two predators—Tegan wasn't giving up so much as giving in, and gladly, it seemed, based on the way his eyes rolled and fluttered when Vic stilled.

And then, Vic began to move, holding on to Tegan's hips and pistoning his own, which caused Tegan to rock into Cade, and the men moved in tandem, a perfect rhythm, until Cade's orgasm hit him, yanking itself out of him, his ass contracting, which caused Tegan to yell out and spill inside of him. Vic's cry was hoarse, almost painful, and when Cade could see again, he found Vic undoing his restraints and the ring around his cock.

Tegan was massaging his arms and legs, and then Vic was helping him up, bringing him over to the glass. Spreading his legs, driving inside of him.

"Have to have you, baby," Vic murmured.

"Yes, Vic," Cade encouraged. "Come inside of me. Please."

Vic growled and pressed him cock-first against the glass. "One push of a button, and they'll see everything. You'd better give me a good ride."

Cade nodded as Vic's hand closed around his throat, his thumb stroking his thrumming pulse point and words spilled out—"*Vic*," and "*Yes*," and "*So full*," and "*More*," and Vic complied.

His palms, flat on the glass, Vic holding him by the throat and hip as he hammered into him, and Cade came all over the glass with half scream, half sob, slamming a fist against it as he did so. The crowd must've heard the vibration, because the wolf whistles started up again, and the last thing Cade remembered was Vic's hot seed filling him before he began to fly.

––––––––

Cade was exhilarated. Exhausted. Wrung out, in the best way possible, and he didn't fight Tegan's hold on him, let himself be carried and placed in a bed. He didn't even open his eyes to figure out which bed it was, but hell, either Tegan's or Vic's would be wonderful. Even the floor would be wonderful now.

He heard a chuckle and cracked a lid. "Am I saying that out loud?"

"Yes, baby," Tegan told him. "You're in my room. My bed, and we're both here."

"Mmmhmm," he managed, then rolled over against Vic's chest. "Fucking perfect. You're both so fucking perfect."

Vic pressed a kiss to his forehead as Tegan massaged his back. "We'll wash you down in a little while."

"No—want to smell like you all night," Cade protested.

"Same," Tegan murmured, and Vic nodded his agreement.

"Thank you, Cade," Vic said finally.

"For what?"

"For letting us fix what went wrong the first time." Vic's eyes were dark, serious.

Cade smiled, pressed closer to Vic. "I want more."

"More what, baby?"

"More of you guys."

With all three of them secure in the comfort of his bed, Tegan watched Vic and Cade pressing together face first as he curled around Cade's back.

"Guess we wore him out." Vic looked down at Cade's sleeping face, a peace in his eyes that Tegan hadn't seen before.

"You don't look worn out enough," Tegan said.

"It wasn't about me tonight." Vic reached out and touched Tegan's cheek, letting his palm rest there for a long moment. "This is what matters."

"You both are what matter to me." Tegan leaned in and kissed him, hard and fast, taking his mouth and letting Vic know, in no uncertain terms, that he was Tegan's.

"Yeah, same." His brogue was heavy tonight. It had been a long day, coupled with a longer week, and the same issues would still face them come oh-dark-hundred.

Tegan wanted to wave a goddamned magic wand and fix all of it. And maybe, with Strider the Insane, that could actually happen.

Of course, working with Strider also brought along its fair share of rule-breaking because laws were optional in his world. Which was why he'd split from them years ago—mainly for their own safety and also, so he didn't have to hear them complain about little things like *prison*.

How he'd avoided it until now, Tegan didn't want to know.

CHAPTER 24

VIC STUMBLED into the war room only to find Cade sitting in front of the monitor, watching the dots that signified Axel and Trevor. He turned when Vic came closer.

"I didn't like waking up alone," Vic said to him pointedly.

"Tegan was gone when I woke up too," Cade told him.

"Then I'll tell him the same goddamned thing." He didn't bother to say that he'd gotten too used to having them close while he slept, that they alleviated his nightmares, that, after what happened the night before, not seeing Cade had freaked him out.

"I'm sorry." Cade was up and touching him, hands on Vic's neck, running down his arms. "You just looked so peaceful."

He softened slightly. "What's going on here?"

"Everything's fine. Oz looked tired, so I told him to get some rest, and I'd call if anyone veered off course."

Vic leaned down and sucked a mark along the side of Cade's neck, making him laugh and shiver at the same time. "Thank you, Cade."

"For what?"

"For taking care of Oz. For watching over men you've never met. For giving all of it a chance." Cade's eyes filled, but he blinked it back. "I'll bring you breakfast."

At the mere mention of food, Cade's stomach rumbled. "And I'll make it quick," Vic added, but he did pause for several moments, watching Cade marking coordinates. The man was so fucking capable. Vic honestly didn't doubt that he could've taken on Courier all by himself.

Luckily, he didn't have to.

When Vic came back with breakfast, Cade ate silently alongside Vic while they watched the blinking dots that were Axel and Trevor on the screen.

"Are they coming home soon?"

"Should be, yes."

"Will they...will I..."

"Like them? Yes, and yes," Vic assured him. "Now talk to me."

His eyes were so full of heat that Cade felt it surge through him.

"I'm just...it was a lot. Not bad," he assured Vic quickly. "It's just—I don't do that."

"What, baby?"

"Give myself over like a fucking slut. I don't do that. The only thing I have is my control, and you and Tegan took that from me."

"I'm sorry, baby. But I fucking treasure every time you give it up."

"I don't trust. I don't know how to."

"But you do. You've been." Vic's arms circled him. "Every time you let me do this. Every time you stayed here and slept instead of going home. Every time you let us take you to the fights. This is resistance's last stand, baby. After this, it can only get easier."

"I'm so broken," Cade whispered, like he was afraid to say it any louder, like that would make it true.

"None of us ever fully heal. We just grow scar tissue over our wounds that's thicker and stronger and makes it almost impossible to hurt in the same place. So you get ripped open in a different spot and you realize it hurts just as much. But hell, sometimes? It's well worth it."

"I know that. And I always felt like that could never be fixed. But when I'm with you both, I feel like all the broken pieces fit together."

Vic held him tight. "I feel the same way. You. Tegan. You both make me whole. And it's scary as hell. But it's a gift, Cade. A precious goddamned gift, and I don't take that lightly."

"I'm not going to let anything happen to either of you," Cade told him. "You have to know that, as much as you're protecting me? I'm going to do the same thing for both of you."

Vic kissed him and Cade was halfway into his lap when they heard a throat clearing.

"Has anyone ever told you that you've got the worst timing, Paulo?" Vic muttered over Cade's shoulder, and Cade turned to see the tall, blond man leaning against the doorjamb, smiling.

"Yes, actually they have," Paulo assured him as Cade slid off Vic's lap. "Cade, I'm Paulo. I'm sorry about the timing."

Cade shook his hand. "I've heard a lot about you."

"That you're a cockblocker," Vic said. "What's up?"

"Law and Styx are visiting with Tegan in the bar. I wanted to talk with Cade."

Vic nodded, squeezed Cade's shoulder. "Go—have a good visit, and I'll wait for Oz to come back. We'll finish this later. Not too much later, though."

Cade snorted and followed Paulo across the hall into the media room. Paulo shut the door and Cade frowned.

"If we're going to talk about all of them, I'd rather them not hear. They have big enough egos already," Paulo told him seriously, and Cade had to agree. "I also wanted to give you an update on Max, and to let you know that you can come hang out and visit him...as soon as all this is over with."

"I'm glad he's in a good place. I know Law was going to talk with Pat—maybe coordinate efforts." Cade sat on the couch and Paulo joined him.

"They've spoken. Law works with at-risk kids. I mean, we all do, but Law started the foundation. He's been in touch with Pat. He's got a house and counselors. Beds. He can take Max. Between him and Pat, they can do the initial assessments. Emergency placements, like they've been doing already but now, Pat and Lee will get paid."

Between that and Oz getting them listed as official fosters...

"Good. That's good." Cade was already emotional to start with today, but this threw him over the edge. His eyes filled and he put his head down.

"Ah, Cade," Paulo said gently. "You remind me so much of Law. So much."

"Is that good or bad?"

"He's the love of my life—him and Styx both. You'll get through this."

"I'm just..."

"Scared. Freaked out. Wondering how you could suddenly have such strong feelings for two men at the same time?"

"Took the words right out of my mouth," Cade muttered. "So I'm guessing my feelings aren't unusual."

"Not at all, based on my experience." Paulo sat back. "Just because it's not something everyone does? Don't let that freak you out. Because not everyone gets something this special. You do."

"It's been a long time for you guys, right?"

"Almost eight years," Paulo agreed. "Never regretted a second of it."

"I never thought..." He shook his head. "I don't want to tell them all about me."

"You think anything you tell them is going to drive them away? Or is that scared part of you that thinks you don't deserve this hoping it will?"

How had Paulo hit on that so perfectly?

Paolo's hand came down on his shoulder. "Tell them everything you need to. I know nothing you tell them will turn them away."

"How can you be so sure?"

Paolo's smile was full of confidence. "I've seen the way they look at you."

"Thanks." Cade smiled.

"I'm going to give you my number—all our numbers, so you can call anytime." Paulo told him, then looked serious. "But there's one really important thing we need to discuss first."

CHAPTER 25

TEGAN CAME up from the gym, the extra burst of energy from the scene the night before making his adrenaline refuse to drop. He'd snuck out of bed early, refusing to wake up the two exhausted men, and he'd wrung himself out with exercise, then showered in Oz's room. Because he knew if he walked into his own room, he'd end up waking the two men up for sure. And he'd grabbed clothes on his way out for that very reason.

He'd already jerked off twice that morning just thinking about Vic, Cade, and Room 4.

Oz came in while he was getting dressed. "Hey, Law, Styx, and Paulo are all here. Law and Styx are waiting for you in the bar. Paulo wanted to meet Cade."

That made sense—when Paulo had first gotten together with Law and then Styx, he'd been considered the outsider since Law and Styx had grown up together. He was probably concerned about how Cade was faring with this newfound...relationship.

Because that was what it was.

"You okay, Teegs? You suddenly got a little pale there," Oz observed.

"I'm all right. Maybe."

"Worried about Cade talking to Paulo?"

"What? No, it's not that. It'll be good for him."

"Yeah, it will be," Oz agreed. "You know, he fits."

Tegan stared into his friend's translucent blue eyes. "Fits?"

"He's us," Oz said simply, and the truth of that hit Tegan like a bullet. Law liked to call them all lost boys. And like definitely gravitated to like—Tegan had seen enough evidence of that over the years. "Law's waiting in the bar. Styx is...wandering."

Tegan smiled at that. Knowing Styx, he was setting up a perimeter of his own, despite the fact that they'd done that long ago, pre-Cade. He went down to the main bar area, where Law sat alone, looking pensive.

"You all right?" he asked Law.

"Just checking out all the ghosts." Law had owned this place with Damon for a long time, and while he'd been more than ready to give it up, Tegan knew this place held a lot of memories for them, both good and bad. "Damon said to say hi."

"Where is he these days?"

"He and Tanner take off whenever the kid's got leave," Law explained. "I think they're somewhere in Bali."

"Sounds nice."

"Sounds like just another jungle." Law shook his head. "But they seem to enjoy it."

Damon and Tanner had fought hard for their relationship. So had Law and his men—all three had a long road back from hell, and they were inseparable. Knowing them was the only reason Tegan could even begin to consider what was happening between him, Vic, and Cade as something real.

There was no denying that the dynamic was explosive. Whether it would stand the test of time was a question none of them could answer. Not yet, anyway.

"So, you, Vic, and Ranger boy doing okay?" Law asked, not even trying to be casual. Or, if he was, he really sucked at it.

"Cade's okay, considering the circumstances."

"Not exactly what I asked, but nice bob and weave."

Why everyone felt the goddamned need to push him, he had no idea.

"Want to talk about it?" Law asked finally.

"Nope."

Law nodded and stared straight ahead. "Club looks good."

"He's a lost boy, Law," Tegan blurted out.

"The one you don't want to talk about?"

"Fuck you."

Law snorted. "You and Damon might actually be the same goddamned person."

"How do you do it?"

"With Damon? I don't fuck him, but I do tell him to fuck off a lot."

Tegan sighed. "You—and Styx and Paulo. How?"

Law shrugged. "I don't think about the 'how' too much. It just does." He put a hand on his heart. "It works here. After that, the rest is easy."

"By the way, Vic is definitely more like Damon than I am."

"You keep thinking that." Law gave a sympathetic shake of his head. "Tougher they are..."

"You fell pretty damned hard."

Law shrugged, his blond hair falling across his forehead. He pushed it out of the way. "I did. Twice. And you and Vic should've fucked a long time ago."

"He was always with someone."

"Yeah, like I said, you should've fucked a long time ago." Law shook his head. "What's the problem, really?"

Tegan knew exactly what the problem was—Vic had so much power inside of him, enough to quell the chaos that swirled around inside of Cade. As for him... "I don't know what the hell I bring to the table."

"Why don't you ask?" Vic's voice came from behind him. An arm wrapped around his chest as Law nodded approvingly. "Baby, you're the calm. You're the one who makes sure we point in the right direction."

"And there you go," Law said quietly as Styx walked in the side entrance. "Where were you? Setting up extra cameras?"

"What? No—I'd never do that." Styx's look said he was doing exactly that. "How about a drink?"

"Nice distraction technique." But Tegan did pour them some drinks—brought the bottle over to one of the tables, and the four of them sat and bullshitted, not realizing that several hours had passed...not until Oz walked in and said, "Are you all planning on keeping that table all night? We have paying customers who'll want it."

Styx laughed and poured another shot, but Law straightened up, looking behind Oz and asking, "Where's Paulo?"

"With Cade," Oz said as he slid into a seat next to him.

"But I thought you were with them." Law sounded...distressed.

"They don't need babysitters," Oz said, frowning. "Well, Paulo doesn't, and he's with Cade so..."

"Paulo doesn't need watching?" Law's voice rose an octave.

"Law, what the fuck?" Tegan asked.

"Paulo and Cade alone is *not* a good idea." The concern on Law's face was almost comical, except for how serious he actually was.

"You brought him here," Tegan reminded him.

Styx stood. "We need to find those two—now."

Law groaned. "It's probably already too late."

Cade was just setting up the food when Tegan and Vic came into the media room.

"What's wrong?" Cade asked because they both looked rushed. And concerned.

"Nothing," Vic said unconvincingly. "We just didn't realize how long we'd been bullshitting."

Paulo moved to the door, grinning. "No worries—Cade and I had a great talk too. We've got a lot in common."

Before Tegan could say anything, he noticed the spread of food. "How many people are you feeding?"

"Shit, sorry. I wasn't thinking that maybe you don't like—"

"I like," Vic interrupted. "But it's enough for a small army."

"Yeah, it's a lot," Cade admitted. "I guess you were right, Paulo."

"What was Paulo right about?" Vic asked.

Cade caught Paolo's eye as he started retreating from the room. "Just that...you guys aren't, um...my age..."

Tegan caught Cade's gaze. "Tell me exactly what he said."

"Just that you guys were older and that you might have different dietary needs."

He looked at Paulo, and Paulo shrugged innocently as he took another step back...right into Law.

And Styx. Paulo glanced over his shoulder at them. "Oh, hey. Thought you guys were still at the bar."

"Different dietary needs?" Law asked him.

"Older?" Styx added.

"Shit, did I get you in trouble?" Cade asked Paulo.

Paulo mouthed, *It's all good*, with a small smile and then turned to Law. "Do you need to see the medical research on diet and aging?"

"I'd really quit while you're ahead," Styx murmured. "Excuse us—we *older* guys need to show this young one a few things. Immediately."

"All the rooms are open," Tegan offered. "Room Three, especially."

Paulo winked at Cade as Law and Styx each took an arm and escorted him away.

Cade looked at Tegan and Vic. "What's going on?"

"Worried about our diet?" Tegan asked him.

"Older men?" Vic said.

Cade looked between the two of them. "Are you two...I mean, you're being all sensitive about your age. Paulo just said that you'd want to eat before five so you could digest..."

From the hallway, they heard Paulo howl with laughter and then Law's words of "You're not going to sit for a week," rang out...and then Cade got it.

Paulo had gotten himself in trouble on purpose. But why would Paulo want to get Cade in trouble?

But the look on Tegan and Vic's faces when they advanced toward him? That answered the last question.

Trouble equaled pleasure.

"I mean, you could just have the white rice if you're worried," Cade told them.

"I was just feeling sorry for you, that Paulo got you in over your head," Tegan said. "But now..."

Vic was behind him, a hand on his waist; the other had a firm grip on his biceps. "I'm not feeling sorry for him at all," he told Tegan.

"What are they going to do to Paulo?" Cade asked, trying to sound innocent and failing.

"To *him*? I'd worry less about Paulo and more about what's going to happen to you," Tegan warned.

Cade swallowed hard.

"But if you're really concerned about it?" Tegan crooked a finger at him, and Vic pushed him forward so they could follow him.

Tegan turned the monitor on and the camera, specifically the one in Room 3, for a brief moment. There wasn't sound, but Paulo was splayed out on Styx's lap while Law watched. And the look on Paulo's face?

Pure bliss. And Law and Styx? The same damned look. They loved this. Like a game they played regularly.

Getting in trouble made things more fun.

Then the monitor flicked off, and Cade realized how hard he was. "So, Room Three," was all he could think of to say.

"Yeah, that was Law's favorite room when he owned this place. They come here sometimes and play in there," Vic said.

"So now, us old guys"—Tegan pointed between him and Vic—"we're going to show you our advanced age."

Paulo's words echoed in his head.

Just give in to it. Because when they're both focused on you, there's nothing better.

Cade swallowed hard. "Did you want to eat before five? Otherwise..."

He didn't get a chance to finish. Tegan swept him off his feet, threw him over his shoulder, and carried him into Room 4.

CHAPTER 26

WHEN VIC CLOSED the door behind them, Tegan put Cade down...and Cade wasted no time in winding his arms around Tegan's shoulders. Tegan started to pick him up and Cade climbed him like a tree, winding his legs around Tegan to keep himself hiked up. But then Tegan put Cade's back against the wall, so the hold on him was leveraged by Tegan's body weight. There was no escape for him, and with Tegan's mouth on his, Cade wasn't looking for an out.

No, he wanted *more*. His fingers dug into Tegan's short hair as Tegan ravaged his mouth, his tongue mimicking what Cade wanted his dick to do.

"C'mon, Tegan—I'm leaking. Gonna make me come all over myself like a teenager."

Tegan smiled. "You issuing me a challenge?"

"Fuck me now."

Tegan laughed and dipped his head to lick Cade's throat, suck on his racing pulse, hard enough to leave a mark and Cade cried out, half laugh and half protest. "You call us old, and you expect to get rewarded for that?"

"It worked for Paulo," Cade pointed out. "I guess he likes it...rough?"

"Sometimes, yes. Law likes it rougher, though," Tegan added. "Law's what we call a switch—he gets off on both roles, top and bottom—with the right top."

"Like Tegan," Vic said.

"Really?" Cade asked.

"Really," Vic told him, leaning in to lick a stripe up the side of Tegan's neck. Tegan smiled and groaned as Vic's hands moved to his ass, as Cade watched over Tegan's shoulders. "You have more questions."

You promised me a spanking. The words were on the tip of his tongue, but he couldn't quite bring himself to ask for it. Instead, he managed, "What they were doing to Paulo..."

And Vic smiled. "I haven't forgotten, Cade. I wanted to make sure you were really ready for it. Sometimes the talk is enough for some people—and that's okay too."

"I want it," Cade managed, and slowly, Tegan lowered him and shifted his body out of the way so Vic could lean in and kiss him—a slow-burn kiss that started sweet and got dirty fast. Tegan was adding his own touches and nips to the back of Cade's neck, and he was overwhelmed with sensation.

"Wasn't anyone ever sweet to you?" Vic practically crooned when he pulled away, and Cade could honestly answer, *No*...not like this.

Nothing like this.

He was losing himself, losing everything to these men who surrounded him with the heat of their bodies, their rough palms flexing along his skin...the drag of their mouths and tongues like fire dancing over his skin.

He'd never had a chance, not the way they were working him over, tending to his pleasure, and this wasn't at all what he'd expected. Not when Vic sank to his knees, freed Cade's cock, and took it into his mouth. Cade's hand stroked the side of his face, feeling the scars under his fingertips.

When he looked down, Vic's dark eyes were staring up at him, and Tegan was at his back, pressing a kiss to his shoulder and Cade wanted to freeze this moment.

A flurry of groans drummed up in his throat and escaped, and fuck, he wanted to last all goddamned night and bask in this pleasure. He was so close to coming, so goddamned close...and then Vic pulled away. "Vic, c'mon," he begged.

"First things first," Vic told him. "I promised to make you scream."

"I was getting ready to."

"Not the way you will once you're over my lap," Vic promised, and Cade swallowed hard. Vic rose from his knees, and Cade was sure his legs wouldn't move. But Tegan was pushing him to follow Vic and he did, somehow, watched Vic sit on the couch and pat his thigh. "I'm waiting."

Tegan was pulling Cade's jeans down farther off his hips, leaving them around his thighs as he helped Cade settle across Vic's lap.

Fuck, this was too much. Maybe he didn't want this. He was lying across the couch, across Vic's lap, bare ass in the air.

You can say no. Say red. Yellow, at least. But when Vic asked, "Ready?" all Cade heard himself say was, "Yes. Hurry."

Vic's arm was on his lower back, holding him in place. Then Vic's hand came down on his ass cheeks, one then the other, a pattern undiscernible to him and after several slaps, he didn't bother trying to keep track. He couldn't—the pain/pleasure line was blurred—so goddamned blurred—and he squirmed and cried out and buried his head, humiliation and pleasure warring with each other.

Intense wasn't an adequate enough word. Exquisite was better, because the pain exploded, his nerve endings sparking at every touch and his only thought was *More*, a drumbeat of a word echoing in his head.

But everything that had been balled up inside of him was slowly evaporating, wrapping itself in the pain and dissipating. He was letting go and floating away with every slap of Vic's palm.

The sensations forced him to focus on the pleasure and nothing else, not allowing him to compare this experience or to sink into flashback. It was all present and presence. He gave more than just his body, offered himself up...and they'd take it all, accept it and give themselves over to him in turn.

And he'd accept it, hold it, selfishly refuse to give any of it back.

What happened in this room might've started as a game, a power play, but now everything had reversed.

Suddenly, he was off Vic's lap, on his knees in between Vic's legs.

"Vic," Cade groaned. "Please..."

He didn't know what he was begging for, but it didn't matter because Vic did. Tegan's fingers speared him as his mouth closed around Vic's cock. He'd heard the term spit-roast, but he'd only ever seen that in porn videos, and fuck, it was hot then. Hotter still to be the one in the middle of it in real life.

When Tegan's cock entered him, he was in the middle,

being fucked and filled, and he felt like he was floating, watching it happen, the sensations sparking through his body. His skin was tight and hot, too small to contain him. Tegan's palm smacked his already sensitive ass as he drove inside of him, and Vic pushed his cock down Cade's throat and held him there for just a second...and the total loss of control had Cade coming in hot, hard spasms, with no one touching his cock.

Tegan held Cade, who'd half collapsed on him on the couch. Vic was next to them as they all recovered, but the energy that thrummed through the room was strong enough that Tegan knew they weren't done in here yet.

"Think he liked it?" Vic asked seriously.

Tegan rolled his eyes. "Are you looking for a compliment?" he teased the dark-haired man, and Vic smirked.

"What are you looking for, Teegs?" Vic asked, his voice dark and a little more than dangerous. His dick had been content until the moment Vic started talking and dammit, the man knew it too. "You need it, too? The way Cade does?"

Cade was awake now...and listening. "You switch, Tegan? Want to see that," he murmured. "Can I watch?"

"Definitely," Vic told him, and Tegan laughed without answering, mainly to hide his nerves.

"What do you like, Tegan?" Cade was asking, but his face was suddenly serious.

"What's wrong, baby?" Vic asked him.

"Nothing, really. It's just...is this—what happened—like what Deran does to Theo?"

Tegan cleared his throat. "I don't know specifically what Deran does to Theo, but Deran's slightly more...hardcore, than what we've done here."

Cade's brows shot up. "What does that mean, exactly?"

"It's different for everyone," Tegan hedged.

Cade climbed deftly into his lap and demanded, "Show me."

"You won't like it."

"How do you know?" Cade sucked at Tegan's neck, hard, then bit and hell, maybe Cade did know.

He pushed Cade back, stopping him for a second, felt Vic's eyes on them. "He's into pain, Cade. Giving pain."

"As in, pain for pleasure?"

"Yes. But it's not a light spanking I'm talking about. It's..."

"Does he hurt my friend?" Cade's voice was quiet.

"If he does, it's because Theo asks for it...wants it. Maybe more than that—he might need it."

Cade nodded. "So the back-and-forth between them, the love-hate thing..."

"I'm guessing it's part of the pleasure-pain thing."

Cade leaned in. "Show me."

"Cade—"

"You and Vic—show me. I need to understand."

"If it's not what you need—"

"How do I know?"

"I'll do it," Vic offered, then his tone softened. "I'll do it, Tegan. Let me."

Tegan shook his head. "Not on him. Show him on me. So he understands."

"Teegs—"

"No. He doesn't need to feel it to understand. He just

needs to see it." Tegan's eyes met Vic's. "We both know it's not his thing."

"But it's yours?" Vic asked, his voice husky, as if he'd finally unlocked a mystery he'd been wondering about and dammit, Tegan wanted to close and relock that particular fucking door...almost as much as he wanted to kick it down.

"Yes," he admitted finally.

Cade was watching him carefully. "I want to feel it too, Tegan. Please. I need to understand."

"Both of you—get moving now." Vic's voice boomed without him having to raise it, and Cade obeyed immediately. But it took Tegan a moment longer while he stared at Vic and everything hung in the balance, and it felt so fucking heavy, like he was drowning.

And Vic was offering him a lifeline. The final piece of the puzzle. "I've got you, Teegs. It's okay. It's going to be okay."

Tegan kept repeating that last phrase to himself as Vic readied Cade.

"I thought I was just watching," Cade said as Vic strapped him back down to a bench with a vibrating dildo in his ass.

"This is more of a participatory activity." Vic smiled and Cade groaned, but it didn't stop him from watching Vic strip Tegan.

Finally, Vic kissed him, hard and fast, and then led him over to the St. Andrew's Cross and strapped him in.

Tegan's dick was rock hard, and he heard his own ragged breaths. "Vic, please..."

"Do I need to gag you?"

"Fucker," Tegan muttered and found himself gagged for

that. Vic didn't play around, and Tegan realized he hadn't wanted him to.

He didn't remember much after that—not once he felt the first blows from the flogger tease and torment him. After the flogging, while his back and ass burned hot, Vic fucked him till he flew, with Cade's whimpers surrounding them, cushioning the roughness just enough.

When Vic unstrapped him, he also supported most of Tegan's body weight as he helped him over to the couch. It would be a while until he got his sea legs again and far longer to come fully back down, but it was the most perfect thing. With the perfect men.

"Did that help?" Cade murmured, his face flushed from his own experience.

"Yeah, it did."

"It helped me too," Cade told him.

"Of course it did," Vic said loudly, and both men laughed. "I mean, if you're both going to question it, I will gladly do it all again."

Tegan stared at Vic, knowing he'd be feeling the session for days to come. "I don't think I'd mind that at all."

Paulo, Law, and Styx stayed in Room 3 for a good part of the night, and Tegan, Vic, and Cade did the same in Room 4. After a couple of hours' rest, Tegan felt much better than he had in a long time.

A little honesty always went a hell of a long way. And Vic was really good at aftercare. Plus, having Cade there, understanding and appreciative, cemented everything Tegan could've hoped for.

Now, he exited Room 4 and stood outside the door, not wanting to interrupt the men at the end of the hallway. Paulo had just exited Room 3. Styx walked up behind him and rubbed his ass, and Paulo hissed and smiled. Styx's arm went around his chest from behind and nuzzled his neck. Law closed in and bent his head against Paolo's chest, and Tegan noticed that each of the men had a hand entwined.

Such a look of contentment...like the three men held the best secret in the world between them.

It echoed exactly how Tegan felt right now. "You guys need anything?" he asked when Styx acknowledged him.

"We're good," Paulo said, still half in space.

"How often does he do that?" Tegan asked Law and Styx, pointing to Paulo.

"Every time he wants a night like that," Law said, looking at Paulo like he was everything. "He could just ask, but he has so much fun doing it this way."

"Reminds us of the old days," Styx added. "Although I think this time he was trying to ease Cade into the whole *three guys* thing."

"Ease? You mean throw him into the deep end," Law corrected.

Paulo simply mouthed, *You're welcome* to Vic, who'd just walked up to Tegan and smirked at Paulo's response.

"I guess we've got our hands full," Tegan said.

"You more than anyone, seeing you're the oldest," Vic murmured.

"You son of a—" Tegan started but Vic was already running away, laughing, calling, "Keep up, old man."

Law glanced at Styx. "Since you're the oldest, think you're going to need a cane soon?"

"I can think of someone who's getting a cane," Styx warned him.

Law glanced over toward Room 3. Paulo, of course, was already in the doorway. "I'll accept my punishment gracefully."

Paulo laughed and hurried them back inside the room.

CHAPTER 27

EARLIER, Cade had mentioned the underground fight Andrei offered him to both Tegan and Vic, very casually, like it was no big deal for him to be asked to do *"an illegal underground death match"*—as Tegan called it—and then Cade had sweetened the deal with, "You guys can take me there and back," as though he were pliant and easy.

"Wow, such an amazing invitation." Tegan had muttered, rolling his eyes and stalking off, but Vic smiled and Cade knew they'd cave.

He also knew he *was* pliant and easy for them, dammit. There wasn't any denying it. So he didn't.

Vic sighed. "He's going stir crazy."

"No one's heard from Strider at all. And Rigs hasn't heard anything more about my case," Cade added, for Tegan's benefit.

"That doesn't mean we're in the clear," Tegan pointed out.

"The fight won't be posted," Cade told them. "It's one of the after-hours fights."

Tegan shook his head. "Illegal, you mean."

Cade shrugged. "It's money. And I need to help Pat and Lee. And pay you guys—"

"Don't use us as an excuse for your illegal activities," Tegan told him.

"Vic did it for years," Cade said.

Vic shrugged. "He's got a point."

"Not helping, Vic." Tegan relented. "No publicity?"

"No one knows who's fighting until they're in the ring. Invite only—total blackout. And Andrei and Dobry know about Courier—he won't be allowed in at all."

"Does Rourke get invited?" Vic asked.

"Cops don't come to the illegal fights. They record the crowds."

"Nicely done," Vic said and Tegan glared. "I mean, how illegal. Bad fight club."

Cade laughed and Tegan shook his head. "Two idiots."

"Idiot who's winning tonight's fight," Cade corrected. "Pat's first, then the fight."

"Then home...until we find Strider," Tegan said.

"Deal."

And so Tegan and Vic escorted Cade to the fight, hawking over him before he got into the ring, as usual.

This wasn't his first underground fight—he'd had several big ones, none of them easy, but the crowd loved them—and him, by extension. But this time, he incorporated a lot of the moves Vic taught him and they worked like magic. He won his fight, bruised and slightly bloodied, but he walked away.

His opponent kind of limped, but hell, that was what this was all about. And after Cade came out of the ring, three men had slipped their cards into the waistband of his shorts and when the fourth attempted to do the same, Vic actually growled like a rabid dog, and Cade almost laughed at the look on the face of the man with the card.

"Hey, you're scaring my groupies away," Cade complained.

"You'll have to settle for us as your groupies, and I think we did a decent enough job fucking you in the alley to qualify," Vic growled again and Cade's dick rose and yeah, jealous Vic was hot as fuck.

So was jealous Tegan—hot and scary. "You looked great out there." His hand went around the back of Cade's neck. "Going to show you how great as soon as we get out of here—put you over Vic's knees. What would your groupies think of that?"

Cade's body responded immediately. He was practically purring against Tegan. "I think they'd like it."

"We definitely need to get him home so we can fuck him," Vic announced and the men around them nodded appreciatively.

Cade smiled at Vic and Tegan. "I think you guys just got me a whole new set of fans."

Cade went to shower quickly and change. On the way to the back, he saw Lonny, a foster kid he'd helped last year, coming in to refill medical supplies. But that was only because they were busy tonight—Cade knew that Lonny had worked his way up and gotten a coveted front door job during the after-hours fights. Now, Lonny loped over to him, grabbing him in a bear hug.

Lonny was a big dude for seventeen. Bigger still now, he'd been working out, but he was the pure definition of gentle giant. "Cade! You kicked ass tonight, man!"

"Thanks, Lon." Cade hugged him, then pulled away to study the now-seventeen-year-old. "I'm hearing good things about you all around."

Lonny looked good. Happy. Way fucking better than he'd looked when Cade had first met him after he'd taken a wicked beating from his foster father. The only good thing to come out of that, beyond finding the start of financial independence, was that the social worker had actually removed him from the home. Now, he was in a group home situation that he was cool with—and if he hadn't been, Cade would've gotten him in at Pat's for sure. Lonny was on his own now, having emancipated, but he'd be okay.

"I'm thinking about enlisting," he told Cade now. "I'm not sure, though. Dobry likes me a lot, so I could definitely do well here."

"I'll take you out to eat, and we'll talk about the Army—next week?" Cade asked.

"That's great, Cade."

"I'll text you." Cade pulled him in for another back-thumping hug and then headed to the shower.

And even though Lonny was doing great, it still put him in an unexpectedly melancholy mood, made him think about Theo and the situation they were currently in.

Christ, how could everything come rushing back that fast? Just when he'd thought he was all better...he should've known that he could never escape his past. One minute he was falling for two incredible men and doing what he loved in the ring and the next, he was that scared, broken kid, just trying to survive.

There were still secrets, ones only he and Theo knew, and if those were to spill out?

He refused to let himself go there.

Maybe you should just tell them. Head Courier off.

He was so tired of thinking about the past. It should stay dead and buried like all bad things...but Tegan and Vic deserved to know what he'd done. What he might end up doing.

It might be the only way they understood.

"Cade?" Tegan was standing in front of him and Cade snapped to. "You all right? Take a hit we didn't notice?"

"No way," he scoffed. "I didn't give him time to get hits in."

"That's right—thanks to my pointers," Vic crowed, and Cade couldn't deny it. "You ready to get out of here?"

"Yeah, I am. Can we just make a stop?" he asked as he shouldered his bag.

"Hungry?" Vic asked.

"Well, yeah, but that's not where I want to stop." He noted that they looked at each other over him, but neither man pressed him any further. Instead, Tegan let him direct the truck to the old building that was a block down from Pat's. Tegan parked in front and Cade got out, waiting for them to warn him that it wasn't safe.

And it probably wasn't, but he needed to do this here. Before he chickened out. So he sat on the stoop and Tegan joined him. Vic remained standing, on alert but no less interested in what Cade was preparing to tell them.

It was quiet out—peaceful, which was ironic, and the snow began to float down in big, fat flakes.

"This was my fourth foster home," he said quietly, like he was afraid that saying it any louder would stir up too many memories. "I was here the longest. And it was the worst. If it wasn't for Theo...I don't know what I would've done without him." He paused. "This was Theo's building. We met in school and we bonded pretty quickly. It's easy to spot another kid who's being knocked around the same way you are."

He glanced up at Vic, who looked like he was ready to beat down any ghosts who dared to threaten Cade. Tegan's hand skimmed his back, but neither man pushed him to continue.

Finally, he said, "We met Pat when he found us sleeping in his truck. We broke in one night when neither of us wanted to go back home." He shivered at the memory of the two of them huddled together for warmth, happy to be without anyone threatening to hurt them—for that moment, at least, and fuck Courier for trying to make him helpless again. "One night...things got really bad. For Theo. I went over to his place when he didn't show up to meet me. That was never a good sign." Normally, when that happened, it meant Theo had caught a bad beating and needed some help getting out of the apartment—usually through the fire escape once his stepdad passed out. Cade stared into the distance and saw the scene unfolding before him. "It was quiet. Too quiet. I went in through the fire escape and that's when I saw..."

Theo, sitting on the floor, holding his arm, his shoulder looking like it was set at a funny angle. Bruises on his face, his lip swollen...and blood all over the floor.

When he saw Cade, he held up his hand to stop him from rushing in and stepping in the blood. And that's when Cade turned and saw Theo's stepfather on the floor, a knife sticking out of his chest, his lifeless eyes staring at the ceiling.

"Theo, what happened?" he asked, but Theo just shook his head, obviously in some kind of shock. He was sixteen, too big to let his stepfather keep hitting him. But this was what he'd been afraid of, not being able to stop himself.

"Did I do that?" Theo asked.

"I don't know. If you did, it was self-defense."

"No police," Theo said and yeah, Cade didn't blame him. But he had no clue what the hell they should do.

"What did you do, Cade?" Tegan asked, concern and zero judgment in his eyes. Vic looked angry—like if he'd been there he'd have killed Theo's stepfather again and again for what he'd done.

"We, ah...took care of it. Theo kept getting his stepfather's checks. We both stayed at his apartment. We went to school so we wouldn't trigger any welfare checks. And when I dropped out and took my GED, I went to work to help supplement our money, until Theo turned seventeen and we both went into the military. That's when I stopped depositing his father's checks into his account." It spilled out, all the memories squashing together. "He's good—I'd never take away his career from him. I'd do anything to let him stay doing what he loves."

"I understand that," Tegan assured him. "How did Courier find this out?"

"I have no idea," Cade said. "No one knows. No one. His checks still come but no one cashes them. Not anymore. He's got no other family."

Vic grimaced. "Where's the body?"

Cade shook his head. "It's gone. There's nothing to find. Trust me."

"Cade—" Tegan pressed.

"Fine," he bit out. "There was a man who lived in the apartment below Theo's. Mr. A. He was older. He worked at a funeral home."

"I don't like where this is going," Vic muttered.

"He knocked on the door and I let him in, because I didn't know what to do."

"Because you were fifteen fucking years old and shouldn't have known," Tegan added.

"Mr. A took one look at us, told us not to move. He came back with a body bag an hour later, and he helped us. We rolled the body into the bag, put that into a rug, put it in Mr. A's car, and never saw it again. Later, he told me that he cremated it all so there was no evidence. He helped us clean up the blood. And then he made us swear each other to secrecy."

"Maybe he told someone?" Tegan persisted.

Cade shook his head. "He left everything he had to me and Theo when he died a couple of years later. There's no way. No way. Fuck."

Vic leaned in. "If there's no evidence, it's Courier's word against yours."

"Courier's CIA gold," Tegan pointed out. "His word carries some weight for sure. He can also manipulate shit, so we need to be careful."

"And we will," Vic said quietly. "You're a good friend, Cade."

"Theo would do the same for me," Cade insisted.

"I believe that." Tegan wrapped an arm around him. "I also figure you're telling us because you're planning on confessing to this. We're not going to talk about that now, because you've already been through hell just talking about it. But thank you...for trusting us with your life, and with Theo's."

"You'll never regret it," Vic assured him, and somehow Cade had already known that.

CHAPTER 28

OZ TRIED to shake the feeling of dread all day but nothing worked. Now, with Cade at the fight with Tegan and Vic, he stared at the computer screen, unable to concentrate on shit.

He hated being helpless. Hated worse that he didn't know if the lack of contact between Gray Ops and Axel and Trevor had anything to do with the email he'd received that morning.

None of your hands are clean.

He'd passed the message on to Strider, who he hadn't seen or heard from in the better part of a week. He was relieved when the man walked through the back door, but he'd never, ever admit that. Not out loud, anyway. "How the hell did you get past the cameras?" Oz demanded.

"Missed you too, Oz." Strider looked...agitated. "I got your text."

"I hope you've got good news."

"I definitely do not." Strider paced. "Nothing from Axel or Trevor?"

"Nothing since yesterday. I'm thinking about sending

Deran after them," Oz admitted. "And I haven't told Tegan yet."

"Oh, keeping secrets?" The old Strider flashed back for just a second before he got serious again, and serious Strider was seriously fucking scary. "Courier's no longer interested in my services. Says he's got an alternate plan that panned out."

"Which is?"

"I'm afraid I'm about to find out." He tapped the keys.

Oz watched over his shoulder, felt Strider still first, the air in the room changed perceptively. "Strider, am I looking at..."

"Yes." Strider glared at the screen. "This entire thing just went sideways. And I'm very good at sideways, Oz. So very good."

After no calls, no messages, and no live sightings of the tall, amber-eyed man, Strider was waiting for them in the war room at Crave.

Cade's gut tightened and Tegan muttered, "This can't be good."

Strider had taken the helm of the main bank of computers, and he and Oz barely turned around to greet them. "About time you guys got back—I tried to send Oz out after you to round you up, but he was too worried about Cade's fight."

"And he punched Colin out," Oz added. "He's lying down in the break room. Possible concussion."

"What the fuck, Strider?" Tegan asked.

"He wouldn't let me in. All I did was come up through a fire escape and through a locked window—which wasn't very hard to pick, by the way—and everyone gets so suspicious."

"We have rules," Tegan told him.

"Those rules don't apply to me, and you know it."

"Start talking," Tegan ordered, and, for once, Strider didn't mince words.

"We've got a major problem. One that negates Cade from leaving this place from here on out."

"Oh, fuck that," Cade told him.

Strider shook his head and swiveled his chair. "Stubborn, stubborn boy. I figured you wouldn't just take my word for it." He pointed at the screen. "Check out your auction. The countdown for buyers starts in sixty seconds."

Cade stared at the screen with the countdown clock, the words *Live Auction*, his first name, age, and stats. And his picture, that he recognized from the video Courier had made of the two of them. "Where the fuck is this happening?"

"Dark web," Vic growled as he glanced between Cade and the screen.

Cade couldn't take his eyes off the countdown. *Ten, nine, eight...*

"Isn't there a way to stop it?" Tegan demanded.

"It would take a great deal of effort, and we'd end up with nothing," Oz said quietly.

Strider pointed to him. "What Oz said. Besides that, we've got a better shot of letting a buyer come forward with a winning bid and then tracking him."

"In order to track him, Courier would need to have Cade," Vic said.

"I didn't say there weren't kinks in the plan." Strider

frowned and Vic growled loudly. "That's the spirit, Vic. Now, can we agree to keep Cade protected and sequestered here? Because once the final bid comes in, someone's been hired to hunt and collect him."

Seven, six, five...

"This guy's a sick fuck." Tegan shook his head and Cade realized the room began to spin a little, almost like this wasn't real and he was floating.

Four, three, two...

"How did this happen?" Tegan demanded.

"I got a notice from Courier that the police involvement negated my job opportunity. I was always just a safety." Strider banged the desk. "He knew I'd bring Cade back to you. He used me..."

"To make sure Cade stayed in one place—to make the arrest easier," Tegan finished.

"Then why the auction?" Vic asked. "Seems like overkill."

"Humiliation? Strider's hot button?" Oz said quietly.

Strider was equally as quiet, but there was no doubt he was fuming. He was crazy but he had a definite code of honor. It might not match anyone else's, but it existed.

One.

Cade's face heated—anger, humiliation, and pain flooded through him, and he refused to run from it. Instead, he remained stock still, in the middle of these men and watched the video clip...and then read the message that followed when it flashed across the screen.

Buy this special boy to have for your very own. He likes pain. Sex. He's a very good boy.

Along with the message, there were close-ups of his face, several of them while he was coming.

His anger threatened to rise, and if he let it go unchecked, it would quickly spiral to uncontrollable levels.

"There are bids," he said quietly instead. "I think Strider's right—this is the best way to back-trace Courier."

"And we will, Cade," Strider assured him crisply.

Cade nodded, pulled out his phone, which had beeped with an email received. He glanced at it because Theo had taken to emailing him—a lot. But the email clearly wasn't from Theo. He saw the subject line and the link itself without having to open the email, thanks to the way his email preview was set up.

Do those men know about your past? They do now.

And if they opened the link, they could be implicated. *Shit.* "This is a setup like...fuck. How did he know? Did he find the letters? The PO box isn't even under my name."

"Letters?" Strider's eyes glittered with a rage that was at once so calm it was terrifying, and it made Cade feel empowered, not scared.

How did Strider know what he meant about the letters? But he did—Cade was sure of it. He turned to Strider wordlessly and handed him the phone. "Me and Theo both."

Strider glanced at it. "Don't touch it. As much as you want to delete it, don't. And I'll need the PO box number as well."

Cade gave him the information and went to take the mailbox key off his key chain, but Strider stopped him. "I don't need a key."

"What is it, Cade—what's Strider talking about?" Vic asked.

"You're going to get an email—from Courier. You can't open it or delete it, because it will infect your phone and your network," Strider answered instead. "Give me your phone and let me take care of it immediately."

"I'll take care of what's on the server," Oz added.

Strider still had his, and Cade noticed that Vic and Tegan handed their phones over without question. Strider knew what it was—and so did Oz—and everyone was going to tell him that it didn't matter, but fuck, it did. And it changed everything.

As humiliating as the auction was—and it fucking was, even if the men already knew about the sex tape—it wasn't the worst of it.

There'd been the beatings. Fucking for money. Getting rid of a dead man. Beating up foster fathers. Excelling in the military and beyond. Needing to submit to the men at Crave, a need he hadn't realized he had until he'd been pushed into it. Courier had known, which annoyed Cade to no fucking end, but he comforted himself in how it made Courier lose all control of his plans.

Until now. Because Vic and Tegan had seen all of him... but this? The last piece to be exposed was so humiliating, so private a shame that was now going to be exposed that his breathing came in short pants and inside his mind felt jagged and exposed.

Courier wanted to put him back in a cage.

Surrounded by his numbness, he walked out.

"Let him go," Strider urged. "Cade needs some space."

"Besides, there are some other things I need to talk to you about," Oz added, and Tegan felt the weight of his friend's voice.

"It's about Axel and Trevor, isn't it?" he asked.

"They haven't checked in," Oz admitted. "It's only been ten hours past time, and normally I wouldn't worry but we got a threat from Courier around the same time."

None of your hands are clean.

"This has always been bigger than just Cade. Dammit," Tegan muttered.

"You couldn't have known," Oz reminded him.

"And we know now—that's what's important," Vic reiterated.

"Yeah, we know when he wants us to know," Tegan bit out. "We're still playing catch-up, and he's very much in charge."

"I put out a call to a couple of friends in the area," Oz told them now. "They're checking in on Axel and Trevor for us. You all know that comms suck where they are—even with SAT phones. This could be a coincidence."

"Or Courier could be tracking them too. He's got a lot of resources." Tegan paced.

"They're professionals. And they're always on the lookout for ambushes," Vic reminded him.

They were. Tegan knew that and still, he couldn't help but worry. "We apprised them of the situation, so at least they know something might be coming."

"See?" Vic rubbed his shoulder reassuringly. "Let's take one thing at a time. You guys work on finding our boys and getting to the bottom of this auction. I'll go check on Cade."

Tegan nodded, his mind racing. Everything Courier was

doing seemed like a distraction more than anything. It would be just like the spook to do it, wanting them to spin their wheels, look in the wrong direction, make them weak. But to what end?

If he's got you thinking in circles, he's winning. Tegan forced himself to concentrate on the fact that everyone here was safe—that Trevor and Axel knew what they were up against—that no one was taking Cade from them. No one was getting past Deran, either.

Courier would ultimately lose, and he had to know that Tegan would concentrate on making sure he went down alone.

CHAPTER 29

VIC COULD FEEL the pain pulsing off Cade when he saw the auction countdown—it was fucking palpable, and he'd wanted to drag Cade away and do anything he could to make him forget he'd ever seen it. But that ship had sailed, so now, Vic was all about damage control.

He knew Cade hadn't left Crave, and he also knew that when Cade was upset, he didn't wallow. No, Cade fought.

Which was why Vic headed to the gym and heard the *thwack* of the bag being punched before he entered. Cade was in the zone, focused on the bag in front of him like it was enemy number one and for a while, Vic simply watched him.

Until Cade turned to face him, and it was apparent he wasn't content with punching inanimate objects anymore. Vic stripped off his shirt, barely had time to get rid of his sneakers and socks before Cade was on him, sparring without words. He was pissed and that made him stronger, more focused at this point instead of less.

It would catch up to him in the end, Vic knew, but for

now, the boy gave him a hell of a fight. And Vic didn't want to hurt him, but Cade needed to feel pain now. And Vic knew how to deliver pain that felt so damned good that it became absolution.

Cade had taped his knuckles under the gloves he threw off before coming at Vic, and Vic went at him bare-knuckled. Cade jabbed, then gave a straight punch that caught Vic in the cheek. Vic hit with a short, needling shot to Cade's rib cage, turning his knuckles like a screw.

Cade didn't make a sound beyond a snort of pain, and he came for Vic harder. It was apparent he was going for blood, probably didn't realize he was snarling.

Vic had been there, needed to let Cade have his way in order for him to come back. But it had to be fair and square. He let Cade beat on him, but he also gave as good as he got, sparred until Cade was exhausted, drained in a productive way. He was using Vic to beat down his demons, and Vic was all about that. He lunged and Cade gave a silent yell, the groan crushing out of his body from the weight of the slam/punch combo. He collapsed on his back, breathing hard. Drenched.

Vic became aware of Tegan watching them from the corner at some point, although he had no idea when Tegan had arrived.

Vic crouched over Cade in a partial front mount position, straddling him but not sitting on him. "Giving up?"

Cade rolled his eyes. "No."

"Looks that way."

Cade shrugged…and then without warning, he twisted and hooked his calf behind Vic's knees in a single-leg takedown and reversed the mount, landing a solid takedown on Vic's prone body...baring his teeth as he did so.

When Vic's back hit the mat, Cade took the opportunity to slam onto him, but they were both sweaty and it was hard to get a grip on each other. Still, Cade managed to hold Vic down, and Vic struggled...maybe harder than Cade wanted to notice. Maybe he wanted—needed—Vic to feel the panic and pain he felt right now.

But when he realized he was doing exactly that, he broke the grip. When he moved away, Vic rolled quickly, and for a long second, stilled, on all fours, a predatory look in his eyes... and Cade saw the haunted, hunted man that he'd triggered.

"Vic, please, I'm sorry." He stilled, not wanting to trigger Vic further. Because it didn't matter that the threat was imagined—for Vic, it was as real as it had been when he'd been held captive for months...because of Danny.

"Vic, baby—it's okay." Tegan's voice was gentle, non-threatening as he bent down on all fours in front of Vic, going lower than the man in a submissive posture. Once Vic met his eyes, Tegan reached out slowly and traced the scars on Vic's cheek first, then continued touching them, following them all the way down his body as Cade watched. It was like a healing, an exorcism. Vic remained stock still, like he wasn't sure what to do, as Tegan's fingers traced the swirling patterns from his cheek to neck, shoulders, down his biceps—along his side to his hip and up his back, trailing back to where he'd started.

Worship. Acceptance.

Vic slowly came back, his eyes warmed, and he nodded at Tegan before locking eyes with Cade, and Cade felt the connection between them, sharp and powerful.

And they're both connected to me.

But he'd hurt Vic, and that was inexcusable. *Fuck.* He stood and left the gym.

Neither man followed.

Once Tegan was assured he was okay, Vic had him go back to the war room to check on the various balls in play. Now, Vic stood on the other side of the bathroom door, giving Cade the time to wring himself out in private.

And when the sobs turned to soft hiccups, Vic took his cue and went in. The water had turned barely warm and he shut it off, wrapped Cade in a soft towel, and carried him to the bed. In his arms, Cade started drifting to sleep, which was the best thing for him.

But then his eyes opened. "Vic, I didn't mean—"

"Yes, you did. You wanted me to hurt the way you hurt. You wanted to show me how you felt, the only way you could," Vic explained, so Cade's mind could shut off and stop spinning with worry over and over about what he'd done to Vic.

"Shit."

"You didn't hurt me. Not irreparably anyway," Vic assured him.

"Let me hunt him, Vic," Cade said finally, what seemed like hours later.

"Not with the police already out to get you."

"They won't catch me."

"And I won't lose you. Do you understand that? I will hunt Courier down myself. I'll kill him with my bare hands. I'd kill Dolentz if he wasn't already dead."

He didn't mention the Nelsons because Strider had already promised him a crack at them after his crack at Courier.

"I know," was all Cade said.

"If it comes down to it, we'll do it together—the way we've been doing it," Vic promised.

And Cade gave the first smile Vic had seen from him in hours. "Yeah, that sounds right. Together."

With that, Vic tugged Cade on top of him, and, as Cade watched, Vic surrendered to him. Kept his arms slack and remained passive against the headboard. "Do your worst. Do whatever it is you need to do to feed your demons."

"What about yours?" Cade whispered.

"They'll work with yours, baby. Plenty of room for all our demons."

Cade's breath hitched. He got rid of the towel and bent down to kiss Vic, his tongue dueling with Vic's, breathing in his scent. Moaning Vic's name as Vic's blunt fingertip probed his hole, teeth bit his nipple, then tugged the barbell and fuck yes, that was exactly what he needed—and how did Vic know? "I want you to pin me and fuck me."

"Cade—"

"Plenty of time for me to ride you, but tonight..." Cade didn't have to ask twice. In seconds, Vic rolled them so he was on top, shrugging off his pants and stripping off his T-shirt. Cade's hands were all over him, his chest, his thighs, his own body arching against Vic's. This would be a fight too, but it was the exact one Cade wanted.

Vic sat back on his heels and put Cade's thighs over his arms. He raised the lower half of Cade's body, held Cade's ass open, and, as Cade watched, he buried his face in Cade's ass.

"Christ," Cade muttered helplessly as he felt the wet press of Vic's tongue against his hole. His hips bucked in response and Vic's hands stilled them as his tongue continued its exploration, licking, laving, sucking. Kissing his ass like he'd kissed Cade earlier and fuck, the sensation was incredible. His dick was hard as glass, and Vic's dark eyes watched his response, which made it that much hotter.

Finally, when Cade was ready to come, Vic stopped and lowered him, turned him and urged him onto his hands and knees. Cade heard the snap of the lube top, felt Vic's fingers open him farther, and then Vic's cock was pressing inside of him.

Cade's mouth opened at the intrusion, but his body knew what it wanted, pushed back against Vic until he was fully seated inside of Cade. Vic rode him so hard that at first, his arms gave way and then his knees, and he was flat on the mattress, pinned, with Vic's fingers twined in his.

"Please...more," Cade begged, his body tensed, strung tight like a bow, then released and everything imploded...and he took Vic along for the ride, his ass milking Vic, who groaned and collapsed on top of him.

Finally, Vic moved, and Cade flipped so he could hold Vic, as much as Vic was holding him.

"Why me, Vic? How'd I get so lucky?" Cade's voice was rough, hoarse. No longer angry, just resigned to what would happen, resigned to fight whatever got in his way of happiness.

Vic smiled. "Because you have war in your eyes...just like me." With those words, Cade's last wall of resistance crumbled. Dissolved. He leaned his forehead against Vic's, and Vic put a hand on the back of his neck. "And Tegan? He's our peace. Our calm. He's come through the war, so he's on the other side."

"Not fully," Tegan broke in. "Never fully out of war. But I'm here."

God, they'd looked beautiful together, Vic on top of Cade, taking him, driving him crazy. Cade doing the same to Vic in return. He'd stood in the doorway, watching, unable to move and yet knowing that, somehow, he was still there with them.

"Is everything okay with Axel and Trevor?" Cade asked hesitantly.

"Yes, they're fine. We got in touch with them," Tegan assured them, and Vic sighed with relief. "I came right up to tell you...and then got distracted."

"I can imagine," Vic said wryly.

"Fuck, he's beautiful," Tegan bit out, his eyes on Cade as he moved close to Vic. "So beautiful, Cade."

Tegan knelt on the bed behind Vic, leaning down to kiss his shoulder, brushing a hand over his chest. Tweaking a nipple, hard enough to make Vic groan. Cade's cum splattered his stomach and chest, and Vic's cock was still half-hard. "I think you need to come again," he told Vic.

"Maybe," Vic managed as Tegan's free hand played along the seam of Vic's ass.

"I think Cade could come again, too," Tegan continued, and Cade's eyes were heavy-lidded, pupils blown, but his dick was at half-mast and definitely agreed.

"Want him to," Vic told him. "Want you, Teegs. C'mon—fuck me. Now."

Tegan knew Vic wouldn't say it if he didn't mean it. So he grabbed the bottle of lube that was next to Vic's leg on the bed, even as he backed away from Vic and licked his way down Vic's spine.

And then he buried his face in Vic's ass, tonguing his hole, listening to Vic cry out his name and buck forward into Cade, whose moans joined in the chorus. He used his fingers too—Vic was so goddamned tight, he'd milk the hell out of Tegan's cock. Vic didn't mind pain, but Tegan would be damned if he made the man regret anything about this. And whatever Tegan did to Vic made Vic thrust harder into Cade, driving him crazy as well.

"Tegan, come on—fuck me now," Vic demanded, but Tegan still took his sweet goddamned time, wanting this to last.

When he finally mounted Vic from behind, he felt the strength in Vic's surrender as Vic's body rippled around his cock, accepting him and fighting him at the same time.

"Tegan, don't you dare stop." Vic's voice was hoarse and begging as Tegan took the man, inch by inch, murmuring against his skin, marking it with his teeth the way his dick was marking Vic's ass.

Cade was palming his own dick slowly while he watched, his free hand on Vic's chest, playing with his nipples, watching the slow dance until finally, Tegan's balls were flush against Vic's ass.

"Yeah, T—c'mon—move. Now. Please," Vic pleaded.

Vic spread his legs open wide, the ultimate surrender to Tegan's pounding, even as he took Cade's ass.

Fuck, Cade was definitely going to come again. This was all about Vic, bringing him to the edge and pushing him over, because Cade knew that Vic was usually the one in control of these sessions, standing, watching or directing. On top.

He was still directing, somehow, but it was so fucking amazing to watch Tegan take Vic.

Vic's eyes closed for several moments as his body took the brunt of Tegan's and passed it forward to Cade. Tegan was definitely in charge of this fuck, and he was watching both of them, making sure they were enjoying every second of it. He reached down and grabbed Cade's hand, making sure all three of them were connected. Touching.

"I'm guessing neither of you...will...call me...old...again," Tegan said between thrusts. "Does this look old to you?"

"I'll have to take a ride, just to be sure," Cade breathed earnestly.

"You're both trying to kill me," Tegan accused as Vic laughed weakly before groaning.

"Close, baby?" Tegan asked. Vic nodded and moaned and Tegan doubled his efforts.

"Tegan...Cade," Vic murmured as he shot inside of Cade, and Cade spilled onto his belly again...and then Tegan came with a roar.

They remained like that, motionless, for several long moments until Tegan announced triumphantly, "I am not done." With that, his hips began to undulate, his eyes closed, his head thrown back in pure pleasure and Cade just watched him, a warmth spreading through him.

He's mine. They're both mine.

CHAPTER 30

CADE WOKE, spooning Tegan. Vic faced them both, looking peaceful, which made him happy. Tegan was also breathing evenly, and Cade eased away quietly. He'd only slept for an hour, thankfully waking before his dreams got too intense.

Maybe it was a good sign.

He headed downstairs, knowing what he needed to do, and he stood in the first-floor hallway for a long moment. Finally, he built up enough courage to go back to the war room. It was surprisingly empty, and he stood in front of one of the monitors for several minutes before leaning in and hitting a key to wake it from sleep mode.

The first thing he did was check the auction. He stared at the bids and it pissed him off, but it wasn't gut-wrenching, because it was adult Cade, and he'd made the decision to let Courier record their encounter. This was shit he could deal with, as disgusting as it was. Adult to adult, it was an even playing field.

But there was something else. Because Courier had

texted him to let him know that this video wasn't the only thing he'd sent the men in Cade's life...and Cade knew exactly what Courier meant.

"You want to look at the email." Strider's voice, low and dangerous, came up from behind him.

"How did you know about the letters?" Cade asked without turning around.

"Because I know."

"I want to look at the email," he finally agreed.

"No, you want to look at the pictures that are attached."

"I don't want to—I have to."

"Why, Cade?"

"Because I need to see them. I need to know that I've gotten past it." He turned to look at Strider. "I know that might not make sense."

"It does. I'm not sure you'll ever be over it, though. I'm not sure I'd like the person who did get over that." Strider's words were blunt, as always, but he was quiet, his usual running monologue MIA. He grabbed an iPad, clicked a few buttons, and then handed it to him with the link intact.

All he had to do was click it.

"This isn't running on the internet connection here. Otherwise, it would infect the entire system," Strider said. "Don't ever open or delete a link like this on a connected computer."

Cade nodded numbly.

"Do you want me to leave?"

"I'd rather you stay." And Strider did. Together, they sat, and Strider held his hand as he opened the link and stared. Photos began to flash across the screen, pictures from another time and place in his life that he'd cordoned off in his mind.

Doing so had entailed putting up thick walls that would need dynamite to blast through. And now, here it was, out in the open...his worst fucking nightmare.

He'd been with the Nelsons from the ages of seven to fourteen, although after he'd turned thirteen, he was basically on his own. He lived at Theo's when his stepdad was away or at Pat's, or he'd rent a motel room for the night—because it was easier to turn tricks in one place. Safer too, because Theo could guard the door and listen in, just in case he ran into trouble. By that point, he'd also been working at the fight club, and they'd let him crash there several nights a week as well in exchange for cleaning the place post-fight. He was also learning the finer points of both fighting and self-defense.

But the pictures were the fucking worst of all of it, the bane of his existence, the reason he received letters from the well-meaning FBI task force every single time a picture of his was taken down. And since nothing ever really left the internet, it was like playing whack-a-mole.

The pictures had been taken in the spare bedroom of the Nelsons' apartment. It was supposed to be his room, but more often than not he'd been sleeping curled in a chair or in the bathtub...anything it took to not have to go back into that room and pretend everything was fine.

They'd started forcing him to pose for these photos when he was seven, and that'd continued until he was nearly twelve, when he got bigger and aged out of being wanted by pedophiles. At least the ones the Nelsons catered to. Because of that, the years between twelve and thirteen had been the worst, because he'd been too young to survive fully in the streets and he was of no further use to the Nelsons, so their abuse ramped up. It was just after he'd turned thirteen that he'd met Pat.

Finally, after his trip down memory lane from hell, Cade handed the iPad back to Strider. He was still holding Strider's hand with his free one, and now, he tugged Strider along with him, out the closest window. With Strider behind him, they climbed up the fire escape to the roof spot they both seemed to like.

"I needed to breathe," Cade said by way of explanation, which he really hadn't needed to do, judging by the look in Strider's eyes now, as compared to how they'd looked when both men looked at Cade's pictures.

But now, Cade almost laughed because Strider had actually spray painted, "my spot" by the chimney, and Cade chose to sit on said spot anyway. "You're not going to kick me off your spot."

"I could, you know."

The thing was, Strider definitely could, but he didn't. "If I didn't know better, I'd think you cared."

"Don't be cute." Strider sat next to him, lit a cigarette and offered it to Cade, who accepted it. Strider lit one of his own and they sat in silence for several long moments.

Finally, Cade asked, "Do you fix things? Outside of killing people?"

"Sometimes—if the money's good." Strider motioned for Cade to continue.

"Look, I want you to clear Vic," Cade said, and Strider didn't ask what Vic needed to be cleared of, so he must have already known about the dishonorable discharge. "Can you do something like that? I'll get you whatever money you need...but it might have to be in installments."

"You surprise me, Cade, and I'm not sure I like that." Strider paused as if to consider it. "No, I don't like it at all."

"Why?"

"Most people are static, easy to read, which makes it easy to figure out what they want...what they think they should have. You're...difficult."

"I've been called worse, but difficult is kind of my middle name. Not for real or anything," he added quickly because Strider seemed interested that it could be an option.

"That's disappointing." Strider frowned. "Let me see about the Vic thing. No promises. I'm sure Oz has already tried, and I don't want to get in the middle of whatever plan he's got in the works. I'll let you know what kind of money I need. Now, what else would you like to discuss? And don't be coy—it doesn't suit you."

Cade sighed. "Why do you care so much...about Courier. The letters?"

"It's not about me caring about what happens to you—it's about my understanding what you went through and your need for revenge. It's best to let me take care of it."

Cade's fists flexed. "I want to go after him. It's taking everything I have not to leave here, find him, and kill him."

"I know."

"But they would follow me, and they'd get caught in the crossfire. Hell, they already are, and so is Theo. And I promised Theo I wouldn't try anything with Courier. Dammit. He knows I won't break a promise to him."

"Maybe you should focus on the good that's come out of this—your fated mates."

Cade side-eyed him. "Are we going to talk about werewolf books again?"

" 'Why wouldn't we?' is the real question. I've sent you several."

"I haven't been in the reading mood. But I understand your point. Despite everything, I got lucky."

"You did. Even though Tegan and Vic aren't werewolves. But I suppose you can't have everything. And speaking of werewolves..."

"Which *we* weren't—that's all you," Cade told him.

Strider ignored him. "Find someone for Oz."

"Just like that?"

"Would you rather me find someone for him?"

"Hell no."

Strider gave a satisfied smile. "Well, I am. So there's your incentive. Find him someone before I do."

"You'd find him a werewolf," he muttered.

"If they existed, I'd be fucking them regularly," Strider assured him. "And Oz would be too."

Cade held his hand up. "I'll find him someone."

"Good. Take your time though—it's too soon, but you need to scout early."

"Any idea when werewolf season starts?" Cade asked.

Strider smiled. "That's the spirit."

Cade snuck back into the room as quietly as possible, but Tegan's head still turned to acknowledge him. Cade climbed in and wrapped around him, chest to Tegan's back.

"Did I wake you?" Cade murmured, his palm moving to Tegan's chest.

"No, I felt you go." Tegan put his hand on top of Cade's and entwined their fingers. "You went to see the pictures."

Cade froze, for just a second, but Tegan wasn't judging him, not at all. It was about resignation—and understanding. "I had to."

"When I was growing up...Deran and I...it was a neighbor."

It was all he said, but it was all he needed to say. Everything suddenly made sense—his own needs, Theo's, Tegan's... even Vic's, to some degree.

He'd known that there were a lot of men and women who'd gone into the military already damaged, to some extent...and Theo had once told him that some people also used BDSM to process trauma.

"I'm sorry," was all Vic said now. He was facing Tegan, and he laid his arm across both him and Cade. "I know what that link was...but what was the talk about the letters?"

Cade took a deep breath, but Tegan answered for him. "There's a victim notification system. We get letters every time our images are seized as part of an investigation. And there can be a lot of them, even if you let victim's services streamline the process, so..."

"So you set up a PO Box, so they're not coming directly to you," Vic said softly.

"But you still have to check them. To know," Cade murmured.

"Not anymore," Vic said. "Neither of you need to check anymore. That's on me. For Deran and Theo too, if they're okay with that." Because of course Vic would know that Tegan would take on Deran's burden, and Cade's, Theo's. Because Vic would've done the same. And now, he proved it.

"Okay," Cade told him.

"The thing is," Tegan told him, "Strider knows now. So I don't think he's going to let any of us see any letters anymore."

"I'll check in with Strider, then," Vic promised.

Cade didn't question any of it. "I'd like to help Strider."

"I know, Cade. But he works alone. It's better that way. What you do, to help others like you...that is enough. Strider will tell you that as well," Tegan soothed him. "Let's get through this...and we'll go from there."

"Yeah," Cade agreed. "We'll go from there."

For several long moments, they just lay there, skin to skin. Breathing. Processing.

Finally, Cade said, "If I don't set Oz up with someone, Strider's going to find him a werewolf."

Tegan snorted softly.

Vic asked, "Do you think Strider might actually be a werewolf?"

"What? No," Tegan scoffed, but he sounded uncertain.

"Right? That's ridiculous," Cade said, his tone just as unsure.

Tegan buried his head in the pillow. "Fucking Strider. He's got to go soon. This is what he does—gets into your head."

"The werewolf books are good, though," Cade added after a pause.

"Really good," Vic agreed.

From under the pillow, Tegan groaned. "We've got to get Oz laid. And fast."

CHAPTER 31

LATE THE NEXT AFTERNOON, Vic saw Rourke's car pull up in the back lot, in full view of the cameras. The detective got out and leaned against his car, checking his phone like he was settling in for the long haul...and letting them know that fact.

"Fuck, this can't be good," Vic muttered to himself. Cade was busy with Oz and Tegan, so he took this opportunity to slip outside to have a chat with their resident detective.

He opened the door and the tall, blond man glanced up, unsurprised. "Are you alone?"

"Yes."

Rourke nodded. "I'm here to arrest him, Vic. Can you have him step outside?"

Vic stared at him. "No."

"If you don't have him surrender in the next several hours, I'll have to get a crew to forcibly remove him. I don't want to do that—to you or to him. He's got a lawyer. I'll get him in, get him booked, keep him safe until his lawyer comes."

"Bail?"

"I don't know yet."

"You've got to give me more than that."

Rourke sighed. "There's a witness to Cade killing Theo's stepfather. And evidence."

"He didn't do this."

"Unfortunately, no one's asking for our opinions," Rourke reminded him. "Go talk to him. Call his lawyer. Deal with it. I'll be here."

Vic nodded and went back inside, dialing Rigs as he did so.

"There's no witness. That's bullshit. And what fucking evidence?" Cade demanded as he paced the war room half an hour later. Vic told him about Rourke's ultimatum as soon as he'd come in, but now Cade was in discussion with Rigs, and Vic and Tegan had been ushered outside.

Vic and Tegan left him alone with Rigs, who'd zoomed over from a wedding two states away, no questions asked. Rourke was still circling outside, trying to be respectful, but Cade knew it wouldn't be that way for much longer.

"You have to tell me *why* that's bullshit." Rigs's shirt was unbuttoned and his tie askew. His jacket was long abandoned, and he had scruff on his face. "I'm not going to abandon you—it doesn't matter what you tell me. It just needs to be the truth right now. I can work with anything you tell me."

"And it's just between us?"

"Yes."

"The only witness is Theo."

"And he'd never turn you in?"

"He was the only one there, Rigs. I walked in on him—and Dolentz was already dead on the floor."

Rigs sat heavily. "Cade—"

"I'm taking responsibility for it, if it comes to that. But right now, I want you to dig into the witness. Because that witness is lying. I promise you that."

"I'll do whatever it takes."

"To protect Theo? So will I."

"That's what I'm afraid of," Rigs muttered.

In the end, Cade walked out to Rourke on his own terms. Vic and Tegan were not happy about it, but Rigs told them that the arrest was inevitable.

"If he's with the police, he's not with Courier," Oz reasoned. "It cuts into Courier's plan."

"Unless this arrest is his plan," Tegan pointed out.

"That's where I come in," Rigs reminded him.

Through it all, Cade remained silent, listening to them talk about him. It didn't matter—he'd already made his decision. He walked over to Tegan and tugged him down for a kiss, then pulled Vic in close and did the same thing.

"I'll be fine," he told them.

"You're not staying in there long," Tegan warned. "As soon as bail is set—"

"I know." Cade stroked a hand down his cheek. "Don't tell Theo. Please. He'll come here and make it worse."

"Don't do what I think you're going to. Please." Vic's

hand rested on the back of his neck. "The evidence won't bear out. Trust that."

Cade nodded but didn't commit fully to trusting the system. They wouldn't expect him to. "I'll be okay," he told them, and Oz and Strider both nodded. And then he walked outside, straight over to Rourke, who didn't look all that surprised.

"Thanks for waiting," he said.

Rourke stared at him. "This wasn't my idea, Cade. But it's my job."

"I know." He put his hands on the car and let Rourke pat him down, read him his rights. And put handcuffs on him.

"Is that necessary?" Rigs asked.

"You know it is," Rourke shot back.

"I'm following you into the station. He doesn't get questioned at all without me—understood? If I find out he was—"

"He won't be." Rourke opened the back of his car and held Cade's head as he ducked in. Cade settled uncomfortably against the seat, his mind exhausted.

Rourke didn't talk to him during the ride, and Cade was grateful for that. What the hell could he say? Cade was angry and humiliated, which was what Courier hoped for.

Rourke escorted him into an interrogation room before he was booked and fingerprinted, but Cade knew he wasn't getting out of this without spending time in a cell. For now, he sat next to Rigs and across from Rourke—and who knew how many people behind the two-way mirror in the interrogation room. The walls were a pale green, peeling and dirty, and Cade remained silent, the way he'd been in the car with Rourke.

His hands were now cuffed to his chair.

"We came in here in good faith and answered all your questions," Rigs started, pointing to the handcuffs. Rourke pressed his lips together but ultimately came around and freed Cade's wrists.

"Thanks," Cade murmured.

Rigs continued, "Cade hasn't tried to leave the jurisdiction and he surrendered willingly to you tonight and we still haven't been made aware of why these charges continue to stand."

Cade had been charged with murder, and there was no statute of limitations on that.

"Cade, you understand that this is a very serious charge," Rourke said, ignoring Rigs for the moment. "Despite what your attorney says, you had motive to kill Mr. Dolentz. We know that your foster family and Dolentz liked to take illegal pictures of both you and Theo."

Cade schooled his expression carefully as Rigs stiffened next to him and addressed Rourke. "So you have a theory, Rourke? I'm assuming you've contacted every single foster kid and child that both families took pictures of, since they'd have equal motives, as you're calling it."

Rourke stared at Cade as he listened to Rigs. "There's also physical evidence."

"Like what?" Rigs demanded as Cade absorbed the lie.

"We were given a knife a week ago—it had Dolentz's DNA...and Cade's."

"I want independent testing," Rigs said. "That means shit."

Rourke nodded like he'd expected that resistance. "Cade, let's go over your story again. Tell me how you met Courier."

"Is he behind all of this?" Cade asked.

"You seem to think so."

"I met him at the fights. I was bouncing the first time. The next time, he came to see me fight. It's not like I saw him a lot, maybe four times over three months. And they were quick fucks in the alley behind the club. After I fight, sometimes I..." He shook his head and stopped. Rourke was watching him carefully, with understanding in his eyes. "Anyway, it's like I told you before—he came to the club. Started getting all weird and possessive. I told him to fuck off, and then he tried to get me to...do things. When I didn't do what he wanted, suddenly, this whole Dolentz thing started."

"Looks that way," Rourke said. "But he says there's proof that you killed Dolentz. A knife, with your prints and Dolentz's DNA."

Rourke held the bag up and Cade bit his tongue so he didn't say, "That's not the knife Theo used." Instead, he looked more closely. "I haven't seen Dolentz since I enlisted."

And that was a truth, one he'd pass a lie detector with.

"Do you have a body to go with that DNA?" Rigs asked as Rourke's phone dinged several times in a row.

Rourke stared at his phone, his expression suddenly dark. "No. And I might've just figured out why." He stared between Cade and Rigs, looking like he was debating telling them something. Ultimately, all he did say was, "Give me a minute," before he got up and left them alone in the small room.

"No speakers," Rigs called after him and Rourke waved over his shoulder, which Cade assumed meant he agreed.

Still, he waited until Rigs nodded before he murmured, "If it comes down to it, I'm confessing."

Rigs shook his head. "I definitely don't recommend that."

"I'm not letting Theo get dragged into this."

"Theo's not here. No one can find him. Right now, he's in the best place possible."

"Don't you think I know that?" Cade stood, paced around the small room.

"I'm not letting you confess to something you didn't do just to save your friend. That's suicide. Besides, when Theo finds out..."

He'll come back here and turn himself in. And he'll kill me for confessing. Cade was suddenly exhausted. He folded his arms on the table and laid his head down. He felt Rigs's hands on his shoulders, digging into his knotted muscles.

"Cade, I'll get you something to eat and drink. You don't talk to anyone without me there—understood? Because they'll try."

"I understand. I won't." Fuck, he just wanted to sleep and wake up in Tegan's bed with him and Vic and pretend none of this existed.

"Vic and Tegan are out looking for Courier—and any information they can find on him. Strider and Oz too," Rigs told him. "You just need to have faith and hold on. Can you do that, for them?"

They were putting themselves on the line for him. The least he could do was stay strong and keep his goddamned mouth shut.

Maybe they could end this once and for all.

And, if they couldn't, he knew what he had to do. With that in mind, he put his head, cheek down, on the table in front of him. He wasn't sure how long he'd slept for, but he woke with a jerk, realizing quickly that he was still in the interrogation room with the dirty walls and peeling paint, and he felt more trapped than he had before.

He rubbed his eyes and tried to get his bearings as the door opened and an officer walked in.

"Everything okay?" he asked. "Can I get you anything?"

Cade shook his head. "No thanks."

The cop smiled. "Your lawyer told you not to talk to anyone. You think I came in here to trip you up."

Cade shrugged, because yeah, he figured that was how it worked, but he wasn't going to challenge this guy.

The officer walked around the table and he stood just close enough to make Cade feel uncomfortable. Even more so when he said, "It doesn't matter how hard the FBI tries. Doesn't matter if the person who put the dirty pictures up goes to jail or dies. Those pictures of you will stay up forever."

He didn't sound upset or disgusted, and by the time Cade realized why, the taser was zapping him, burning his skin... and Courier's face was the last one he saw before everything snapped to black.

CHAPTER 32

"THE AUCTION'S ENDED, and we have a winner." And Strider was still typing.

"Find him, Strider," Vic said through gritted teeth. "Find both of them."

"All I know is, the amount of money Courier has is mind-blowing. He could buy his own island with that money," Strider told them. "I'd like my own island."

Oz mimed banging his head against the desk in front of him. Although maybe he wasn't miming it, because Tegan actually heard banging.

He put a hand on Oz's shoulder. "You can't afford to lose more brain cells."

Oz kept his head down but shot him the finger. Tegan would've told Strider to focus, but the man's fingers hadn't stopped moving over the keys, his talk no doubt a product of nervous energy as he surfed some of the darkest places on the web.

Tegan's phone rang. *Rigs.* "How is he?"

"He's gone, T."

"What do you mean?" Tegan put him on speaker and hoped against hope that Rigs meant released, but the feeling of dread increased too rapidly.

"Someone took Cade out of the interview room. They're running video feeds. It looks like he was tased," Rigs told him, and Vic was out of his seat, ready to go find him.

"That's the only way they'd get him out of there," Strider murmured. "Courier had a man in the police station."

"Officer Reece," Rigs added. "Now, he's unaccounted for. Rourke is bringing hellfire down on everyone here."

Oz was pulling up Reece's file. "Did Rourke send someone to Reece's house? Because I'm betting Reece outlived his usefulness before his shift started today."

"He's got uniforms on the way there now, but he's betting they find the real officer's body there." Rigs sounded resigned. "Listen, I need to talk to you about the evidence."

"Can't it wait?" Tegan asked.

"No—it might be important," Rigs insisted. "Courier's evidence was a knife that supposedly had Dolentz's DNA on it. The DNA evidence came back as a match to Dolentz first, but Rourke sent it for more testing, because he started working a theory. Turns out, it's a familial match for a sex offender."

"Wait, Courier screwed with the system to have the DNA match Dolentz's?" Vic asked.

"Turns out, there already was a sample of Dolentz's DNA in the system—except the name attached to it is Harry Stanton," Rigs continued.

Tegan saw a flash of pure, white-hot anger. "If Dolentz is really Harry Stanton, then Courier is Jamie Stanton—Harry's biological son."

Strider stared. "You know him?"

"I think what's worse is that he knows me."

The whir of the camera woke Cade. The ceiling fan was blowing softly on his overheated skin, and he tried to cover his face but found he couldn't. When he turned his head to look, he realized that he was bound with BDSM leather restraints on his wrists and his ankles, naked, save for his boots, and spread-eagle on a bed.

There was also a ball gag in his mouth, and Courier was taking pictures of him. "So pretty, Cade. Just like those first pictures of you I found. I knew my father's taste. I knew I'd find him by looking through the pictures, but I never expected you. He didn't have you, did he? So you're all mine. My prize."

He brushed hair from Cade's face and then reached around to take the ball gag off. Cade's jaw ached, his throat was bone-dry, and Courier put a bottle of water to his mouth.

Cade turned away until Courier took a long drink of his own from it. "See? It's not drugged. But you are already. Heavily."

Cade accepted the water, drinking greedily, because it would be stupid not to. But Courier's hands were all over him as he drank, and finally, Cade swallowed...and then spit in Courier's face.

Courier's first instinct was to raise a hand at him, but he stopped himself as Cade watched. "No. You fetched good money. Can't mess you up. Granted, the man who bought you definitely will. It'll make your childhood look like Disneyland."

"You're a sick fuck," Cade bit out. His head was so foggy from the drugs....His body felt like lead...and how the hell had he gotten here?

Courier shook his head and prepared to put the ball gag back in. "Your new owner's been following your pictures for a long time, like I have. He's a fan of Theo's too, but there's time for that. You needed to be owned. You know it as well as I do."

Something ugly replaced the panic in Cade's gut, something he hadn't let take over for fear he'd never come back from it. But now, it uncoiled, bloomed, and everything else took a back seat to it.

Vengeance ran through his blood. "I don't care how long it takes—I will end you."

"I'm sure you'll try. We'll always be connected, just the way I'm connected to Tegan and his brother." Courier smiled at Cade's confusion as he shoved the ball gag back in his mouth. "They'll figure it out soon enough, but it'll be too late by then."

———

Yes, Tegan knew Harry Stanton all too well. He'd been the man who'd molested Tegan and Deran when they were younger, and he'd taken pictures of them too. He'd done it to the brothers separately, though—preying on young boys whose parents were too drunk most of the time to notice anything. Stanton took two boys who needed affection and gave them the worst kind of attention.

Stanton had also killed his youngest son, Eddie, and both Tegan and Deran had testified against him. But Eddie's body had never been found and ultimately, it had been the word of two preteen boys against Harry Stanton's. Jamie Stanton, aka Courier, had refused to testify against him, instead claiming that a stranger had taken Eddie, that his father had never touched him, that his neighbors were making everything up because they were angry about their own dad.

Add to that the fact that no incriminating materials were ever found in Stanton's possession, that there was nothing incriminating on any of his computers, and he'd been found not guilty. Ultimately, Harry Stanton had been forced to move away from his family, and Tegan and Deran's father had left them, and their mother moved them away. Things continued to go downhill for her, but Deran and Tegan had each other.

And when they'd been old enough, both Deran and Tegan had continued their search for Harry Stanton—Tegan especially had been all about revenge once he'd gotten the means to search the man out, until he realized it was eating him alive. Strider was the opposite—he ate the vengeance alive, not the other way around, and he waited for it to find him. Probably because he understood how much evil there was in the world—he took it on in manageable chunks. He was built differently, and Tegan respected the hell out of him for it, which was the only reason he was allowed back in Crave. The only reason he was still part of their lives.

He'd never been able to find Stanton, but he'd been close. So goddamned close.

It started with Stanton, but it would end with Courier.

"You know what he is then." Strider's tone was measured,

the psychotic anger hiding just below the surface as it broke into Tegan's thoughts.

"Deran and I looked, once we were old enough to do it, we looked."

"You don't need to seek absolution from me, Tegan. Know the kind of man you are. And I know how hunting monsters can be."

And Strider did know. It was why Tegan had ultimately decided he'd have to let him go from Gray Ops to begin with —and why Strider left before that could happen and didn't hold a grudge. "Help me find him."

"I'm going to take Cade's auction winner out," Strider told him, pointing to the screen. "You and Vic can find Cade. Think, Tegan. You knew Dolentz—or Stanton or whoever he is—well. Where did he live?"

"Next door to our old house."

"Sounds simple, right? But have you checked to see who owns the title for his old house?" Strider asked, which meant he'd checked himself.

"He still owns the house?"

"Either he does, or Courier," Strider confirmed.

"That's got to be where he's holding Cade." Tegan was on his feet, paused when Strider frowned and stared at the screen. "What's wrong?"

Strider's gaze met his. "We need to move fast. Theo's auction just went live."

Tegan swallowed back his rage. "Where's the first auction winner supposed to meet up with Courier?"

"Our winner hasn't heard from him yet, but I know where he lives too." Strider smiled.

Tegan didn't bother to ask what would become of the

auction winner—he didn't deserve anything better, and not knowing for sure? It was plausible deniability at its finest.

Strider put a hand on his shoulder. "Go—get your boy, Tegan."

Tegan was in the passenger seat, with Oz driving and Vic in the back, getting their weapons ready. Tegan's old house—and Stanton's—were twenty minutes from Crave, the irony of which wasn't lost on any of them.

"I'm going to call Deran," Tegan told them now. "I've got to give them the heads-up. I don't know if this psychopath wants to hurt Deran or Theo more than me—or Cade."

Vic met his eyes in the rearview and nodded in acknowledgment. "It's not going to get that far, but don't let Theo come back here. Not until this is resolved."

"Agreed." Tegan dialed Deran, who picked up on the first ring with, "What's wrong?"

He didn't bother to deny that anything was, because Deran also lived and died by his gut instincts. "Cade was arrested on suspicion of killing Theo's stepfather. Courier got to him when he was in jail and he's missing."

"Fuck," Deran bit out, and Tegan could picture his brother, pacing, running his hands over his shaved head.

"We're not sure if Courier's got people after Theo...and they might be after you, too."

"What the fuck, Tegan?"

"Remember Stanton?" Tegan tasted the bitterness of the name on his tongue.

"I'll never forget him, Teegs. But what's he got to do with this?"

"The guy who's been after Cade and Theo is Jamie Stanton."

There was dead silence on the other end of the phone, and then Tegan heard a loud crash. "Fuck. Tegan, you're fucking kidding me with this."

"I wish I was. The DNA proves it," Tegan said. "I'm on the way to their old place—it's under Jamie's name."

"What else do I need to know?"

"Courier started a live auction a few minutes ago...for Theo."

He heard Deran's sharp intake of breath. "He's not leaving my sight, Tegan. Call me the second you have more intel. I'm not telling him this...not yet." He paused. "I never thought the stuff with Harry would come back to us like this."

"I know."

"Stop feeling guilty."

"You first."

"We were ten and eleven."

"But we never forgot. Not really." Tegan rolled his shoulders. "He's coming after us. You know that, right?"

"Feel it in my bones."

"And that makes it just as dangerous for Theo to stay with you."

"I suppose it does."

"And maybe that's exactly why Theo should know it."

"But then he'll try to protect me."

"Yes."

"And he'll stay here."

"Are you catching on now, or do I have to draw you a picture?"

"Fuck you, smartass." But he could hear the smile in Deran's voice before it went serious again. "Please, Tegan, call me the second you know something. Anything."

Tegan knew what it was like to sit on the other end of a phone, helpless. "You'll know it the second after I do."

Oz got them to the house in record time. He went past the house at normal speed so they could scope it out, telling them he'd circle around again.

"Looked quiet—driveway's empty. What do you think, T?" Oz asked.

Tegan's old house had been painted. The lawn was cut. It looked like someone had finally cared for the place. But Stanton's? It was as if time had stood still. The same dirty white shutters. The sagging porch. The window on the second floor with the broken screen, where Harry Stanton would do his dirtiest deeds.

If Tegan had his way, he'd burn the fucker down. Today. "It looks deserted."

Oz parked a couple of doors away. "We'll go in and scope it out, Teegs."

Tegan nodded, got into the driver's seat, prepared to back them up. It was definitely better for him to not go inside, emotionally, at least.

After what seemed like hours, but was no more than five minutes, Vic came to the front door and gave the all clear signal. After contemplating for a few seconds, Tegan grabbed the keys and got out of the truck.

He'd never be satisfied if he didn't vet the house himself— and both Oz and Vic knew it.

"You sure about this?" Vic asked once Tegan walked into the house, gingerly, like the floor was on fire.

Tegan nodded tightly.

Oz came down the stairs. "We looked everywhere. Was there any place secret? Hidden?"

No, there hadn't been, and he'd known the house like the back of his hand. That didn't mean that Courier didn't make a tunnel, but after searching, tapping on walls and hitting ceilings, there didn't seem to be any new additions. By all accounts, no one had been to this house of horrors for a long while—the only dust that had been moved was from their footprints.

He stood inside what used to be Stanton's office. Nothing had changed—the desk remained. The couch with the washable denim cover. The rough rug on the floor. Bile rose in his throat.

Nothing good came of memories. He turned away. Because Cade wasn't just a memory. And Tegan would make sure they brought him home.

In the darkness, they left the house quietly and got back into the truck. Oz started driving, not wanting to draw attention to them any longer, and Tegan called Deran again, his head swimming.

"I can't find him, Deran. He's not at the house," Tegan said when Deran picked up.

There was a long pause, and then Deran's words came like they were swimming in molasses. "The boat, Teegs. Remember the boat."

"The boat." Tegan shook his head, trying to shake the memories loose.

"The boat. That's why we picked the Navy," Deran was

saying.

The boat. Tegan recalled his first boarding exercise in BUD/S, how he had some kind of panic attack the instructors wrote off as dehydration. All these years, Tegan had agreed with that assessment...until right now. He'd been on it twice —and those two times gave him some of the worst memories ever. "Oz, there's a boat. We've got to get to the marina."

Oz didn't hesitate.

"Deran, do you remember the name of the boat?" Tegan asked now.

"No. I was never on it. You told me about it. After." Deran sounded half-broken.

"Tegan." Vic's voice was commanding, grabbing his attention that had started to spiral into panic...a place his mind rarely went. "I want you to put Deran on speaker."

Tegan did so.

"Now, I want you to tell me everything you remember about this guy and his son. No matter how small or insignificant it seems."

"It was so long ago, Vic," Tegan started.

"You were just at his house. Think of what you saw there," Vic instructed. "I saw pictures. Fishing rods. But not a picture of a boat."

"No, there were no pictures of it. He said..." Tegan shook his head as the memory grabbed him, seemingly by the throat.

"No one knows about this place...especially not the wife." Harry Stanton had winked like they were sharing the best secret in the world.

Looking through his then eight-year-old eyes, he scanned the cabin of the boat. The blue carpet. The bed. "I don't remember the outside of the boat. Not many people knew about it...not even his wife." Tegan closed his eyes as silence filled the car. "His wife's name was Naomi."

"Is that important, Teegs?" Vic asked.

"Yeah, very. The boat's name is *Omie's Dream*."

CHAPTER 33

IT TOOK Cade several seconds upon waking to realize he was now in a fucking dog cage, bound, on his side, staring out the side of the open stainless steel design that allowed him to check out where he was, which was in a room that only had a rug and a bed in the corner. It was dusty and dark, and it took him another minute to orient himself.

What the fuck happened?

He had to think hard about how the hell he'd ended up here. That he'd been drugged was obvious—the foggy feeling in his brain and the heavy feeling in his limbs told him that. He focused on remembering...

The cop coming in to ask him if he needed anything. Cade telling him he didn't, and the cop leaning in to remind Cade that his pictures would stay up forever...and then the electric shock hitting him hard...

His head ached—he might've hit it when he fell after being tased, and his chest hurt. He'd no doubt have burn marks there from the prongs. Fucking cop was in on it...if he really was a cop or not remained to be seen.

The auction.

Courier. Photos. Ball-gag. More drugs.

No. That word was the strongest. He closed his eyes and just breathed and reminded himself to calm the fuck down and remember his training—childhood, Army, Fight Club, Theo, Vic, Tegan, and finally, Strider. Because Strider had taken him aside and bound him and made him get out of it as a surprise ambush. In those moments, Cade fucking hated him, hated that he stood over him and whispered all the horrible things that were going to happen to him after the auction...all the awful things that would happen to him if he didn't escape before that happened.

With those warnings in his head, he knew this wasn't a drill. This was the real deal, and he was his best chance of survival.

He always was. Didn't mean it wouldn't be great to have help.

As he shifted the cuffs on his wrists, he checked for cameras and saw one in the corner. There was no real way to break out without being seen, so he'd do it fast and prepare for any possible onslaught.

Wrists first, behind his back. He angled the cuffs the way Strider taught him and snapped the chain in the middle, and then he did the same thing to his feet. He was still naked, his clothes sitting on top of the crate, but Courier must've had a thing for boots because those were still on. He felt for the thin ceramic blade he always kept in the false sole of his boot. It was a spot that Courier wouldn't have found unless he'd already known it existed, and it was a modification Cade made to every pair of shoes he owned in one way or another. He'd definitely benefitted from Theo's time in Delta—his friend had saved his goddamned life, even from a world away.

There wasn't a lock on the door beyond the one that came with the cage, so he simply reached around and pinched the levers together to open the door, and he was out fast, on his feet, facing the door. Waiting.

And nothing.

This is too easy. Had to be a trap—somewhere. Some way. He stayed still and surveyed the room. Then he knelt so he could get a different perspective...and that was when he saw it—the wire that ran across the door.

Trip wire, wound from the bedpost to the doorknob. Thin, almost undetectable in the darkness. He reached up and grabbed his clothes and tucked them under his arm before he moved forward. It took him several more minutes to crawl to the door, slowly, in order to make sure no one came through it.

He listened to the silence, needing to hear something—anything. But fuck, it was too quiet. Was he really alone? Or was Courier's plan to send in Vic and Tegan after him so they'd all be blown to shit?

As he sat there, he realized that the floor seemed to be moving, which added to the queasy feeling the drugs had left him with. He put his ear to the floor and quickly realized that they were on the water. He was on a goddamned boat. Was it drifting? Was that Courier's plan? He couldn't even check the blacked-out windows because he'd blow up, and maybe waiting on a rescue was a hopeless thing.

No. Vic and Tegan will find me. He was sure of it. And because of that, he sat there, overriding his natural instincts to do fucking something, beyond getting dressed.

Finally, after what seemed like forever, but was probably closer to ten minutes, he heard footsteps, and remaining quiet was no longer an option. The boat was still docked. "Don't open the door."

"Cade?" Vic's voice. "Baby, you okay?"

"I'm fine—and so are you—unless you touch the door."

"Trip wire?"

"Yes."

"Is it the only one?"

"I'm not sure—it's dark as fuck in here. The window's tinted."

"Are you free?"

"Yes. And I'm alone but there's a camera in here."

"Tegan's looking for a monitor. Don't go near the window —Oz is checking it from the outside. And I'm staying right here." Vic's voice was calm. Steady. Soothing.

"How'd you find me? Where am I?"

"You're on Courier's father's boat."

Cade frowned in the dark. "Why?"

"Because he knows Tegan. It's all connected. We'll talk about it once you're out of there."

Cade nodded as though Vic could see him. "Tell me what to do."

"Besides staying still and not touching the door?"

Cade rolled his eyes. "Yeah, besides that."

"Keep rolling your eyes, Cade," Vic said and that made Cade smile. "Are your eyes used to the dark?"

"I think so, but the wires are thin."

"The floor didn't click?"

"No—no pressure plates on the path to the door." He glanced at the window. "I see Oz's flashlight."

"Good—check the room while he lights it up."

He squinted out of habit, even though that didn't help shit. But finally, he was able to focus, and the light glinted off the wire...the wires. "The walls are all wired."

"Okay, anything else?"

"You want more?"

"Yeah, a lot more—with you, Cade." Vic's voice warmed him and in spite of everything, he smiled again.

"Tegan's mad at me."

"Tegan's not mad," Tegan said, and Cade forced back the tears that threatened. Because fuck, Courier was not winning this one.

He looked up and saw the cutout in the ceiling, which was probably an access point for heat or AC. It didn't have a molding, so it would've been easy to miss. "Can you ask Oz to shine the light on the ceiling near the door?"

A second later, Oz was doing just that. Cade pointed toward the access panel and Oz's light went directly to it. "I don't see any wires," he said. "It's an access panel—I can move the wood aside."

"It could be wired from the inside," Vic said.

"But how would he get out?" Cade asked.

"Oz says there's no outlet for it on the outside. Let me check something," Tegan told him.

Seconds later, Tegan confirmed that there was no outlet anywhere, so the access panel was self-contained. The perfect spot for the bomb.

It was the only other way out. The window would trigger the walls, and the entire room—and most of the boat—would blow. What did Courier expect? That they'd leave him in there and wait for him to come back?

"I think the camera and the bomb mechanism are both in this panel," Cade said. "There's no other way to set it to blow. He couldn't have closed it without blowing himself up if he wired it. Let me get in there, and you can tell me how to defuse it."

"Do you have anything on you to cut wires?"

"A knife."

"I'm not seeing a lot of other options, T," he heard Vic say.

"Cade, I'm going to walk you through this. Are you ready?"

"No choice but to be."

"Does it freak you out? Because I'm willing to lie," Vic said.

"I'm good. I'm okay."

"Good. Do you have a way up?"

Shit. "Hang on." He crawled toward the dog crate. Slowly, he checked it—if it had been wired, he would've been dead on exit, so he wasn't worried about that, but he wasn't moving fast in here. He dragged it across the rug and upended it. "Okay, I'm going up."

He had to balance along the edges and move fast—the crate wasn't meant to withstand his weight on it. First, he reached up to the panel and gingerly pushed it aside. And he breathed. "Moved the panel. I'm jumping up."

First, he felt around and there was nothing in the immediate area. He didn't have a lot of leverage, and he was never more thankful that his hands and forearms were strong from fighting as he was when he jumped and caught the sides of the open space, holding on for dear life as he pulled his own body weight up. Finally, his shoulders were in, and he dragged himself in a little farther, so his body was half-in, half-out.

And that was when he saw the timer.

T-minus ten minutes left.

He slid farther inside the crawlspace and saw a vent that probably led into another room, but it was too small. And probably wired as well. "There's a timer. Nine and a half minutes."

Vic's voice drifted up, still calm and steady. "Are there batteries you can see?"

"They're wrapped in the wires. Looks like they'd be tough to pull out too."

"Okay, tell me the colors of the wires."

"Blue, brown, yellow, white, and green," he said. "Two of them wind all the way around, and one of them looks like it's nestled in with the batteries."

He was sweating. He forced himself to keep his hands steady, drew the knife out of his pocket, and waited while Vic and Tegan talked.

Finally, Vic said, "Do you have anything to put on the other side of the wire and the knife? For leverage?"

He looked around and saw nothing. *Shit.* But he checked his pockets and found a card in there—a credit card he'd slid in for emergencies that no doubt had gotten washed and forgotten. He slid it out and cut off a slice that could fit easily on top of the wire. He'd cut up into it. "I'm ready. Which one?"

"Green, baby. Cut the green in one shot, okay? Clean through."

He didn't have to ask what would happen if he didn't. He put his head down on his arm for a few seconds, wiped the sweat from his brow and said, "I love you both. So goddamned much it hurts."

He didn't know if they could hear him and it didn't matter—he'd said it, out loud. He reached out and sliced through the wire, holding his breath.

The timer stopped. Three minutes and twelve seconds. His new favorite numbers. He collapsed his head onto his arms and realized he was shaking. "We're good," he managed, and it sounded faint to his own ears.

"We're coming in."

"No!" he called. "No, please. I want all of you out of the way. And then I'll open it. Please. You have to do this for me. You have to let me..."

Save myself. Prove myself.

"Okay, Cade. Give us two minutes and then please, come out to us," Tegan said.

"I will. Love you both," he called.

"Love you, baby." Vic's voice, followed by Tegan's, "Love you. Hurry out."

He nodded. Counted the two minutes in his head before shimmying down, avoiding the crate. He put his hand on the doorknob, turned and opened it.

Nothing.

He hurried up the stairs and onto the deck—and into Tegan's arms. Vic was at his back, saying, "Come on, let's get into the truck," moving them along to the dock.

That was when the bullets rang out.

"Sniper." Tegan's voice was clipped as he shifted his body efficiently to cover Cade's before hustling him behind another boat as shots whizzed by his head. "Stay down."

While Oz fired back, Vic managed to get into the water and swim around to get behind Courier. It came naturally once he heard the gunshots, something he hadn't been sure would happen until this moment. It was the first battle he'd been a part of since his capture at the hands of his best friend and lover, and he'd been putting off helping on any Gray Ops missions because he had no idea if he'd be ready.

Fuck it, he was. Always had been.

Now, he swam quietly. Tegan would be pissed at this, no doubt would be extra wounded that Vic had taken the water route away from the former SEAL, but Vic wasn't letting anything happen to any of his men. Not to Oz either.

This came back to him as naturally as breathing. There was no panic. Just adrenaline and focus, the kind he'd grown up with. The kind he'd trained for.

The kind he'd been born with.

Oz held the sniper off on his own until he was sure Cade and Tegan had enough time to get to the truck. Tegan would turn right around to help Oz, and sure enough, Vic heard another gun join the battle.

Now, the gunfire gave Vic coverage as he snuck up behind Courier, but it wouldn't be that easy. No, Courier was good, and just as Vic expected, he turned at the last possible moment and attacked.

Vic held his battle-ready stance, turned, and kicked the gun out of Courier's hand. It clattered along the deck, and Vic dove at Courier, taking him down to the ground. He felt the blade slide through his side, but he wrenched away to try to stop it from going too deep. He gave Courier a punch right below the sternum—it would have completely taken out a lesser man, but Vic knew it would only slow Courier down enough for Vic to get the knife away and do some damage of his own.

He felt the blood dripping along his side as he slashed across Courier's ribs, drove the blade in, but it would take more than that to kill him. Vic didn't want Courier dead—not yet. There was time for that, but Tegan needed closure. Answers.

Instead, Vic would subdue him until Tegan came to get him.

"You think Cade's yours? I've had him too," Courier managed.

"No, you never had Cade," Vic sneered. "And now, you definitely never will."

Courier came for him, jabbing and bleeding, and Vic did the same, managed to get an arm around his neck to choke him out...and that was when Tegan came up from behind them, dripping wet.

"About fucking time," Vic huffed. He let go of Courier, who sank to the ground.

"I didn't think the SAS knew how to swim," Tegan told him as he caught Vic around the waist while Oz dragged an unconscious Courier a safe distance away. "Let's get you out of here."

"Stay and question him," Vic commanded, his voice sounding far away to his own ears.

"Still giving orders?" Tegan asked, gently cradling the side of Vic's face.

"Still damned good at it, too."

"How do you manage to be smug, even when you're bleeding?"

"It's a gift," he told Tegan.

"You're going to be fine."

"Now who's giving orders?" Vic managed. "Listen to me. He's still alive—I did that purposely. Get...your closure. You have to, T. S'important." He smiled up at Tegan, because there was also something else important to say. And now. "Fuck, I love you, baby."

Tegan touched Vic's cheek. "I've been falling in love with you for a long time, Vic. And I'm finally here. I love you, Vic. So don't even fucking think about dying on me."

"Fucking...romantic," Vic huffed.

Tegan glanced over at Oz, who had his boot on Courier's neck. "I'll talk to Courier. I'll get you into the truck first, so Cade can take you to the hospital," Tegan finished, and Vic couldn't argue with that.

Cade had gotten safely to the truck, started it and waited, at the ready. He couldn't see much, but finally, he saw Tegan and Vic heading toward him, Tegan mostly carrying Vic.

"Shit," he muttered and drove as close to them as he could.

Tegan opened the passenger's side door and helped Vic inside. All Cade saw was the blood. "Go, Cade—get him to the hospital. Oz and I pinned Courier down—he's restrained, and we'll wait for the police to come grab him. Go."

Cade didn't hesitate. When the door shut, he took off. He

used one hand to put pressure on Vic's chest, encouraged Vic to talk to him.

"M'fine, Cade. Christ, you drive like a fucking maniac," Vic mumbled.

Cade didn't stop to talk, or for stoplights. No, he prayed for a cop because he'd follow them all the way to the hospital. But finally, after what seemed like hours but was actually less than five minutes, he was in the emergency bay, door open, yelling for help.

People hopped into action and Vic was on a stretcher, Cade walking with him.

"I need to talk to his family—I need consent for surgery," a doctor called, because Vic had passed out.

"I'm family," Cade said. "He's my brother."

The doctor didn't question it, motioned to the nurse. "Sign these—we're taking him right in."

"Is he going to be okay?" Cade asked the nurse.

"I think it missed his lung, so that's good. Dr. Holden's the best. Trauma surgeon in the military. He's got this," she reassured him.

"Tell him Vic was military too," he said. "Please. *Please.*"

"I will. Have a seat, honey. You look like hell."

He didn't bother to tell her he'd lived through it.

Tegan went back to where Oz had dragged Courier to guard him. In the distance, he heard sirens, and he knew time was limited.

He kicked Courier viciously in the ribs and the man curled into a protective ball, the blood pooling underneath him. Vic had given as good as he'd gotten, that was for sure, and Tegan pushed down his panic at that to finish this. That was what Vic wanted.

It was what Tegan needed. He bent down. "I guess your plan didn't work out so well, did it?"

"You think you're free? You'll never be free of me—or my father." Courier spit blood and smiled. "You know I'm right. Even now, I know you remember everything. Cade does too. Deran...Theo..."

Tegan backhanded the smile off his face. "Your father was scum, just like you. And you're going away for a hell of a long time."

"All these years, you could never get my father out of your mind," Courier taunted. "If it wasn't for you, he wouldn't have moved so far away from me. That was your fault—yours and your brother's. There was nothing unnatural about what he did to you. You asked for it, the same way Cade and Theo did, and then you turned around and blamed him."

"You sick fuck." Tegan slammed the side of his head with the butt of his Sig, but Oz stopped him from a second hit.

"Let him rot, Teegs."

"No, Oz—I'm taking him out so there's never a chance of this happening again."

"Let natural selection take its course in prison," Oz reasoned. "You know what they'll do to him in there."

Tegan looked back at Courier. "Tell me where Eddie's buried."

Courier gave a laugh/cough. "He didn't kill Eddie. Eddie took up too much of his time, so I found a perfect way to get rid of him. Cade's auction wasn't my first."

If Tegan closed his eyes, he could still see Eddie's cherub-like cheeks as he smiled and ran after his brother, trying to get his attention...

Wait for me, Jamie. "What did you do with him, Jamie?"

When Tegan used his old name, Courier smiled. "It wasn't as easy as it is today, but I still managed. My father found the dark web and I just logged into his account and met a friend who liked them young. Eddie was at the park at the same time every day. It was easy."

"Did your father know what you did?"

"I did it for him. I never thought you and your brother would get involved to throw doubt on him. If you hadn't done that—"

"The police investigated him," Tegan said through clenched teeth.

"It took me a long time to find my father after he was acquitted, because he'd fallen off the face of the earth. Once I found that stupid slut who killed him and I found out that he was connected with Deran?" Courier laughed. "What a small fucking world."

With that, Courier levered his upper body off the dock in a last-ditch effort to cause pain, smashing his forehead against Tegan's. Tegan saw stars from the hit, but a minor concussion wouldn't be enough for Courier to gain advantage. Tegan had lived through far worse.

He held Courier down by his hair and hammered his face with his fist. "Where is Eddie?"

"You'll never find him. It's too late." Courier smiled. "By the way, sorry about your brother."

He closed his eyes, his breathing shallow, and Tegan got Deran on the line. "D, get out of your safe house, now. Now!"

CHAPTER 34

"WHO'S THE DOCTOR?" Tegan was demanding of the same nurse who'd helped Cade sit down and get some food into him. It was two hours later, and Cade shot her a sympathetic look as he went over to corral the angry, worried man. "Tegan, it's okay. Dr. Holden's operating."

"Trace Holden?"

"He and I aren't on a first name basis, babe," Cade said tiredly. "Can you please come sit next to me and stop being all fucking growly to the nurses?"

"Growly?" Tegan asked but he let Cade lead him over to the bank of seats near the OR. It was late—sometime after three in the morning and fuck, Cade hated hospitals. Anytime he'd absolutely been forced to go, he'd also been forced to lie about how and where he'd gotten his injuries. He'd hated the look of pity in the staff's eyes, because they knew they should report him...and they also knew how much worse they'd make things for him if they did.

"Want some coffee or something?" Cade asked, finally looking at Tegan's face. "You need stitches."

"It's fine." Tegan waved off the cut in his eyebrow that was bleeding—heavily—under the piece of T-shirt he was holding against it. "That fucker Courier? He's in jail. I wanted to kill him. I tried to, but someone stopped me."

Oz—who was no doubt that someone—was striding down the hall, looking equally as dirty as Tegan, but he didn't appear to be bleeding. "How's Vic?"

"Still in surgery. The blade just missed his lung, the nurse said, but he'd lost a lot of blood."

"He's going to be pissed as fuck when he wakes up," Oz said and then pointed to Tegan. "You—with me. Stitches."

"I'm staying right here," Tegan said stubbornly.

"He's out of surgery and he's doing fine. Lost a lot of blood but otherwise, he was damned lucky," Dr. Holden said from behind them. "He's in recovery and he'll spend the night in ICU. You can see him in an hour or so. I told him you were here." He spoke that last part to Cade. "You just going to sit there and bleed all over my hospital?"

"Your hospital? You fucking own it now?" Tegan rolled his eyes. Well, the eye that Cade could see, because the other was blocked by the dirty piece of fabric.

"That's not sanitary," he mentioned, and Tegan's eye gave him a dirty look.

Dr. Holden sighed like he was deeply put upon. "Come on, you asshole—I'll stitch you up myself."

"You'll probably scar me on purpose," Tegan muttered, but Oz was yanking at him and forcing him to follow Dr. Holden. He mouthed, *Be right back*, before they disappeared into a room.

Cade wondered what their history was as he sagged in relief that Vic was okay. That Courier was behind bars.

"I'll take care of Courier," Strider assured him.

Cade turned to look at him, not bothering to ask where he'd come from. "He's in jail."

Strider snorted. "That's nothing you should concern yourself with. The fact that he kidnapped you—and held the auction—has been reported to Rourke. Looks like the investigation against you and Theo is over."

"What do they think happened to Dolentz?"

Strider shrugged. "Who knows? They'll probably end up thinking Courier killed him. After all, he's been using the house and the boat, all without transferring them to his name."

Cade put his head back against the wall and closed his eyes. His head had begun to throb like the adrenaline had left his body all at once. "Fuck."

"Cade, you all right?" Oz was leaning over him, a concerned look on his face.

"Yeah, I think so. Is Vic okay?" He tried to get up, too fast, and got woozy.

"He's okay, yes. But I think you might have a concussion." Dr. Holden leaned in and shined a light in his eyes. "A definite concussion."

"Dr. Holden, I need to see Vic," Cade told him.

"Call me Trace. And he's as stubborn as you are." That last part was directed at Tegan, who was at Cade's side, a bandage over his eyebrow.

"You okay, baby?" Tegan's hand slid over his and he nodded. "Let's go see Vic, and then you can go home..."

"Not leaving without Vic." He looked at Tegan. "You're not planning on it, am I right?"

"Even with a concussion, he outsmarts you," Oz said. "Told you this one was trouble."

"I told *you* that," Tegan protested.

"Hey, I'm right here." Cade started to get up again, but Tegan had an arm around him. "I'm not fragile."

Trace shook his head. "Pathetic, all of you. And I don't even want to know what the hell you were doing tonight. Just follow me."

They did, up the bank of elevators, down the hall and into the private ICU room behind the glass door where Vic slept. But his eyes opened when Cade and Tegan both touched his arm. He gave a sleepy smile at them, then back at Oz and Trace. "I'm good, guys. Really. Just tired."

"We got him," Tegan said.

"Good." Vic closed his eyes and Cade wanted to crawl into bed next to him.

"I'll grab you guys some scrubs. Go shower off before the nurses admit all of you," Trace ordered.

"Not the boss of me," Tegan muttered after him.

"I'm going to need this story later," Cade told Oz.

"Deal."

"Not," Tegan told both of them, and in his sleep, Vic snorted a soft laugh.

Tegan was running on adrenaline, coffee, and fumes. Still, he kept checking on everyone, as if to assure himself that everyone was really safe. Deran and Theo—and all Deran's men—were fine, but Deran was pissed about his safehouse being blown up. And Tegan woke Cade up often through the night to make sure he was okay since Cade refused to let himself be admitted. Still, Trace came to check on him and Vic both, which was nice of him, considering what an asshole he was. Rigs came by too, as did Rourke...who did not look happy.

"Where have you four been for the past few hours?" He pointed at everyone but Vic, who was finally awake and drinking the ginger ale that Tegan held for him.

"Here," Oz said simply, although, to be fair, none of them knew where Rigs had been before he'd shown up an hour earlier. But he was a lawyer and could presumably deal with his own shit if caught.

"Who saw you?" Rourke demanded.

"The whole staff. The doctor. Vic," Tegan said.

"He's not a reliable witness," Rourke pointed out.

"Go fuck yourself," Vic managed groggily, then looked pleased with himself. "How's that for reliable?"

"What's the problem?" Rigs asked.

"The problem is that Courier's not in his jail cell," Rourke started. "The other problem is that we found him, dead, in the alley behind the police station with his neck broken."

"So what, he fell out of the jail and died?" Vic asked.

Tegan glanced at him and frowned. "What kind of drugs do they have you on, babe?"

"Because I want some," Oz added.

"I still don't see why we should care that Courier's dead," Vic said.

Cade began to stir and Tegan went to him and rubbed his back until he drifted off to sleep again.

"You should care because he was killed," Rourke said through gritted teeth.

"Unless he fell out of the jail—escaping," Vic repeated.

Tegan shrugged. "Seems legit."

Rourke pointed at all of them in turn. "None of you fuckers leave town."

"Because a criminal is dead? You going to his funeral, Rourke?" Oz asked, his voice taking on a decidedly deadly tone.

Rourke just pointed to him, hard and left the room.

"Don't forget your crayons!" Vic called behind him. "Fucking jarhead."

"Fuck you too, Vic," Rourke called back.

"You know, Oz *did* take a long time getting coffee," Vic murmured. "And Rigs only got here a little while ago. They'd be my top suspects."

"Asshole," Oz muttered at him.

Rigs shook his head. "No one talk to him without me, got it?"

"Strider," Cade said sleepily.

"What's that, baby?" Tegan asked.

"Don't ask him again, dammit. I want plausible deniability," Rigs told him.

"Like we all don't know it was Strider," Oz said with a roll of his eyes.

"Can I go home yet?" Vic asked.

"Yes, baby. We're all going home," Tegan promised.

CHAPTER 35

ROURKE SLAMMED out of the back entrance of the hospital. He hadn't wanted Cade to get blamed if he was innocent, but nothing had been proven. And now, Rourke's key witness was dead. Granted, his fingerprints were all over the cage and the houseboat where Cade was kept imprisoned, but beyond that, there wasn't any other evidence beyond a "he said, he said" scenario.

The chief was going to have his ass...and Rourke never handed over his ass willingly.

"You look like someone stole your doll."

The voice went through him like a shiver. It was...lilting. An accent Rourke couldn't quite place, and when he turned to face the tall man standing in the shadows, all he could focus on was his strange, amber-colored eyes that glowed under the poor lighting in the parking lot.

He'd seen pictures, but the real-life version was far more devastating.

"I don't play with dolls, Strider," he growled. "You should think twice before sneaking up on a police officer."

"Don't worry, I did. And then I ignored it." He didn't move away from the wall, so Rourke moved in closer. "I'm flattered that you know who I am."

"Every police officer and FBI agent in the country knows who you are," Rourke shot back.

"How...exciting."

"I could drag you down to the station right now. Question you. Forget you're in a room and leave you there for the FBI to pick up."

"Eventually, all of you would have to release me. Even the CIA and the NSA never could find solid reasons to hold me. Mossad, either. But if it makes you feel better..." Strider held out his wrists. "Give it a try."

The warnings on Strider were a mile goddamned long. Dangerous. Deadly.

Killer.

Psychotic.

Shows no mercy. The list was endless, as were the unsolved murders that many had tried to pin on him.

Tried, and failed. Miserably.

"You're going to arrest Cade again, aren't you?" Strider asked now.

Rourke refused to confirm or deny. "Last I looked, you weren't a member of this department."

"Thank the good lord above for that," Strider murmured. "You're going to arrest Cade—and Theo—when you find him."

"The investigation hasn't ended. Because we can't find Dolentz."

"So a drunk pedophile disappears, and you're going all

out to find him. How fucking predictable." Strider sounded bored.

"I hear you know something about drunk pedophiles disappearing."

"Big ears, Mr. Rourke."

"Detective."

"My apologies." Strider sounded completely unapologetic and like a complete asshole, in fact. "The *mister* makes you so much more interesting, like you're part of a fantasy."

"Is that what you're looking for—a fantasy?"

"You certainly aren't at the end of it." Strider's look was withering and if Rourke didn't have confidence, *he'd* be withering.

He turned on Strider, who'd gotten way too close, ended up with a hand across Strider's throat as he leaned into the man. "You need to back the fuck off."

"Do I?" Strider tilted his head, unconcerned with the threat. Rourke was a big man—he frightened a lot of people just by being in the room...but Strider was obviously fucking nuts. "I'd like you to reconsider your plans to keep this case open."

"I'd like you to fuck off."

Strider laughed, a low, dangerous sound. Rourke backed away like he'd touched fire. "Get the hell out of here."

"But I've got a proposition for you. One that would definitely be beneficial to both of us."

"Not interested."

"For a detective, you're not a very good liar," Strider challenged. "You're intrigued."

Rourke couldn't deny it, but he'd replace *intrigued* with *horny*, and maybe he did need that vacation his chief was always talking about. Because he wasn't fucking a known psychotic killer. "What do you want, Strider?"

"I'll give you definitive evidence that Courier killed his own father."

"I'd rather know who killed Courier," Rourke told him.

"I heard Courier killed himself."

"Right. And then he escaped from jail with his broken neck."

Strider smiled, his eyes glittering and fuck, this guy was scary. And handsome. And yeah, Rourke was *definitely* going on vacation. "So you'll give me evidence to prove that Courier killed Dolentz—"

"And you'll leave Cade and Theo alone. Cease investigating them."

"Are you fucking Cade too?" Rourke asked.

"Sadly, no. But I'd never say never."

"What happens if I say no to your deal?"

"I could blackmail you."

"With what?"

"It doesn't matter. I could take a little nothing from your past and blow it up."

"You're really fucking terrible at this favor thing, you know that?"

"Do you think I don't know everything about you, Rourke?" Strider asked seductively. "I know your likes. I know about that suspect that went missing. Does your immediate supervisor? Your chief? Your old partner? But I won't tell anyone that...and all you have to do is pick your favor. Stop wasting time questioning it."

"You don't make any goddamned sense," Rourke muttered, frustrated.

"You like putting innocent men in jail?"

"How do I know Cade and Theo are innocent, Strider?"

"You know what Courier—and Dolentz—were. What they did to those boys, and many others." Strider's voice was a hiss. "Besides, it's not like you've never looked the other way in an investigation. The Hart case, for example?"

Rourke's blood went cold. *He doesn't know shit—he's just fishing.* But still, if he did... "Fine. I'll take the favor," he ground out.

"I knew you'd see it my way."

Let Strider think what he wanted. In the meantime, Rourke planned on digging up as much shit on the man in front of him as he could. "How will I get in touch with you to collect? Because I will collect."

Strider rolled his eyes. "And I'm sure a thrilling time will be had by all."

Rourke leaned in close and licked Strider's neck, because fuck it, crazy wanted crazy? He'd get it. It'd been a long time since he'd let that side of himself out, but now? It wanted to play. "Bet on it."

For the first time that night, Strider looked intrigued.

CHAPTER 36

AFTER A COUPLE OF WEEKS, Vic was up and around and bitching about having to take it easy...which was how Cade knew he was going to be fine. During the day, Cade helped Tegan and Vic with Crave and learned more about running both the club and the mercenaries of Gray Ops.

They were only too happy to let him help. All of it felt right, like coming home...to a home he'd never known he'd needed so badly.

Now, he stood inside Room 4. It was empty, the walls retracted so he could see down into the club. Crave hadn't opened yet, so he just absorbed the memories, the ghosts, that this space held.

"I never thought it could be this good," he said finally, because he felt Tegan and Vic behind him. They moved silently, but he'd begin to feel it inside of him when they arrived, a connection that still managed to floor him.

"This is the rightest thing I've ever done," Vic told them both.

Suddenly, the three of them were standing together, looking out into the club.

"It's the best thing I've ever done," Tegan echoed.

"And when people ask what sharing is like, what will you tell them?" Cade asked.

"It's not sharing. Sharing implies you don't own it, and I want to own both of you. Got it?" Vic told him.

Cade smiled. "Is that an order?"

"Consider it one, yes." Vic swung an arm around Cade. "I guess you need to convince us? Over and over?"

"Takes two of us to satisfy you. To control you." Tegan smiled. "Same here. Maybe that's why it never worked for me before. We needed more."

"I guess it means we've got a pretty big capacity for love," Cade said.

"Yeah, we do. Makes sense. We tend to live big. Need more, seek more," Vic told them. "Do you think Theo will be okay with it?"

Cade smiled. "He's the one who told me how lucky I was to find double the love and that I'd better not screw it up and push you guys away...or he was coming back to kick my ass."

"Yeah, I like Theo a lot."

"I don't like the idea of Theo coming home without me there," Cade told them now.

"Don't you guys have a third roommate?"

"Yeah, we do. Sway's away a lot too. He's been gone the better part of this month, which is a good thing, because he'd be all worried too."

"Theo's always welcome here, and so's Sway—we've got plenty of room," Tegan told him. "But if you want to stay with Theo when he's home, that's okay too."

"Thanks." Cade turned and kissed Tegan and then kissed Vic. "Love you."

"Love you," Vic murmured back.

"Love you both," Tegan added. "So fucking much."

They drew together. It didn't matter that they'd been together since being in this room. Didn't matter that everything had changed, and for the better. For Cade, this was an exorcism of sorts, his taking back control of his life, this room, these men.

His men.

It didn't matter what—who—had brought them together. It only mattered that they were. "It was good then," Cade said of his first memories that seemed so much farther away than they really were. "But so much better now."

And Tegan and Vic? Knew exactly what that meant, which was the best part.

"This is our room," Cade told them. Where they'd met. Where it all started.

"And you two? Are mine." He grabbed each one possessively, hands fisting the fronts of their respective shirts. "Got it?"

"Yes, Cade, we've got it," Tegan told him, his smile relaxed. "You've got us...and we've got you."

"Can I fuck both of you now, if we're through with the sappy shit?" Vic asked.

Cade's body heated. "I thought you'd never ask." He leaned forward, pressed his lips to Vic's first, then Tegan's, and then Vic manhandled him toward the couch, Tegan following with a husky laugh, to their couch, in their room.

ACKNOWLEDGMENTS

I always say that writing a book takes a village, and I'm very lucky to be surrounded by so many wonderful people who help me so much.

First, thanks to Frauke from Croco Designs, who does everything from websites to book formatting to covers to ads and more (and you always answers all my millions of questions so patiently!)

First, to my wonderful beta readers, Jill Corley and Melinda James Rueter—you're the first people to see this book and your feedback (and cheerleading) is invaluable.

To Hope Vincent and Jess Rose from Flat Earth Editing —I mean, I cannot say enough good things about both of you. From copy edits to proofing, you've had my back on this book...and we laughed a lot in the process, which always makes work more fun.

To Michelle Slagan from Vibrant Promotions, who put together my blog tours and so much more for this release— you made everything streamlined and simple and took so much off my plate in the process.

As always, to my readers, because you guys are really just awesome. You hang out with me on Facebook and laugh, you support me, celebrate the book releases and make everything about this job so much more fun. I'm lucky to have you all in my corner, and trust me, I know it!

Last but never least, for Zoo, Lily, Chance, and Gin—thank you for letting me escape into my fictional worlds for long periods of time and always being there for me when I return.

UP NEXT FROM SE JAKES

**SAVING SWAY: Book 2 in the CRAVE Series
Coming June 2019**

And, if you enjoyed meeting Law, Paulo, and Styx in *Keeping Cade* and want more, you can read all about them in the following books:
Bound By Honor: Men of Honor 1
(*Kindle Unlimited*)
Bound By Law: Men of Honor 2
(*Kindle Unlimited*)
No Boundaries: Phoenix, Inc. Book 1

<<<<>>>>

MEN OF HONOR

BOUND BY HONOR

SEJ

NEW YORK TIMES BESTSELLING AUTHOR
STEPHANIE TYLER
WRITING AS
SE JAKES

Don't miss the Men of Honor!
BOUND BY HONOR:
Book 1 in the Men of Honor Series, on sale now!

A promise forces two men to bare themselves...completely.

One year ago on a mission gone wrong, Tanner James failed to save the life of Jesse, his Army Ranger teammate. Before dying in that South American jungle, Jesse extracted a promise that won't let Tanner rest until it's fulfilled—no matter what it costs him.

Damon Price loved Jesse, but problems in their relationship had come to a head right before Jesse left on his final mission. Now a reluctant Dom and a man still in mourning, he's not happy when Tanner appears at his BDSM club. And even less happy with Jesse's last request—that Tanner sub for him for one night.

After a rough start, Damon realizes that the tough soldier, despite his protests, aches for someone to take control. And Tanner senses a hesitance, an insecurity in Damon that makes him wonder if he's simply a placeholder for Jesse, or if their tentative connection could grow into something more.

For Jesse's sake, they agree to try one weekend together. Then duty calls, and a series of attacks that have been happening near the club hits too close to home, making both men wonder if giving their hearts is a maneuver fraught with too much risk...

Warning: Contains rough language, rougher sex and warriors who fall hard for each other.

CHAPTER 1

TANNER JAMES HAD BEEN to hell and back more times than he could count over the course of his twenty- six years and was always pretty sure he'd live to make the trip again. But this time, even as adrenaline raced through his body and every muscle tensed for battle, hell beckoned with a one-way ticket and without a goddamned firefight in sight.

No, that would've been easier, *much* easier than this slow crawl to the door of Crave—a BDSM club with the reputation of being both accessible and safe—the week before Christmas.

He looked up at the dark sign with white lettering at the entrance and thought about turning back and going home.

If he hadn't promised Jesse that he'd do this, that he'd look up Jesse's former boyfriend, he'd be home right now, having just returned from a month-long mission, not about to offer himself up like some bondage sacrifice.

This wasn't his scene. Not really. He was all about rough sex, was bisexual with a definite preference to men for as long as he could remember, used to having to *don't ask, don't tell,* thanks to his military career—but this? Having to go in and greet the owner with a message from his dead lover? Well, that was fucking weird and could get him thrown out on his ass.

Jesus Christ, this was going to suck.

The man checking patrons who entered was dressed in bright, loud colors. Tight black leather pants. Guyliner. And he flirted in an over-the-top manner with anyone he deemed hot enough.

Tanner knew he'd be the subject of the man's flirtation. Although he'd shrugged it off his entire life, the looks and stares and come-ons he'd been on the receiving end of forever told him he was handsome.

He was more interested in being the best Army Ranger he could, spent most days knee-deep in jungle crap with paint on his face and men who only cared that he could shoot an M-14 with dizzying accuracy.

"Hey."

"Hello, gorgeous. Please tell me you're alone." The man peeked behind Tanner, saw no one and clapped his hands. "Alone. There is a God."

"I'm looking for Damon Price."

"I'll bet you are," the man said with a shake of his head. "Shame, really, that they all want what they can't have."

"I just need to talk to him."

The man erupted into peals of girlish laughter and Tanner rolled his eyes. He'd never been into queens and this was why. If he was going to fuck a man, he was going to fuck a man. "Tell him I've got a message from Jesse."

The man stopped, nearly choked, but before he could answer, he was elbowed out of the way by a much taller blond man—ruggedly handsome although unsmiling, and Tanner wondered if he was face to face with Damon himself.

But rather than introduce himself, he asked, "What did you say about Jesse?"

"You heard me," Tanner bit out.

The man nodded slowly. "I heard you. I just don't know how Damon's going to feel about this." He paused. "Are you sure you want to go there?"

Tanner reacted before he could stop himself. "Why the *fuck* would you care where I want to go?"

The man raised a brow and held up a finger, indicating for Tanner to wait a minute, before disappearing down a back hallway.

Last chance to head for the hills. And despite the ease with which he could do so, Tanner remained rooted in place.

He couldn't see very far into the club at all from where he stood—it was designed purposely to let the incoming patrons hear the familiar sounds of sex occasionally rising over the music. The smell of sex was also unmistakable, partially hidden and mixed with whiskey and smoke. It was meant to beckon, to lead men astray...and Tanner didn't bother to hide his hard-on.

A few minutes later, Tanner was being led by the blond man who introduced himself as LC back to a private office with a big *Do Not Disturb* sign on the door.

No doubt, *this* counted as disturbing Damon, but it had been eating away at Tanner for a year now. He had to rid himself of this burden, do what Jesse asked and then go home and pretend none of it ever happened.

Before going in, he glanced at his watch. Just after midnight. Exactly the way Jesse had wanted it.

A hard growl of a voice called, "Come in."

LC stared at him, and Tanner, in turn, stared at the floor for a long moment. And then he opened the door and realized he'd been anything but prepared for Damon Price. Tanner was big and broad and strong, stood six foot three and turned heads wherever he went. But Damon—he was well over six foot five, with jet black hair and chiseled features. He stood, hands at his sides in a deceptively casual stance, dressed in full black leather and looking like a fucking badass.

Tanner nearly hyperventilated, because Jesse hadn't mentioned this part.

"He's my boyfriend and he owns a club," was all Jesse said. *"He's strong—reminds me of you. He's a Dom."*

"I'm not a Dom."

"No. But you could probably use one. It would be the only kind of man who could handle you."

Jesse had closed his eyes then before Tanner could tell him he had no interest in being anyone's bottom boy. Because Jesse had been talking to him about boyfriends and Doms when he'd been dying, slowly and painfully in the middle of a jungle in South America where he and his Ranger team had been on a mission, and Tanner had been fucking helpless to stop it.

Fuck.

He shoved his hands in his pockets so Damon wouldn't see the fists he couldn't uncurl and hoped the pain didn't show in his eyes.

This was supposed to bring closure—to both Damon and Tanner. There was no way to break a promise to a dead man.

Damon studied him for a few minutes. Tanner wasn't the type to squirm and he wasn't about to start now. Finally, the man said, "I hear you have a message from Jesse. And I swear to Christ, if you're fucking with me, I'll put your head through the wall."

Tanner snorted in spite of himself. "Okay, sure. I'd like to see you try."

Damon pushed away from the desk and stood toe-to-toe with him. "Talk."

Talk. Yeah, like it was that easy. "Jesse told me to come here—to ask for you. To tell you that..." Fuck. He shifted, aware that the proximity of Damon was freaking him out. If he hadn't been Jesse's, Tanner might've made a move without a second thought.

As if he knew what he was thinking, Damon arched an eyebrow at him, his lip curled into a half sneer.

Fuck it all. "I'm supposed to tell you to have a session with me. Jesse wanted it that way." "A session?" Damon repeated.

"Yeah. I'm supposed to let you Dom me. It was Jesse's dying wish."

Damon paled, took a step back from Tanner, and then another. "Is this a sick joke?"

"Do I look like I'm joking?"

"You little fuck." Damon had Tanner's shirt bunched in his fists, was slamming him against the office wall hard. "You sick bastard. You think you can ingratiate yourself to me by using Jesse?"

Tanner ground his teeth together hard and tamped back his anger. He'd known Damon wouldn't take this well. If Tanner had been in the same position, he doubted he would either. "He asked me to wait a year before I came here. He died after midnight."

"How do you know that?" Damon demanded. "Even I don't know that."

No, he wouldn't. The mission was deemed classified—and Jesse's time of death a closely guarded secret. "I was with him when he died."

Damon let out a long, hissing breath and let go of Tanner's shirt.

"I'm sorry—I didn't know how else to tell you. Jesse made me promise—"

"Stop saying his name," Damon growled hoarsely.

"He made me promise I'd wait the year. Said you wouldn't be ready before that. That you'd need to be dragged back into the land of the living, kicking and screaming. He said to tell you...to use the skull- and-crossbones collar with the broken latch." He spoke fast, stopped to catch his breath at the end. Gauged Damon's reaction.

The man hadn't moved a muscle during Tanner's speech. Simply stared, and Tanner tensed more, wondering if he was going to have to fight tonight.

Fighting and fucking were definitely two of his favorite things to do, sometimes all in the same night—or hour—or hell, the same time, but he had a feeling that he'd be pushing his luck taking on this guy.

He was in way over his head. And he couldn't remember the last time—if ever—he'd felt that way.

Damon's features relaxed slightly. He sat back on the top of the desk, folded his arms and stared Tanner up and down. A hard, assessing stare that was enough to make Tanner hard with desire and anticipation.

He wasn't sure why the sudden thought of Damon taking him got him hot, but that was short-lived, because he saw the tension in Damon's stance, the pain in his eyes. Tanner wanted to apologize, but he wasn't sure what for. Wanted to tell Damon that he was scared to fucking death that the Domming would actually happen—and also scared that it wouldn't.

He was so fucked up he could barely see straight.

Damon finally spoke. "I wouldn't touch you. You're not man enough to handle me."

Jesse's words echoed in Tanner's ear. *It would be the only kind of man who could handle you.*

Tanner hadn't been able to handle a relationship—or being touched, really, since what happened to Jesse last year. And so he nodded and he said, "You're right about that. This was a mistake."

The failure hanging on him heavily, he pushed out the door, went through the club and headed for the parking lot.

Jesse.

Damon had mourned over that man, cried over him, beat his fists against the wall, up until three months earlier. Things had eased, but he still wore the cloak of grief that sometimes threatened to choke him.

Now was one of those times. He'd waited until the gorgeous man left his office before he fell apart and tried his best not to hyperventilate.

Use the skull-and-crossbones collar with the broken latch.

The boy who'd just left his office would have no way of knowing that—wouldn't have known that Damon kept that collar in his loft, had fixed the latch right after Jesse died because it was one of the only things he could do.

Damon wouldn't be able to use the damned collar on this boy—Jesse knew that collaring meant something—that it didn't happen on a first night together.

You don't even know the boy's name.

He shuddered involuntarily that he'd thought of him as *the boy*. Because that's what he'd called Jesse—and only Jesse.

Jesse had been the first to ever thaw what Damon had considered a heart of ice. First, and the *only*.

But something tugged at his gut.

He could've been lying. This could be part of an elaborate scam.

The only thing was, the man had definitely been military. A Ranger, like Jesse, or so he said. Damon didn't doubt it, had a nose for those things, having been in special forces himself what seemed like a lifetime ago. And the timing was exactly right. Jesse had died a year ago, nearly to the hour, although he'd lied to the boy about not having that information.

Fuck.

He called through the open office door, "LC, grab that guy who just left."

"I'm not your bitch," LC drawled, and no, LC was no one's bitch...not since Styx left. "And he's already in the lot."

"Dammit."

LC held his gaze for a second and then called to one of the bodyguards. "Renn—grab the guy in the brown leather jacket who just left. And bring a few guys—he won't come willingly."

LC didn't say anything more, didn't have to, and just headed to the front of the club to supervise. And Damon waited in his office, trying not to pace. Trying not to picture what the boy would look like, bound and spread for him.

Trying to pretend he wasn't hard at the thought of it.

He shifted but could do nothing to hide the erection in the pants he wore, and when LC barged back into the office, it was the first thing he noticed.

Thankfully, he didn't comment on it, just said, "They've got him and he's not happy."

"Makes two of us."

"Did he really know Jesse?"

Damon nodded. "He says that Jesse sent him here—wanted him to have a session with me."

LC's eyes widened, but wisely his mouth remained closed. He was part owner of Crave, working mainly behind the scenes. He was also Damon's best friend—the only person Damon confided everything in. The only one he trusted enough to let him run the business in those months after Jesse died, when Damon couldn't get out of bed most days. LC had finally gotten him up and functioning.

Just then, the boy was dragged back in by three men—he was pissed for sure, but not fighting as hard as he could. Damon knew that, and whether it was grief or curiosity or both, he couldn't tell yet.

"Let him go," Damon commanded, and the men dropped him and left the room with LC, the office door shutting behind them as the boy stumbled forward until Damon caught him, held him hard by the biceps and stared at him again.

He was handsome as hell—all-American-looking, a blond haired, blue-eyed devil, even with his lips twisted into an angry grimace.

"What the fuck do you think you're doing?" The boy jerked out of his grasp and yes, he was strong. Damon had suspected as much. Earlier, when Damon had him by the shirt, backed against the wall, he hadn't flinched. It was the calm of a man who knew how to fight—who knew how to kill.

"What's your name?"

A jut of a chin, a glint of wild eyes and he ground out, "Tanner."

"Why did you come here?"

"Because I made a promise to Jesse when he was dying. I don't break promises like that."

"And you're willing to follow through on what he wanted."

Tanner pressed his lips together—he wanted to say no, that much Damon knew. For some reason, this handsome, strong, brave man wanted nothing to do with being Dommed, and it didn't appear to be for the usual reasons.

No, he wasn't uncomfortable, either in this club or with Damon and his leathers. But something was most definitely wrong with him.

"I'll do what Jesse wanted, yes."

"But you don't think you're man enough."

He waited for Tanner to snap an answer back, but none came. Instead, he shrugged.

"Well then, there's no time like the present. But no collar." He motioned for Tanner to follow him, out the door of the office, down a small hallway and into a room marked Room Four.

Once inside, Damon pressed a few buttons to bring the lights up and to remove the shading from the plate-glass divider that separated the room from the rest of the club.

As soon as he did so, the bar began to cheer. Damon activated the two-way speakers as well, so the sounds went from muffled to completely clear.

Tanner's eyes widened. "We're doing this here—where everyone can see?"

"Yes. That's what Jesse would've wanted."

Tanner couldn't have known that was the furthest thing from the truth—that Jesse understood the value of privacy at the start of a D/s relationship.

That Jesse would hate him for this.

Well, Damon hated Jesse for dying and leaving him. For refusing to quit the military and let Damon take care of him for the rest of his life.

For recognizing that Damon had been slowly dying inside during the last year of their relationship and continuing to satisfy his own needs instead.

Tanner swallowed hard and then he nodded.

Yes, let's see if this man is for real.

NEWSLETTER

**Sign up for the newsletter of SE Jakes and her
alter-ego Stephanie Tyler!**

Be among the first to learn not only about new and upcoming
books but also appearances and signings as well as special
promotions and giveaways!

http://stephanietyler.com/newsletter/

ALSO BY SE JAKES

MEN OF HONOR SERIES

Bound By Honor

Bound By Law

Ties That Bind

Bound By Danger

Bound For Keeps

Bound To Break

PHOENIX, INC. SERIES

No Boundaries

INKED SERIES

Hold The Line

Thirds

SINNERS

Sinners

THE CRAVE CLUB SERIES

Keeping Cade

Saving Sway (June 2019)

Taming Theo (September 2019)

Axel's Accord (TBA)

BLUEWATER BAY (MULTI-AUTHOR SERIES)

No Easy Way (novella) in the *Lights, Camera, Action* Anthology

WRITING AS STEPHANIE TYLER

SHELTER SERIES

Shelter Me

Pieces of Me (*forthcoming*)

MIRROR SERIES

Mirror Me

Rule Of Thirds

Walk In My Shadow

Double Blind (coming soon)

SKULLS CREEK MC SERIES

Vipers Run

Vipers Rule

HARLEQUIN BLAZE

Coming Undone

Risking It All

Beyond His Control

ABOUT THE AUTHOR

Stephanie Tyler is the *New York Times* bestselling author of romance novels spanning multiple genres, including Romantic Suspense, New Adult, Paranormal Romance and Contemporary Romance. She's a hybrid author who writes for multiple publishers, including Random House, NAL/Penguin, Harlequin, Carina Press, Mammoth Books, Belle Books and Samhain Publishing, as well as Riptide (as SE Jakes) and indie publishing. Her books have been translated into half a dozen languages, nominated for an RT Readers' Choice Award and garnered top picks from *RT Books Magazine* as well as starred reviews from *Publishers Weekly*. She's a frequent workshop presenter and has contributed stories for anthologies for charities, including *SEAL of My Dreams*, which has raised over 150K for the Veterans Medical Association.

Visit Stephanie Tyler at www.stephanietyler.com.

SE Jakes is the pen name for *New York Times* bestselling author Stephanie Tyler, and half the co-writing team of Sydney Croft. First published in 2011, SE Jakes has quickly risen to be a bestselling author in the LGBT romance genre, as well as a fan favorite. Her books are frequently highlighted in *USA Today* and have been reviewed by *Library Journal* and *RT Books Magazine*. She's been nominated by several sites for Favorite M/M author and has finaled in the Goodreads M/M Romance Readers Choice Awards in 7 categories. She's a hybrid author who writes for Riptide Publishing and Samhain Publishing, and she indie publishes as well.

Visit SE Jakes at www.sejakes.com.

Sydney Croft is the alter ego of Stephanie Tyler and Larissa Ione, two *New York Times* bestselling authors who blend their very different writing interests into adventurous tales of erotic paranormal fiction. Together, they developed a world where people with extraordinary abilities, like the power to control storms, could live and work with others like them. The series has been described as "Erotica meets the X-Men," and is unique in its own "erotic superhero romance" niche. Larissa and Stephanie live in different states and communicate almost entirely through email, though they often get together for conferences and book signings.

Visit Sydney Croft at www.sydneycroft.com.